Miss Abracadabra

Miss Abracadabra

(*As the World Turns*)

Tom Ross

DEEP VELLUM PUBLISHING

DALLAS, TEXAS

Deep Vellum Publishing
3000 Commerce St., Dallas, Texas 75226
deepvellum.org · @deepvellum

Deep Vellum is a 501c3 nonprofit literary arts organization founded in 2013 with the mission to bring the world into conversation through literature.

Support for this publication has been provided in part by the National Endowment for the Arts, the Texas Commission on the Arts, the City of Dallas Office of Arts and Culture, the Communities Foundation of Texas, and the Addy Foundation.

ISBNs: 978-1-64605-354-4 (paperback) | 978-1-64605-366-7 (ebook)

LIBRARY OF CONGRESS CATALOGING-IN-PUBLICATION DATA

Names: Ross, Tom, 1957- author.
Title: Miss Abracadabra : (as the world turns) / Tom Ross.
Description: First edition. | Dallas, Texas : Deep Vellum Publishing, 2024.
Identifiers: LCCN 2024033013 (print) | LCCN 2024033014 (ebook) | ISBN
   9781646053544 (trade paperback) | ISBN 9781646053667 (ebook)
Subjects: LCSH: Ross, Tom, 1957---Family--Fiction. | Franklin
   family--Fiction. | LCGFT: Autobiographical fiction. | Novels.
Classification: LCC PS3618.O84694 M57 2024 (print) | LCC PS3618.O84694
   (ebook) | DDC 813/.6--dc23/eng/20240805
LC record available at https://lccn.loc.gov/2024033013
LC ebook record available at https://lccn.loc.gov/2024033014

Cover art and design byJen Blair
Interior Layout and Typesetting by KGT

For Patti, who watches over me.

CONTENTS

All In Good Time, My Pretty

Rain could stand sitting up front when she rode with him. She could even take a look out her window on and off here and there and not get that dizzy sick feeling. It's not like the one you get just before you fall down, she thought. It's more like being sucked down from the inside out into a big hole somewhere. More like getting sucked out of herself by the world flying through her eyes and she could not stop it. Motion sickness, vertigo, Mother so-called it, but she called it sick and tired of commotion, and she was sick of that too. But when she was riding with Zorro Casanova, one of the things she admired most about him was how he was so steady and easy behind the wheel. She could snuggle up close beside him and lay her head on his shoulder and somehow then it didn't get so bad. But then again, there was the sight of this one thing that they always passed right then. That sign. As they approached it like always she read intently, lingering as though it were filled with words, too many words to capture at a glance, a dangerous distraction for drivers on that precarious stretch of highway running beside the ice-bound river, precarious too for her because like always she could feel that terrible suction feeling coming again from all the other blurry stuff around it rushing past to sneak in around the corners of her eyes as she read, and she held his hand even tighter and wanted to look away, but already it was too late. Because the sign held not only words, but a picture. A picture with three simple words, one  naming the ground on which it stood and two announcing its welcome to travelers. Words framing three maned heads poised in silent confirmation, keeping watch from a realm beyond that portal over an ever-receding future, staking their persistent claim on memory. Words which her whole life long had held her passing vision just long enough to let them leap through her eyes into the upended space behind them, leading in their wake all their kindred, prancing in thereafter. Besides what she had heard and could not quite remember, she was certain that for the town to have been given such a name there must have been a once upon a time when there must have been more. Even more than all those once counted on that trail lined in defiant fashion with the bleached skulls of the exhausted pack-bearers which General John Sullivan had, after marching across that ancient flood plain to lay waste the longhouses and fields of the Haudenosaunee, summarily laid to rest.

But it wasn't just those pitiful lost ones even way back in the old days, she was certain. Sometime once it must have been so, that there must have been not just a herd but a gang of mad wild horses, that they must have been running everywhere they wanted to run then, that they must have run wild and were never roped, never broken, never ridden nor spurred nor laid to rest then, a mad gang wild and running just because they loved to run and play and chase after one another wherever they pleased. And she dreamed sometimes of how they must have danced and pranced over the plain which cradled the river running from time immemorial through the valley, the river which its first, ancient children had named Chemung. That plain now shattered by the highway called 17 East and West, subtending the arc of the sun in its miles of asphalt, into which nothing could ever grow and onto which no living thing could ever venture without being struck dead and ripped into a bloody heap beneath the wheels of cars and trucks racing ever faster to their fleeting destinations, whose drivers and passengers grew ever more indifferent to the fact of that ancient lowland, to the blurring hacked green of the passing mountainside, to the clumps of poisoned weeds crowding the guard rails, to the sound and sight and fragrance of the river to which the horses had once come down to drink now ever more suffocated and muted, indifferent to the blood-red sunset staining their faces and drenching the horizon of the winter sky. And from this ancient trail gone berserk branched the thoroughfare named 14 North, onto which they had then turned through the first traces of an evening's falling snow to enter the quiet streets of the town. And all the wild horses cavorting through her head stirred up a sparkle in her eyes which she noted, to her secret delight, in the rearview mirror when she discovered her absent face there, and that cute hightop hairdo Pearl had done up for her, just for him. And precisely then she wanted to keep them and the secret delight which they unfailingly brought to her safe from harm. To shelter them so carefully and cautiously that no one not even this presently attractive one could ever enter in to strike them dead or break them or take them away from her, just as this or that one had taken so many of the few small things which she had ever delighted in away from her, to keep them hidden so carefully that they would never know, and for the sake of that secret delight she would pretend not to care. Yes, Lord knows Pearl had been right all along when she'd told her and told her, Listen dunderhead, she said, sometimes the worst thing to do about anything is to care. Yes, Lord knows, she was certain, if He would only admit it once in a while.

He pulled into the parking lot, at the same spot as the first time, right in front of the door. They were nearly in the dark there, lit only by a streetlamp that had just switched on back out by the road. A dark, out of sight, out back kind of place, she thought again, like one of them way-out places where folks too crazy for each other go and rendezvous and park to do all that stuff they can never let on about in broad daylight. Now she knew all about that too. A place where no girl with a lick of sense is supposed to be at night, but come to find out of course some crazy girl always winds up there because she's hardheaded or entirely too curious anyway, and so then walking alone out there out of sight all at once she feels a hand from behind touching her shoulder and then, talk about what killed the cat. Crazy and hardheaded, she thought, sounds like me. But looking up over the office roof she could see that that motel sign was one of those flashing neon types, with nothing pretty on it like wild horses, it was actually one of those tall arrow types, funny she hadn't noticed the first time, it was kinda like those ones she'd seen on Sunset Boulevard in her favorite sneak-to, Confidential-type movie shows, the ones where the light keeps jumping from the top down to the point at the bottom, kinda like a thermometer cooling off in a hurry, but this one looked like it kept pointing straight to them and broadcasting to the whole town that she was here so it felt like here she was, putting her business in the street. And she figured she was already bound for trouble by the time she got back home, at which time would be scandalous, so Mother like always would keep on saying to Father, Scandalous till he got tired of hearing it and then he'd start in preaching, and then the both of them would jump on her like white on rice and never finish with it till she wound up in jail in my room, till she felt like what business did she have even wanting to stay alive and she could almost kill herself if she could find a way to get it over with quick and that didn't hurt too much. They acted like she'd been painting the town red all that time, she wished. But that was already then and she was sure it was different now like she kept telling herself, since she'd already decided once and for all that, whether same or different, that's right, who cares. But just what that business of hers was going to be that night, well she was thinking very hard about it, maybe too hard about it, so she guessed she wasn't sure, or if she would be sure any time soon, time, not that she ever had much of that.

They sat still together in the shadows without exchanging glances, watching the falling snow dust the windshield, leaving silent that small space between them which they had so often before filled with small talk and laughter. Just for something to do she buttoned up her coat, and at last mustered a comment.

Bet it's still like an icebox in there, she said.

No ice. He fix it good, Zorro said.

We'll see about that, she said,

knowing well to keep track of his face, shapeshifting with each gesture propping up his halting speech, appearing and disappearing like the moon into the dark.

Ok, vámonos, he answered, waving a hand.

Like I said before, it's not nice like the Red Jacket.

For me, is good. Nobody know, nobody bother me.

He jumped from the car quickly, like he was tired of hearing about it, but then walked around to open her door. That was one of the things she admired about him, that he was a gentleman. So, nobody else knows it? Shoot, that's only what he thinks, Mister All-Star. He's sure known for that, you're darn tootin', he ought to at least realize that, maybe he's already one of them *personalities*, come to think of it, she thought. Of course, lots of folks around there and all over Elmira where his first place was and over in Big Flats and Corning too, they recognized him even behind those sunglasses, and especially once he opened his mouth and talked for more than a hot second. And they'd be proud just like she was to say they could pick him out of the crowd, because they were his fans, on account of all the wonderful miracles and such he'd performed that summer out on the diamond, like the papers call it, stealing home base and knocking in runs and all that stuff. Tell the truth that's how come he found a way to stay here off-season and got himself that night shift job and find a poor old room like this one just a hop, skip, and a jump from the stadium in the first place, because folks around did know, and why they'd had time to go steady and practically fall for each other. And folks liked to have somebody around that they could be proud of just like she was. Shoot, he's practically a local yokel if you think about it, she explained to Jenny. Fine, if you must say so, she answered, like she couldn't be bothered to think about it, but maybe she might be jealous too. Even if he is a foreigner, he's A good example, like Father says, Good for them and good for us, and that's just how she saw it too. He is kind of a little famous, she mused with satisfaction, whether he knows it or not, even though she kinda liked him from the start for not or pretending not to know who he was even after they put his picture in the *Star-Gazette* and all, still he ought to be grateful for it, and for her whatchamacallit, affection, well at least that's what she thought she was feeling, if she could spell a word on it.

They went in, she hurrying in first. Right away she sat down in the chair by the window, he at the foot of the bed. Both sat there with not a word for the other for a while once again, but were nonetheless drawn helplessly to cast sidelong glances at one another, then turn away. Certainly not at all like their last time here, she recalled, when right off they just jumped on each other and everything after that had happened so fast. Recalling for a moment the excitement of those hours, his face came into her eyes as he had looked to her then. The light brown razor-bumped skin, still pimply here and there, not so long ago worse like hers, but with those baby wide eyes and that adorable nose cut like a perfect slice of spice cake, and that high forehead with that soft half-good hair looking down on it, all fuzzy around its edges and floating ghostly in the dark. She smiled a little, until it faded with the memory. She noticed the hands on the nightstand clock starting in to glow a little. Tick, tick, tick. Seven-thirty. She unbuttoned her coat, happy to let in the heat. She could still taste that chili dog, well the two she'd eaten at the diner, so she felt like she needed to, anyhow she ought to, go back in the bathroom and wash her mouth out, not with soap, but, you know, never mind. He bent down to unlace his boots, Which doesn't bother me none, she thought. But as the mentholated scent of foot powder and unbound sweat rose between them she remembered how the last time before she'd been overjoyed to find, after jumping, that doing it was like falling, but not like really falling but more like drifting down slowly and gently like a falling leaf, to settle down onto his lap, to draw tightly against him, to breathe his atmosphere, to at last reach his tingling surface, her hands and feet and limbs and everywhere touching pressing to discover a delight like a secret kept from her that she'd never known, Like a thermometer heating up in a hurry, she laughed, surprised by merriment once again. Guess even I can get a clever notion once in a blue moon, she thought. And when she'd at last done away with herself, she recalled happily, it had been quick, it had not hurt too much. Aw shucks, here you are again, might as well go on ahead and get comfortable, she told herself, that's easy enough. One of the things she admired most about him was, he sure was a pretty man, all over. But still, here he was, in a shabby place like this. With different ways how she could look at it. A shabby room with a pretty man stuck in it. A pretty man stuck in a shabby room. The room, all around him. Him, in the room. Pretty, shabby, shabby, pretty. Stuck. Back and forth, both ways she could look at it, with two feelings, the same but different. Funny how you can look at everything, she thought, and still not find the answer. And what about me here too, what about that feeling of me. In his mind, does he keep me in the pretty part, or do I get stuck in the shabby part, or maybe I'm from the part that hangs around the edges, the part that's dust-heaped and seldom cleaned, it's back all up underneath and behind where the cockroaches crawl and the spiders spin and where you find all the rest of them nasty critters you can't stand getting on you, where all them lost ticket stubs and phone numbers and fancy earrings which your hired snoops come and rummage up to seal the fate of the guilty lay in wait, unnoticed, hopeful of discovery, it's out at the edge of the shadows pressing in against the face of the clock, it's frightened to notice the passing time, it's dumbfounded to find itself in the light, but then again it knows very well what it's hungry for, what it's hunting after, knows why it's not anywhere but here, at last. Oh why can't I just keep that little old part of me out of it, she thought, like Pearl says, and do like the smart girls do who go on and keep doing it again and again and forget the last man before the next and just have themselves a good time because they know better. But then she looked into his handsome tired face and his eyes cast down to no place in particular and she saw he was sick of it again, them sick-of-it moods he'd get in sometimes from looking around but finding nowhere but the same place every time so far from home, and she longed to find him some kind of quiet little corner of the world where he could put his feet up and rest and she would be near and sweet and tender to him and calm his nervous mind. Folding her hands in her lap, she looked away. Cause maybe the answer is, I can't, she worried, cause I'm too stupid to know how or something else is wrong with me, I can't.

He got up and went to the window. Looked out into the empty lot then back toward the office neon sign, its rosary of lights leaping spastically into the dark. Then closed the drapes and turned on the nightstand lamp and sat back down at the end of the bed. His bony hands crossed the distance between them to clasp her own.

Buenas tardes, linda, he said with a smile,

She shook him off. As much as she wanted to, this time she wasn't going to put up with it. Not so fast, not so easy.

No buenos, I'm mad with you, she said.

Mad, one more time, por qué? he replied.

She sprang from the chair to the bed beside him, pushing him onto his back. Easy to push around now, she thought. He lay limp and still, his dark eyes wide and staring into her face.

Last week I still wanted you to be my Valentine, but you flew the coop. Cause maybe you're just plain old chicken. Least you should remember what a little old Valentine is, cause I told you all about it, she said,

lifting her pointing fingers together to trace in the air before her, first parting ways to arch and fall and, once fallen, join once again.

BE MINE, she cried, stabbing her heart. Mine, it could have been you.

Maybe, I forget.

Wasn't just I forget, you think I don't know where you went?

Yes you know. I fly to Miami, I told you he said.

You sure told me, called from the airport, she replied,
giving him an itsy-bitsy tap upside the head and thereby surprising
herself yet again,

Coño, man! he muttered, flinching back,
some kind of bad cuss word which she'd never wanted to know what
it meant. But that's another thing she admired about him, he never
cussed in American words.

You better tell all or I'll give you something to whine about,
she answered, not saying what she really would have wanted to say,
which was nothing at all, but could not. Not doing what she really
wanted to do, which was to give herself to him carelessly, pretending not to be even the least little bit frightened like any smart
girl in the know who's getting no more and no less than what she
wants, just as she'd done the last time before. To drift down slowly
and gently, like a falling leaf, into his atmosphere, to give herself to
his hands and mouth until the whole world passed over her like a
wave instantly taking her breath away and laying her to rest without hurting anymore, until overtaken by that secret delight whose
name she could not bear the shame to utter but which filled her
up everywhere like the prancing and rearing of wild horses never
broken, never laid to rest. No, she thought, they can't take that
away from me.

And who, pray tell, did you run to see down there?
she asked, almost whispering, as if frightened that her words might
be heard, and frightened, yes, of the answer.

Mi gente, mis amigos. Es mi vida. Life, you know? he said,
rolling over to face her once again.

See what you've done? Rain scolded herself. Thought it was real not a movie. That someday he'd take you back to his own Special Island. That someday you'd ride the *Queen Elizabeth* down to his old hometown Havana and cruise on into the harbor, and all them tall dark handsome fishermen would come out in their boats to meet us. That even whatshisname General Fidel Castro would rush to the crowded pier to lead the celebration of the long-awaited return of their superhuman Shortstop. Thought you'd see more folks looking like you in one place than you'd ever seen before. That you'd have a chance to relax once in your life and start to straighten out your brain which has never worked right. You had all kind of sweet daydreams like that. Now what do you have? Stuck here Saturday night like waking up from a bad dream, with no Valentine.

And she understood then that her scolding had come home to roost, that now she must turn to face what had been in the back of her mind, not a secret which she had kept to herself but from herself, what sometimes when she least expected it would leap from its shadowed corners to run berserk and terrify her with doubt, what had lurked there from the beginning of their time together, from that Saturday afternoon at Dunn Field when she'd first looked mooning up into his handsome face as he sanctified her strayed baseball with his autograph, what she wanted to not be there and now here it was, sneaking up behind her like an unwelcome stranger tapping her on the shoulder.

Maybe I don't,
she answered nonetheless, pushing the words out from the shadows onto her lips.

Ok listen. Then somebody, like what you say, mi Valentine, he replied, very softly.

What's that? Say what? she said,

Not hearing even though actually she did hear it, Funny, she thought, wanting to hear him say this awfullest thing again. All she could think of and all that she could feel in that instant was that one of the things she admired most about him, all that she could bear to think of right then, was how much she loved the ways he found to say things, the way he could cobble up some small talk, because it wasn't some kind of broken English like mother and some picky folks called it, heavens no, it was unbroken and perfect like a song, a love song that said I can't find the words to tell you how much, and that's how she felt too. I see you've gone perfectly overboard for your Ricardo Montalban there, Jenny said, like it was some kind of joke, and one which she herself would never fall for, no not citified Jenny who'd, to hear her tell it, had never once had to play the fool, but it certainly was no kind of joke for her. And it made her feel not at all stupid then it made her get all hot and bothered and romantic sometimes then, just to get an ear full of his sweet mannish talk, she who had hardly ever said or been permitted or able to say what she wanted, who had tried and failed again and again to say even one stupid thing sometimes until she was shut up or got confused or short of breath. And that's one reason why she thought that they could be so good together, be looking out for each other and each day learn to speak better but still speaking in both their own special ways to the world, and especially in each special moment of each day together cobbling, cobbling up words in their own secret language that only they would speak to each other, delightedly together. That's why I say, she thought, he can be so quiet like just now, but boy, when he's determined to open his mouth for more than a hot second, Lord it can be such a hoot, always it's Delightful to my ears, that's just what and all and the only thing that she needed desperately that very instant, to hear him say it again no matter what it meant, and even no matter if it were funny or not, in that instant she would not and could not care.

En Miami, she is there, he answered. For a long time, es mi novia, mi enamorada. Maybe, mi Valentine, he said once again. And before she knew it, she felt the almost irresistible urge to act stupid just like she was afraid she couldn't help that she would. She wanted to cry and jump on top of him and kiss his face all over again and again and say Don't tell me who she is, or anything please don't, she would sigh, Just tell me you'll stay with me and just *BE MINE*, oh please stay. But not this time, not so fast she thought, catching her breath and gathering her gumption, she wasn't doing that stupid dramatic stuff anymore. This time she won't act like the foolish girls who'd got written up as *found dead* in the POLICE GAZETTE. She decided to get tough and smart right that instant, just like Pearl and her other girlfriends who knew how and kept poking her to go on ahead and just have fun without a care. So, she said

Well that's all right by me. I figured you'd run off sooner or later. Most likely you ran off to me from this Novia gal this so-called supposed to be old girlfriend or wife or whatever them mystery words I never heard come out of your mouth before now are supposed to mean. You know what?

she said, pointing and spitting out each word in the stupid broken way he would be sure to understand and that would make him feel stupid and broken like something that makes no sense just like she felt then,

You no good. No damn good.

Si, maybe no good, he replied faintly, looking away.

Boy, do I know how that whole deal goes she told herself, rehearsing all the jaded dignity of a woman of the world, but secretly fascinated in the midst of her humiliation, sensing in its dulling sameness a wild newness, tingling with the danger and wonder of a place she'd never been before. She looked out as she entered its first precincts, she watched as it grew like a sign unfolding into another picture in her mind, of a place taking the place of another at long last laid to rest, of the remnants of its exhausted time.

And by the way, for your information, she added, that's why I've been seeing somebody else myself, since even before you left to gallivant around *Mijami*. Because Mother didn't raise no fool, and I've been getting ready. And furthermore, he is my new Valentine

even though this was the first time it had ever occurred to her to think of him in quite that way.

So then why you came back with me tonight?

he asked, and with that rolled past her out of bed.

Soy cansado, I going for shower, he said,

stripping off sweater and shirt right in front of her, looking down at her with the slightest little half-tired smile on his face, like he knew she liked it, just as bold as he could be. She looked away, shaking her head.

Good for you, go on back in there then, she said.

He shrugged and headed for the tiny bathroom, but stopped and turned back at the door.

You come in with me again? he asked, again with that devil-may-care grin,

Fine for the devil, she thought.

Nice to relax, he said,

rolling his wide eyes toward the shower stall and turning away to leave her there.

She lay back across the bed, arms crossed tightly over her chest, head sinking into the pillow. With a pillowcase that probably hardly ever gets changed in a dump like this, she thought. She could still smell everything from the time before. The *Blue Magic* in her hair, her *Tabu*—entirely too much, her girlfriends said. And the at-first unfamiliar odor which she then recognized as the trace of her own self she had left behind. And his fancy *Club Man* after-shave with that top-hat dandy on the label, hinting of lemons and baby powder, That's why I call it *Baby Man*, she reminded herself, like I do him, more every day, in my mind. Now the cat's out the bag for keeps, she thought. Cause the other reason for that name, one which still even then made her feel brokenhearted though not much lately, was how he kept turning every time she'd turn around, from one back to the other. Such a curious critter, this so-called Casanova. Coming but going, appearing but, disappearing, somewhere but nowhere. Baby, Man, and both at once in between, who knows which or when. Very confusing and aggravating, ain't it? Yep, she answered herself. But shame on me, quite frankly, I was a push-over. This one's been quite clever, she thought, now that she saw the whole deal quite clearly, quite clever at getting what he wanted. Pushed her over with hardly a tiny tap, hardly a puff of air. Jumped on and got himself exactly what he wanted, never cared a hoot for the rest. It's the same old story, she thought, it's just like that one girl wrote in her True Confession, But you don't tell it till it happens to you. But soon that bed and all that she smelled and felt and remembered as she lay there upon it began to work on her. It felt more and more stupid every second to try to remember what was clearly what she should try to forget. She could no longer keep her arms crossed tightly over her breasts like a straitjacket, What for, she was starting to feel antsy and couldn't stand to lie there any longer and just had to get on up, so she did. Peering back into the bathroom she saw that he'd disappeared behind the half-open door, gone to the beat-up medicine cabinet and rust-stained, leaking sink. She heard the creak of the opening cabinet, which tried her nerves because she knew good and well that the mirror on there, right in front of where he was standing and probably looking himself over in it, Mister Pretty Boy Rotten Tramp, always stuck on himself she thought, that the mirror on there was cracked, and it bothered her every time she'd come here and had to go in there and then had to notice it, patched together with tape which had already yellowed and started to work loose, which the last time she looked was ready to let go of the corner that had held it there for who knows how long, like a hand steadfastly cradling its fragile burden through long years. But now, exhausted from its relentless efforts and daunted to be utterly taken for granted, it would soon give way and the glass would tumble down to shatter in the sink and scatter, of course, everywhere, and couldn't ever be put back together again. It especially bothered her to imagine that, because it wasn't just glass, but a mirror which, if that happened it could be awful because maybe it was true that it was terribly bad luck to be involved with breaking a mirror or even to look into one broken, she wondered if maybe not only now but sometime long ago she'd been mixed up, and not even known it or forgotten about it, with a broken looking-glass, and that that explained all her rotten luck and misfortune, not just for seven years but since forever, At least my forever so far, she thought. But Mother had often warned her that such a belief is only superstition, a Worldly Seduction were the fancy words she called it, which anyone truly faithful would pray for and receive the strength to resist, she insisted. Because in the end there is, Mother added, smiling sweetly like she was supposed to believe that she was feeling so nice and sweet toward her for a change, Yeah right, in the end there is, Mother explained, only the acknowledgment that so many things in life, For instance why, since you ask, it seems like folks who lie and steal and cheat and murder, why the Lord does not lift up his hand to *smite them* like in the old days anymore, Since you asked, why not only are they never really punished or made to really pay for their rottenness, That's a real word, right? but instead they get away without a scratch, they keep on getting more and more in life while most of the rest of us keep on losing what little we've got. So that's why, Mother, she went on, she could really understand, she thought, thinking that she would be proud of her finally understanding that one Bible verse after all her life before being an idiot, of her knowing why the Lord said that on the Mound because he had to admit, *To everyone who has, more will be given, but as for the one who has nothing, even what they have will be taken away.* But not only that, please Mother rescue me if I'm just confused as usual, not only do the rotten thrive and prosper but it is strictly required, It's not a request, it's the Lord's order, she reminded herself, also to forgive them for all the lying and stealing and cheating and laying waste and all other kind of rotten stuff they do and have done from the beginning and keep on doing, to just forget about it like none of it ever really happened, to believe that all them fine things in life they get from doing horrible things are what they look like, actually a blessing which proves that they aren't really horrible after all, to just snap your fingers and feel like Oh all that was the past, but this is now, stupid, there's nothing to be done, nothing to be set right. Yes, Daughter, she replied, there's nothing for a body to do but to let it be, to watch and pray, to know our place in this world which will one day pass away and leave all that mess in His hands, because really so many things in life not only lie beyond our power to make them different, not only those things she was troubled and asked about Mother said, but also how you're made in your whatchamacallit, makeup,

25

including what or who a body has no business, that *you* have no business wanting to be or to look like or to do in life, for better or worse, even beyond our understanding why, because all things seen by man are seen but dimly until revealed, It's the Lord's plan, a mystery to us all, Father says. So ever since then she figured that she never would and never even could understand, There's no understanding then she thought, really, no knowing, she had no place, no business knowing why she should get treated, no, dumped like garbage, this way, why there was nothing to feel but just lonely, excuse me, cheap and dirty, stuck in this little room, no in this filthy stinking hole, that might have been a bright and warm and cozy place, or at least a nicer place like the Red Jacket if he hadn't been such a cheapskate while saving up to run off behind her back to Miami, why there was nothing to be done, why all that she could do was cry, no go jump off into the deep end like a backwoods heifer, and why that's nothing more than stupid, the stupid crying of a stupid chubby pimple face gal who has no way on her own to get around in the cold and snow, to get back to get the awful she is certainly going to get when she gets home when even what little she has left will be snatched away. Funny, she thought, how you can look at everything in the world, and ask everything Please tell me what you are, and nothing ever answers, it all just keeps flying by faster and faster till you can't keep up, until you shut up asking let alone trying to say anything yourself, till you're sick again, sick to your guts of everything and of yourself going on Blah blah blah till you're short of breath, it's like a broken record. Sorry I asked.

She could hear him rustling and rummaging and running water in there. Maybe taking some of those strange roots and powders and potions he kept in little blue and red and brown bottles and matchboxes there, a fresh dose sent every month from his mother to keep him healthy, he had said. But maybe it's just super-stitious stuff after all, she suspected, because no good Christian would have treated her like he was then, or like he had turned out to be doing all along, like it was some kind of joke, Funny for him but not for me, she thought, this was not the kind of fun her poking girlfriends meant. She heard his belt buckle jingling open and the rustle of his slacks as they slipped from his legs, which she didn't want to hear, and even to imagine it made her start to feel dizzy. It was like he knew it too, because right then he stepped out into view, unclothed, no, naked as a jaybird, well just like she'd seen it, him at last, and kept on seeing cause she couldn't stop looking, the last time before, once he had taken off his pants and folded them along the creases and laid them over the back of the chair, then lay down beside her and kissed her, his tongue pressing insistently like a delectable serpent against her lips until she opened her mouth to let it crawl inside her head, to drive her out of it, let it in. She looked away as he leaned out to see if she was watching, with that devil-may-care grin on his face again, and of course with that tight stomach rippling like water and broad chest and million-dollar legs and everything else of him just hanging out in plain sight there that had looked so different that last time before, Heavens no, I don't need to see that, she thought, and turned her back to him and sat down on the edge of the bed. She felt his bare footsteps coming up through the floor into her as he came over to stand behind her, felt his hands come to rest on her shoulders. And though those hands lingered there as tenderly as they often had before, she felt that they now held something quite different from before. No longer that old unadulterated tingle of excitement, she thought, Heavens no, now there's the trace, the taint, the current of the stranger, creep-ing within, the shadow of the hunter who stalks wayward girls out alone in out of sight, out back places, the one who approaches unseen, unheard, the one whose face is glimpsed dimly, darkly, the one who strikes without a moment's notice. Another worm in the apple, she thought. Sweet on, with a rotten tramp trick stuck in it. Rotten trick hid inside some kind of supposed-to-be sweetness, like I'm supposed to believe he's all of sudden acting so nice and sweet on me for real, she thought, like he must do with his little Novie Chickadee down there, yeah right. Rotten, sweet, sweet, rotten, makes me sick.

Perdón. I, he said, I sorry,
like he was sorry he was too damn stupid to explain,
I, perdón.
She held very still, waiting for him and for everything to stop, not giving the least little sign or signal, she could hear the breath drifting from his still-open stupid mouth, unable to cobble further words fit to speak. But as for me, she thought suddenly, I'm ready.

Sorry? What for? she heard herself reply quietly, I don't need you to be sorry about a thing, she said,
Like they say, it was fun while it lasted, she thought, ain't that the truth. She smiled to herself, delighted to think that she'd turned out to be so smart, so tough, so careless, after all. And the sickness in her stomach she'd felt all that evening seemed to break in the midst of the deep breath she took. Waves breaking with each breath taken until, giving way, it dissolved, melting and falling away from her like the tears she tasted running over her lips, draining from her head and limbs and belly like water from a broken bucket, whirlpooling through legs down to feet and out of her to sink into the floor beneath them and then beyond, down to the dark steadfast center of the earth. And as it left her, she returned by slow degrees to herself, descending into her own atmosphere, revisiting long-untenanted

nooks and hiding places, filling up the empty space inside herself, like one once lost, returning from a time she had never before remembered.

But it's not really the good old earth, she thought, it's this nasty old linoleum, Girl it's about time you get back in them shoes she thought, so she stood up and went back to the chair and put on her dear fur-trimmed red boots, delighted to feel the coolness at first surrounding her feet inside them getting warm as she stood up and then stood still there, pressing her feet into the floor. It seemed to her that for the first time since forever that she stood firmly upright, like that first time she had felt herself certain of that narrow steel edge upon which she had glided in her new skates over the school-yard ice, neither held up by another nor staggering nor short of breath, knowing her place there on top of her own feet, keeping her own feet her own self after all, sufficient at last. She heard the water streaming down and splashing and draining out and suddenly recalled that this was not the sound of her miraculous release, but that he had gone on into the shower. At once she turned around to watch him there, not caring what she might see of his figure, blurred and fragmented behind the curtain, a shape shifting under the light like a restless ghost, softly singing his habitual shower-song, but tonight with, yes, incomprehensible words, and to an unfamiliar wonderful melody, that made her sad to listen,

    Son de la loma

    Y cantan en el llano

    Mamá ellos son de la loma

    Mamá ellos cantan en el llano

She couldn't help herself. She looked hard at the curtain, yes in a way trying to look through it, to follow those blurred shapes as they moved and yes, to fill in the details, bring them back to the land of the living, to familiarity. Those arms ruffling like wings to soap down the tautly muscled chest with skin so soft and hairless just like a girl's, the round bump pressing against the curtain when he bent over to pick up the soap he'd dropped, and what part that lovely bump was. Shameless, Mother would cry if she could see her, she was sure of that, but Who cares, she thought, she can't see me now, and she would go ahead and get both her eyes full, cause now it didn't faze her one way or the other, now she was, what-chamacallit, detached. Just like her next-door neighbor and wish-she-really-was-my big sister, Petra Koch (alias Mother Superior, or sometimes invoked in whispers over cokes and phosphates in Sugar Bowl booths by starry-eyed timid admirers as first ever in the Valley to get a 100 on the Regents and best figure skater in two counties to boot, or by envious or upright citizens as The Notorious Pearl) says, sooner or later, whenever she tells her battle stories that make Favorite Little Sister here and the other girls blush. But this here Sister's too big to be blushing anymore, she thought, not even if she comes out with that C word or that P word, or even worst of all that F word. That one's the worst of all cause it's not just a nasty way to call certain body parts like those other words, it's calling what you do with somebody, but it's not even how it ought to be, so they say, when you do do it, shouldn't be like what you can see dogs doing in the middle of the street, that it should be another way called something else with some other nicer or fancier word for it you know, but never that word, FUCK, so there, I said it, and maybe it's not the first time she thought, that's for me to know and for them to find out, but in fact folks say nobody should ever do what that word really means with somebody who's not there, that's a no-no, even though they still do anyway. Anyway, that Pearl, she thought, for-tified to recall her inspiration and shaking her head with a smile, she's just as terrible as she can be, always ready to bust right out loud or just matter-of-factly with them C, P, F words at the drop of a hat. Notwithstanding there, that is, all of them listening, shame and delight in hearing them, stirred to such transports of shameful delight that none among them would ever dream of snitching on their beloved MOTHER SUPERIOR, or of their Saturday afternoons lounging around her as she reclined across her bed beneath her framed HOLY OF HOLIES (a dog-eared poster of Miss Dietrich as Lola Lola, reclining on her barrel center stage in Pearl's favorite old-time movie which she woke them up one sleepover night to sneak-watch on the *Late Late Show*— her sole keepsake from the glorious days of Berlin before the dark days fell, the one thing her widowed *Mutti* had been able to recover from the rubble of their bombed-out family *Altbau,* on the same day that Barney, the brave American sergeant, had rescued her from the thieves seizing the heel of stale bread she had purchased for her toddling daughter with *Oma's* bridal necklace), catechizing her timid proteges in the rites of self-preservation and self-indulgence. Green eyes alight with mischief, she'd grin at the sight of their wide-eyed faces or beg *Oh spare me* in a husky whisper from a scandalized moan or scat-sing some old-time show tune no one's ever heard or cobble up a snippet all her own on the spot like she could with her perfect pitch, one grace among others which they'd had to hear gush about, like her exquisite hands and on and on that Mother and others were all the time praising her for till she blushed and couldn't stand to hear another word. But blush was one thing she never did when reporting for instance I *als ich fickte* his brains out, she'd begin, then regale them with mouth-opening details of nights she'd lived through in some motel or faculty flat with some Tom Dick or Harry or Real He-Man from such and such never-to-be-named town or institution of higher learning but never hometown, or the next one after him or the same him one more time until she tired of him too, like Finally he proved he was trash when he told me to jump in the back seat, and so on. And how sometimes smack dab in the middle of it all she'd wind up Utterly Bored, *die arme Mädchen*! Feeling everything but at the same time almost not feeling, almost not remembering a thing, as if she were watching herself go through the motions and carry on like it was somebody else and she wasn't there, like when she'd float up in the air to Look down like a fly on the wall from where the whole show looked so corny and useless that I could've died from the sight, I certainly declare. Sometimes it gets so bad that to make myself laugh I make Loud Moaning Sounds No Sane Person Would Ever Make, which they of course brag about to their buddies after. Sounds? For instance? asked Gina Sindoni, eyes wide with instigation. Like this! cries our Holy Mother ... and there she goes, and we almost pee our pants half from laughing and half from terrified to wake the neighbors, and there we are all in one place, going hysterical.

But don't you care that everybody knows? demanded her gathered novitiates, to which she asked in return, *For what?* Caring not a hoot who thought the worst of her, *What else is new?* or if none of the boys in town respected her now, *Who never have,* or if all those married louses and sad old geezers make passes at her when nobody's looking. Listen up, Daughters. Like Barney, my once *lieber Vater,* she says, I've walked through this valley of the shadow of death from one end to the other, and what dropped dead, and I left behind was that monkey on my back that still cared. So ever since Daddy kicked me out of heaven into the garage loft, I've been Faithfully Careless of course. Let's begin with some PRECEPTS, BY WAY OF EXAMPLE. And Rain was ravished by the sad sparkle in her eyes like the sunshine that she said shows up to flim-flam you after the rain, and adored the brazen tilt of her head, and it positively took her breath away when she'd puff a good riddance kiss just like Saint Marlene would to her latest Brainless Wonder, and almost wept from thankfulness to watch her long limbs twining along the sofa in her fitful laughter, and with such loving inspiration was quite certain of her answer to *What's a girl to do?* Well if our Mother Superior can do all that, she thought, so can I, except shoot I don't need to float in no outer space or crawl up no walls, I can stand right here, cause none of this is gonna faze me, I can look straight all up in there right at that rotten mush-mouth, look dead at him like he ain't nothing not even a true human body but some kind of piece of meat, which anyway really's just what all he is, since he doesn't know how to treat anybody decent anyhow, especially a stupid girl like I was before the last time I came here she thought, recalling how she'd get dizzy and Start wishing I could be a wild horse which was stupid too cause I'm a human girl and don't need four feet to stand up but only two, stupid like I was before when he could get away with murder, but now I'm *stupid like a fox*. Just listen to him in there she thought, singing some silly song like he's king of the world, like somebody wants to hear all that mess, all that stuff nobody with a lick of sense would even try to understand, because half the time they all talk so fast anybody'd have to wonder if they even understand each other, and it's positively rude to do that when he's nothing but a guest here in my country besides. And she babbled some more random sounds to herself that probably weren't any kind of words at all, that sounded more like some kind of wild animal trying to talk even though it doesn't know it, to remind herself what he sounded like until she got scared that she might be getting too loud, They all talk a blue streak like that and half the time don't make a lick of sense, she

33

concluded, at least most folks don't believe they do. Come to think of it, that's one other thing she hated about him a lot of times, that half the time he'd deliberately start talking in *Espanyol* just to cut her out of the conversation, just to make her feel even more stupid than she did most of the time, and she had a sneaking suspicion which she was sure about now that he was even cursing her out sometimes just for kicks, Yeah I get a kick out of you too. Damn nasty mushmouth, ain't no kind of decent human just a piece of meat, shoot so I can stand up here and lick my lips like there's nothing behind that curtain but something to eat and have myself a time. I'll show you detached, she thought, cause if I don't get up out of here soon I just might catch my appetite and who knows what I could do then. I just might go off the deep end like them crazy folks in them whatchamacallit, mass murder stories, except it won't be mass this time, just exactly one. I just might act like the whatchamacallit walking dead, like them zombies folks say sleep up in that graveyard. Cept I won't be sleepin', I'll be creepin'. Sneak up in there like that PSYCHO man did on poor Janet Lee and look out then, forget about some big old butcher knife and scary music, I ain't got no need for all that cause I'll just go berserk and jump up on him in there and start in to bite off and chew and swallow. Betcha he'll get sorry quick then, beg me to turn him loose. Ha! Soap Gets In Your Eyes don't it? But too late for sorry now. *Mira* hold still while I get another good taste, she thought, and laughed and laughed. But she reached up to touch her face and found out she'd been crying like a fool the whole time anyway, and that's when she decided that the most careless thing she could possibly do was to leave, put one foot in front of the other and walk out that door and make a clean getaway.

Quietly, so quietly that she heard only the rustling of her scarf and filling coat sleeves, of her fingers closing buttons, of her breathing, hearing only that gnat-swarm of nameless sounds marking the incessant collisions of the human body with the torrent of objects coursing through the world, sounds which are given only to oneself to detect at the edge of silence and, just as what the body itself is and what it is not, just as incomprehensible words running into one ear and out of the other, come into being and pass away unremembered. Well except when, she thought, but such exception is hardly at issue at this moment, she thought, in fact It's all kinda rather over, she mused, with an intimation of elegance, slipping into her hat and gloves while glancing backward again to the shower stall to find that ghostly figure still softly singing that unfamiliar melody under the falling water. He's taking his sweet time in there as usual, though it's all quite unusual, she thought, then turned back to press the curtain aside and peer from the window into the parking lot, into the darkness covering the blanket of new-fallen snow, and the spark of neon light flashing through it like the trace of an invisible creature darting over the bottom of the sea, and the distant streetlamp like an unfamiliar star offering only uncertain direction, and the headlights of passing cars impotent to reveal what lies unseen within the distance to cross quickly, out alone. She tiptoed to the door, stretched out her gloved hand to unhook the chain, then grasped the knob, turning, turning, And no fingerprints, how about that, she thought, but it's not because I'm the one who's done wrong, I've made up my mind about that, she thought, even though she wondered then for a moment why she would have to make up her mind about that at all. But I've got to be quick about it, she thought, get the heck out and shut the door behind me before I let in a draft, and get across that parking lot in a hurry, without slipping on the ice. For she knew very well what such moments demanded from the true stories she'd read about foolish girls out alone who had nearly fallen into the clutches of maniacs, girls who had come to their senses in a nick of time before the terrible worst that could have happened, who had had the inexplicable good fortune to be granted rescue by divine intervention or to discover a way out of danger. And from the too many other horrible stories she knew equally well, how in the spine-tingling parts, the parts she could hardly finish reading except they were so exciting, what happens to the victims it's because of the tiny little details, the ones you wouldn't even notice most of the time and probably couldn't even keep track of, especially if you're scared to death, the ones your Dick Tracy's and County Corners find to take pictures of after they draw that chalk line around what they find left of you, knew that these other girls didn't make it out alive precisely because of that tiny little something that didn't go their way, Oh please don't let me mess up, she thought. But it would be just like her all the time rotten luck to get out there and slip and fall, and that would be the one little detail that would be her downfall, yes, while she was running like crazy trying to get away she would slip and fall and not be able to get up, inexplicably, just like the girls in them monster pictures when they fall, not hurt enough to be crippled but the hurt reminds them how exhausted they are from screaming their heads off and running for longer and faster and farther than they ever ran before and still not a soul has heard or comes to the rescue, so they give up because they can't go on and you think No it just can't be, you holler Get up you stupid fool, don't just sit there crying, in a daze, you know what's coming around the bend. She pressed against the door to push it open, just enough for Chubby here to squeeze through, she thought, slipped out into the evening chill and shut it gently but firmly behind her, then fell back to stop still there, suddenly exhausted, not yet daring to make way. *Feet, don't fail me now,* she breathed deeply and thought, But if they do then I'll crawl away from this dump if I have to, just like every time with them same monster picture girls once they fall down they start to crawl even though you know they know they should get their behinds up and run but they just can't catch enough breath to even stand up and it's already too late, But it ain't too late for me just yet, she thought, No crawling, I'll jump into that old highway picture in my mind, I will stamp the cold ground with my hoofs and rear up like a mad wild horse, I will run with the river, all the way home. Shoot. Or not even home, she corrected herself, just run wild without guide or destination, just because I love to run and play, just run off to wherever on earth I please.

She heard the fresh snow crunch and grow compact underfoot, and felt the uneven, unyielding hardness coming after. I'll have to put on my skating legs, she thought, brightening with recollection, at least that's one thing I've got the know-how for. She moved along now, putting one foot in front of the other, recalling to comfort herself, with each careful footstep there in the dark, the light of winter mornings of days long before, when the sun climbed above the gabled schoolhouse rooftop into a cloudless sky and, glinting through the bare elms vaulting overhead, glowed like a streak of fire across the unblemished ice. Mornings of days long before she found out for sure, while reading those old Bible stories for Father, that words confused and troubled and would never come easily to her like they did to Mother, on those Sunday afternoons when she tried so hard to take her time and be careful with the GENESIS and then the PSALM but kept making stupid mistakes cause she couldn't help it, not only mispronouncing strange beautiful words like *Gilead* which she could also never remember the meaning for, but even messing up on the simple words which she kept turning around as she read, saying the one after before the one that should have been said before, like when she read it *I will awake myself early* even though she meant to read it right, *I myself will awake early*. Bass-ackwards, Mister Sonny Boy Fun-Maker calls it. She's got to read everything her special backwards way, not like the rest of us, Mother agreed quickly, sucking her teeth. Now that's enough, Father said. But when he stopped her again halfway through the verse and for the last time, and she saw the distance veiling his eyes as he drew apart from her, flashing that delicate *maitre d'* smile he'd perfected through endured years of exhaustion, ill-mannerism, and acci-dent, an arabesque with which he hoped to fix himself there for her despite his disappointment, but which proved once again a failing anchorage in the face of Mother's gesture of infallible disgust, that glaring look with the sharp sound she'd make that folks always think sounds like *Tisk tisk*, oh quite refined they automatically think, but for her Oh no, it's wasn't like some kind of high and proper English whatchamacallit which they always have to go behind and spell dif-ferent from our good old U.S.A. word for it, it always sounded to her like spitting, a spitting meant to hit her. Tsk, Tsk she'd say, if you can call that saying, but to her it was more like noises nobody with a lick of sense would even try and understand to be words, first she'd suck her teeth and then take a drag on that cigarette and then blow the smoke hard at her, that smoke that was to her mind really spit too, a kinda sneaky signifying way to spit on her. And surely, even before those awful days she would start in to sing any old song she could just because then she could forget her miserable self a hot sec-ond, until Mother, For your own good she said, reminded her that she could not, could not even though she could try till she was blue in the face and nobody would be kind enough to tell her to stop, because all that trying would not change a thing because she could not carry a tune to save her life, and Seriously you need to stop humiliating herself she added, Rainie you may be but Ma Rainey you ain't, she said, let's face it, since she had no kind of voice worth hearing, not even worth just hearing herself, about all that half-tin ear she had, she threw in too, was good for was Honking on that clarinet which thank the Lord never has to be tuned, which had been a scandalous waste of good money anyway, she said, because there was only so far she was going with that too. And most definitely, long before she blew up without shooting up, that is to short and dumpy, her teeth rusting from an unceasing torrent of Dr Pepper and jellybeans, her face revolting into thickets of pimples which she could not resist spending lost hours squeezing until they coughed up their plugs and bled in misery, and to boot finding neither miraculous remedy nor MAGIC BLEACHING FORMULA discreetly hustled to the sisterhood of brown-paper-bagged despair in six-point type ads boxed into the back pages of 50-cent magazines which, once trusted, would not fail to rat her out for whitewashing the atrocity of her complexion. And quite clearly, long before she learned to take comfort in God's incomprehensible wisdom which blesses the rotten folks as they use up and lay waste to the good folks and all good things on earth and then hit their knees for a hot second and get saved before they kick the bucket so they all go to heaven in a little rowboat, before she learned that when the world outside her own head moved fast enough for a busy day it was too much for her to stand and made her sick of it and sick of herself and sick to her stomach, and way before she learned to go numb at the thought that getting lovey dovey and necking and smooching, not to mention the worst, were things that would probably never get done to her.

Yes, her footsteps recalled, it was long before those dark days, on those bright Saturday mornings under the bare winter trees, when she had so quickly learned to glide across the schoolyard rink on her brand-new skates, discovering there a certainty and grace she had never suspected in herself, a shy brown girl of nine promptly standing out from the rest, remaining nevertheless unseen but not yet knowing it, and also not knowing but already hoping that she too might be someone somebody remembers is there and is not nobody or nothing. But happily, she recalled, Petra Margarete Koch had already noticed her next-door neighbor, even though at age twelve our Pearl was already the most fabulous skater girl in town, one with no stake whatsoever in attending to a timid third grader. But how quickly, after flashing past and overhearing her cries neither of alarm nor dizziness but of delight, she had spun around to rejoin her! How deftly she had whirled around and between all the crowd to come back to her, how her blades had etched an urgent arc upon the face of the ice, how instantly she had appeared there before her and taken her arm in hers and led them on the round together. No falling for us! she cried to her new protégé and partner, another foolish lonely creature like herself. How they laughed together, two small show-offs, prancing and swerving like wild horses across a wasted plain, loving to run and play and chase after one another wherever they pleased, careless of the envious stares of their playmates, careless of the rancor of the crowd glaring in the unforeseen distance. Round and round they went, two fools rushing in where angels feared to tread, carrying on bravely across thin ice, outshining the sunlight on that cloudless winter morning, now only a fond memory, now devoured by the dark.

It was then that she heard in the distance the door she had closed, opening again behind her. She felt her body slowing to a stop, felt something tying her into knots, like something thrown into the spokes of a wheel, like something jumping up inside her and taking over. It's just like the Holy Ghost, she thought, how it jumps up like a shock inside folks when they're baptized and cut loose from the weight of their terrible sins that we're all supposed to forget they did from then on, or praying through long-suffered sorrows, how they fall out and start shakin' and twitchin' and talkin' a blue streak of angel-talk nobody can make head or tail of except maybe another one gone plumb crazy too and supposed to be whatchamacallit, interpreting the other, they can't help it. Because way back when she and Father (Mother, never) still went up to Elmira to the colored folks' church in that leaky upstairs dance hall back behind the projects, she remembered how she too had sometimes been grabbed by that current, even though she'd been too scared to let on she was feeling electrocuted, but she was certain, and even if most of them with all their monkeyshines and loud nonsense were Only cutting a hog to be seen, Mother says, acting just like white folks expect us to act, showing their behinds in the house of the Lord, Mother said, disgraceful. Even though I'm not particularly tore up over anything right now, especially not that rotten cheat, rotten tramp, she thought, half of her keeping on and the other half scared of the dark with half a notion to turn back to all that foolishness she'd just walked away from, And it sure ain't holy. Oh please not that again, sure enough I'm acting the fool now, she thought, but felt helpless to keep her head from twisting back, even though she longed to strike a careless pose, hands dipping into her pockets, chin thrown aloft in utter indifference to a swarm of flashing cameras like a temperamental starlet on the red carpet. But instead her head twisted around while the rest of her kept pointing forward and, looking over her shoulder across the gray distance, she found him standing there in the doorway, in the light from the room beyond, covered only with the towel wrapped around his waist, the steam rising from his open mouthed breath and his bare head and naked chest to dissolve into the dark. She saw his head turn and stop once his sharp, fielding eyes had sorted her out there in the distance. Both then stopped still there, she staring back into the light and he out into the dark, without gestures of concealment or surprise or beckoning, with neither cry, nor call, nor whistle to mar the silence. Just stupid, she thought, shivering down to her feet. After a while, after too long, after not deciding to keep going but just standing there shivering, she turned and kept on, now at a patient, steady pace. Don't look back, she warned herself, because with nowhere and no reason to run to quit all that was reason enough for now, Don't look back, because to stop running scared like those foolish girls who never get away was how to keep on moving, Don't look back, cause I know that the sight of my sweet backside rolling away on my red boots says *So long, baby. I don't care what you do.*

And in that very instant the perfect story to recall welled up from the dark into her mind's ear, the one that had always been to her the most frightening and most delightful of all, especially told the way her terribly bad big brother Sonny had told it once when Papa wasn't around to overhear. Dig it, Sis, here's how the whole deal went down way back when, he said. Once upon a time in Shit Town, there was this old cat, and his whole family, his main squeeze and two foxy daughters, they all worked for the Town Boss. Hell no not some clown of a Mayor I said The Boss. They worked their asses off and even though they got the short end of the stick a lot of times mostly they couldn't complain, even if they did what difference would it make anyway. But it came to pass that some rough hombrays from parts unknown moved in and took over the town and started to raise hell running their rackets and rubbing guys out and so on and made it even more of a shit town than ever. So this guy calls up the Boss in a panic he says Boss I don't know it's getting pretty rough down here in the valley. These bad hombrays what come in here have took over and ruint this town and now they got their beady eyes set on my wife and daughters. Well turn em out I guess, what else? *Turn out?* she asked. Think about it, you'll figure it out. Anyhow the Boss says What're whining to me for why don't' cha just rustle up a posse and ride in and take and string em up? Well I would have back in my better days the old guy says but I finally threwed my back out last year and also my poor feet hurt so bad these days I can hardly stand let alone stand up and fight and as for the rest I'm sorry to say that more than a few of my fella towns men are likewise out of commission Sir. Good thing you've helped remind me he says as I had almost forgot why I had given your town its name. But being as this is where it's at, I hear you definitely that's the pits but you know I got just the thing. I'll send my boys over in the morning just do what they say and you'll be all right. Next day crack of dawn two gangsters roll up to their front door in a pickup truck, layin' on the horn. Rise and shine knuckleheads driver says. So right quick they all come out and climb in the back and get hauled clear out of town, way out to the edge of the desert. The old cat stands up looks around every which way then he asks them, Where's this supposed to be? And one gangster answers, Where's it look like? Nowhere, says the old cat, and in that case I'm ready to call it a day, plus I think you guys owe us a round trip. You're thinking bass ackwards, pal, the other gangster says. You'd best forget your business back in town he says, it's time to run for your lives, starting here and now. Right about then the wife she sucks her teeth and gives the guy a look that could curdle buttermilk and says Now I know you're nuts. You think I'm gonna dump all my stuff I got back in the apartment and hit the road with nothing, like some tramp.

Mister, you got another thought coming she says. He just laughs. Go the hell back then, the first gangster says, so those so-called neighbors of yours will come out of their bubbles can rob you blind, jump your daughters' bones, knock you upside the head and bury you alive in your own backyard, which they will when we ain't there to protect you like we did last time. The old cat cuts her off quick before she gets started again. All right then, run to where? he says without batting an eyelash. The guy points way off to the mountain-top on the other side. Up there, that should be far enough. Wrong direction right back at ya, pal the old cat says, doin' some pointin' of his own, On these two tired dogs, I'll never make it. But how about that wide spot in the road down the way? It's a truck stop, see, and the missus and me, see, we hear they're hiring in our line, how about that? Finally the other guy throws his two cents in, he says Hey, that joint's where we stopped on the way in. The eats weren't all that bad, right? Good enough to keep down, I reckon, the other one says, then he eyeballs the sky a second. Well, I guess a guy's gotta make a living, he says. Ok, you can go pitch your tent down there, we'll spare that greasy wide spot and cut you a break. But make it fast. Which means, haul ass. So the old city slicker and his whole crew shove off in that old Chevy to their new life in the boondocks. He floors it nonstop all night and they reach the diner about sunrise and not a moment too soon, cause they barely had time to sit down at the counter and check the specials before they heard a big sound filling up the air like a hurricane and saw fire light up the sky, that's right. Cause first thing that morning the boys called in the Bosses' B-52's to nuke the whole stinking country. Of course then it was just like when we finally fixed the Japs, the city and all the lousy bastards in it were either blown to smithereens or burnt to a crisp or both. But wouldn't you know it, wifey there, knucklehead till the end, she runs out to look back just like they told her not to do it and, wham-o. Nobody ever knew for sure, but hey, whatever that dame saw scared her so far out of her wits that she flipped out and froze up like a mummy on the spot, and that's how she stayed, never moved a muscle or opened her trap to be a pain in the old man's or anyone else's ass again the rest of her miserable days. So the moral of the story is, DUCK AND COVER. And that means you, Amen. Even though he hated to go to church and every time Mother would drag him in there he'd jump up and run wild doing and saying whatever he'd please till the deacons got tired of putting him out and Father got tired of whipping him for it and he'd take off fishing instead, even though he was a wild man up in the house of the Lord she still loved to hear him tell those old Bible stories, because he told them better than any preacher she ever heard. She especially found such comfort in this one because at least this time the rotten folks get what's coming to them and get it good, which is so different from how it mostly is today in the world, but she didn't like, and to tell the truth found it horrifying, that the poor wife who, you could understand, must have been mortified to have to leave all her favorite outfits, shoes, jewelry, little doodads and whatchamacallit, gewgaws and such behind, when it takes forever to find and pay on the layaway plan for the fine quality flattering things that can help a girl to feel pretty, well even if only a woman can really appreciate how awful it is to have every silly precious whatnot that lightens your heart snatched away in life, she found it horrifying that she got paralyzed or flipped out or turned to stone or whatever for just doing what, anybody else with a lick of sense would do, The same I bet, she thought, if they overheard a hurricane blowing way out in the desert, if they happened to notice fire lighting up the sky. Maybe she was just curious, she said to him then, but he was having none of that, And that means you, Killjoy, he repeated, because Sonny Boy was perfectly happy with that story just the way he had told it, and that's because he's just plain terrible. Plain sinful, Father says But the truth of the matter, she keeps reminding him, is that he doesn't really mean to be sinful, mostly when he winds up sinning it's an accident. Anyway, if it had been me in the middle of all that commotion, she thought, Shoot, I'd be curious and, I'll admit it, I'd be rubbernecking over it too. All right then I'll admit I'm a knucklehead too, don't know what else to call stopping here in the middle of getting out of the cold in the middle of nowhere and away from a mushmouthed cheat, to look back for what, but I guess that's me, she confessed to herself. Guess if I stick around here too long I might just freeze up like she did, she thought, but instead of course I'd turn into a snowman. Or if I had my druthers, as she preferred to imagine under the circumstances, a snow woman. Frozen, but not into ice, frozen in rest. A snow woman, rolled up and packed into life in a child's adventure, gazing out through two coal eyes too tired to blink, breathless with a carrot nose too benumbed to sniff. And she'd have to have that ostrich-plume hat, the one that Grandmother wore in her first and last picture, the one she'd jumped from her bed and chased Father to the grave for filching, feathers ruffling, too tired to fly. A snow woman, too tired to kill joy or resurrect sorrow, resting to her heart's delight, careless of the enduring chill. But like Father says, No rest for the weary, and none for me now, she thought and, abandoning the proud resolution she'd made only minutes before to ignore the gangsters' advice, promptly started to run. And promptly thereafter, as legless as a snowman, keeping hope alive for the worst, she slipped and tumbled down.

She stared upward for a moment from the tangle of her limbs into the sky, where the ever-restless clouds opened to reveal the implacable stars. Looking herself over she noticed the tear in her stocking, and the bloody knee. Here I am, she thought, laughing to herself, on two left feet, and I'm the one who's supposed to can dance, out of my no-dancing family the only one, and look at me now. But I've had my little moments of glory, she thought. Wouldn't you know it, here I am going back to him in my mind, again. Back to that Saturday she went up to Elmira for the Pioneers' double-header. Hot as the dickens. By the end she was tired and felt like going home but he had run up to the bleachers straight from the dugout and took her hand and asked her to stay and wouldn't let go and nobody had ever given her that stray-puppy-dog look before and the very thought that somebody in the world could really be making eyes at her plain old messed up her mind, so she went on ahead with them with her fool self. They went back to their so-called fixed-up dump they stayed in back off Oak Street, him and his partners playing the field. They got there and she expected that they must have rooms upstairs in the house, but to her surprise they took her out back to the garage. So, why're we back here? she asked, scared to hear the answer and even more scared to wonder what if they don't answer, Am I finally in my own crime scene? she wondered, Will I live to tell? At least they went in through the side door. Is nuestra casa Zorro said. Please go ahead I prefer not to be a lady right now, she said. Zorro stepped in and pulled a long chain with a rabbit's foot on the end. ¡Pasa! he said. She looked in, and up to the hanging shop lights casting their fluorescent fog over the curtained emptiness, heard the drone of a fan coming out of the shadows. She didn't want to embarrass them but she had to ask about all the sheets waving on the clotheslines, If y'all hung all them up outside they'd dry faster, she cried. ¡Coño! he laughed, is no laundry, is how we make our own room. He pointed and turned in different directions, Aquí

Miguel, allí Jesus y Pedro, junto a la cocina yo,, like a talking weathervane. Reminds me of that movie about that spoiled rich girl and the reporter, she thought, when they're in that hobo motel and he hangs up the sheet between the beds. So what do I have on my mind? she wondered and moved along to other things there to think about. The rest was laid out like a living room and so-called kitchen, more like Mister Barney's workshop with a sink and stove in it, a beat up picnic table that looked like it had walked from Eldridge Park, and way in back the shower and that toilet which she'd soon be terrified to use. There she was one poor gal and nobody else knew she had run off with the four of them, still whooping and hollering and talking trash, since they'd won both games and sixty dollars to boot. Quite frankly she wasn't trying to hear all that, but one of the things she used to love hearing him talk about as best he could was, he sure could cook a thing or two, and each time after that when she'd come and he'd cook for her he'd point to each dish in the pot or on their plates and teach her them tasty new words that unlike others seemed to stick in her mind like glue, like ropa vieja and frijoles negros and such. And even on that first day, instead of breathing in the leaden traces of the disused junk that had once been heaped up in there, of the leakage from the run-down cars that had once been parked in there, with that stale sweat smell coming up in the heat and the other smells like over on that couch that had dropped down from her nose to the back of her throat so she tried not to guess what they could be of, she kept near the stove with him, kept her nose stuck up over the arroz con pollo, and watched the sweet corn he'd fixed just for her take forever to boil. After he got that much on the stove there was almost nothing left in that icebox except beer. But up in the cupboard they had every kind of rum and whiskey she'd never seen, on which they'd all started in on soon as they got through the door. First he poured some out the bottle onto the floor like it was the most proper thing you could possibly do, she was kinda shocked. Para los santos, he said. I'm scared I'll catch on by and by, she thought, checking around her feet. All three of them kept loud-talking and rough-housing and such, except for the third-base guy. Except for that shiny bald head he looked kinda like Frank Sinatra, sitting up at that picnic table mouthing nary a word. Sippin' from some kind of fancy flower vase which she thought at first Ugh, why in the world would he drink that nasty water, till he filled it up again from the bottle. And then to her surprise he asked her in nice plain English, Care for a round, Miss? She looked back at Zorro then answered, Thanks, but I prefer fine wines to hard liquor, but Zorro said Pero maybe you like esto, and he reached up in the cupboard and pulled down this bottle of yellow stuff. Looks just like a big old bottle of pee, she thought, with a fat worm laying down at the bottom of it. Only try it, he said, and poured her a glass, and just when she was about to take a drink she thought what if that thing crawled down your throat, but she took a taste anyway just to be polite, and boy she was sorry about that cause it tore her up quick and she had to run and grab a ginger ale, the last bottle left. And didn't they laugh at her then, including those three other gals who had just walked right in without a knock like they had the run of the joint and she could tell right off, no notion to even give her the time of day. They all gathered around the table waiting to eat and get pestered by the menfolk and right off took up all the places to sit, but she felt so catered to, almost like royalty, when he came out with folding chairs and set them side by side at one end, just for the two of them. Oh she was quite thrilled to be there. It felt like she'd suddenly stepped right onstage into a TV show, one she'd never seen but only heard about, like one of her girlfriends saying Oh boy that's my favorite show, you have to watch it, but still never having seen it until right now when she's suddenly in it, Almost like how it happens when somebody in the audience, she thought, you know the ones where folks always laugh at the same time right together, somebody gets picked out for something, and it's the cute smiley sparkly dressed-up girl in the front row, so they stop the show to do a commercial and a guy runs downstairs from up in the balcony, Hey you there, he shouts and it's the director, he smiles back at you and points with his big cigar, Please go on, sweetheart, get yourself up there, you're such a cute sparkly smiley girl and heavens to Betsy in such a flattering outfit, we want the whole viewing audience out there to see you, we're sure you're going to be a hit. Well, it must happen that way sometimes or else she couldn't be imagining it, she thought. So she sat down and crossed one leg over the other and smiled and perked her head to listen very carefully when any of them spoke, even to what she couldn't understand and stuff she didn't particularly care to understand. She made sure to laugh right along with them when they all laughed, even if she wasn't sure what was funny about anything right then, even though most times it was all but one of them laughing at the one not laughing, just like when the worm drink had torn her head up for a hot second, which she quite frankly had had a lot of experience of, being the unlucky person left that is, and was quite used to it, so she wondered when it would be her turn again. Two of them were colored girls too, who he said lived over in them Jones Court projects. They kept looking her up and down, Like some folks can't help but do, she thought. So who you? Ain't never seen you around here before, the busty brown skin one muttered, like a detective speaking out of the dark into a blinding light. Well I was invited to the party, so here I am, she replied, too politely. Her skinny redbone girlfriend grinned and nudged her in the side and said, She new on the block. And that scrawny redheaded white girl in a big Pioneers shirt and tight blue jeans, probably no more than fifteen, not paying them any particular mind, but she sure kept after that Bacardi and they sure helped her, poor thing. Then everybody sat down and ate up that good food, except it was too hot-peppery even for her who loved her Tabasco sauce, so they all had an excuse to drink up even more along with it, while the boys (except for him, which she was relieved about) talked dirty to the girls who talked dirty right back, along with all kind of slurping and lip smacking and burping and breaking wind out loud right there at the table without excusing themselves and footsy playing underneath it and such types of uncouth behavior till it wasn't funny. So what am I supposed to be doing here, she thought. But with one look into his soft brown eyes and persistent smile, which seemed to attach themselves to her every word and gesture, and the scary exciting way the project gals giving him the look-over kinda seemed to pick up on it too, How's that for new on the block, she almost said, but for the moment let her misgivings go by.

Of course they kept right on drinking and the other Cuban fellas put some of that whatchamacallit, *Machito* music on the hi-fi and kicked up their heels and the girls jumped right in. It looked like a big old mess to her, everybody dancing a different way, maybe the boys really did dance their own kind of step but what kind of step it was she had to wonder. Course the other gals certainly knew how to boogaloo and twist, hully-gully and jerk and all that but it looked to her like none of them really knew them Latin steps either, of course they still strutted around like they did even though she bet they hadn't been around any more than five minutes themselves, and the guys didn't give a hoot anyhow, just dragged them around squeezing and grinding all up against them and so forth, but none of them were feeling any pain by then either, not that they weren't the type to go along with it. *Ven acá,* Zorro says, holding out his hands. I don't do all that, she answered, looking over at the others, and I don't know any of them fancy steps you all do, she said. He smiled and shook his head.. I show you, he replied, standing tall before her, his left hand taking hers to lift her arm high, his right hand reaching up to rest lightly on her shoulder. *Damas y caballeros* do the same, he said, This way. *Mira, los pies. Uno,* slide, *y dos,* bring him over. *Y tres,* shake your *culo* like this, *y cuatro,* shake it back, he said, and she could not help but blush a little. *Otra vez.* Is slow, quick quick, slow, and quick quick. Slow, quick quick, slow, and quick quick. Oh my, that's, she said. Yes is nice, right? See, you got it, muy *bien. Me gustan con carne en los huesos!* said the left fielder, at that moment twisting hips with the brownskin gal. What's that? she asked. He say, I love all pretty girls, Zorro said. Lucky for all them, Rain said, not knowing how to say any more. They danced through the whole side of the record, without gestures of provocation or seduction, with neither idle chatter nor laughter mocking the invitation to silence pouring from the music, his left hand holding hers firmly but gently, his right hand now resting lightly at the small of her back, her other resting on his shoulder, but nevertheless conducting, through her arm and into her heart, the spark of his turning, thrusting hips. So close together but not, not yet dare she say, touching, Dare I say, she thought, it's so nice just this way, with the thrill of it without the awfulness of when it really happens, but what's awful about it after all? And not just because I like it, there I said it, I like it. *Me gusta también,* he answered, before she realized that she had not kept her own secret. And the last song had seemed to her to be the singer's confession, mournfully pronounced, perhaps as he walked alone along a deserted beach glowing like a white-hot ember in the sunset, against the waves darkening to ghosts under the evening sky, above the falling waves the distant conga beating its own unrelenting time, the flute and strings sounding a too-persistent memory. *Inolvidable*, he whispered, and again they fell silent, moving in concert, at one remove from the braying voices, the shuffling feet, the clink of over-toasted glasses and the hollow ring of overturned bottles surrounding them, now without fixed step although, she thought, each seemed to sense how and when and where the other would move to the music. No, it wasn't magic, but something more generous and transparent than mere magic, at one moment one leading and at the next the other, at each moment the other would follow or pursue with a delicate playfulness which was, for this their first dance together, one of the few she had ever danced with, With a man, at least seriously, she thought, well maybe seriously, And quite frankly, she thought, rising out of herself to the cobwebbed rafters to watch herself dancing below in the midst of the rest and comforted to have retained her deplorable dignity, that their interlude had been all that she'd dared to hope for, delightful and thrilling and whatchamacallit, self-indulgent, certainly in keeping with Mother Superior's sage counsel. The music stopped, and they separated, and she opened her eyes to look for him and there he was standing before her, in the fluorescent glow, but differently now, like the way she had so often seen him stand in the chalk circle, waiting to step up to the plate, swinging the bat into thin air with downcast eyes, then with a sudden fierceness lifting his head to gaze into the distance as facing off against the whole entire world. In the stillness falling thereafter she too returned to her flesh and bone and, swept away in her ecstatic daydream, sought the tether of his eyes, but in finding them discovered instantly that there was none, that he was not with her as she'd felt so certain he'd been just before, but suddenly departed, as if he'd turned and run, Shoot I should've cared less right then, she thought, as if he'd turned and run to a shadowed, hidden grove beneath the gathered palms, a place to which she instantly knew she could neither follow, nor enter, nor bear to discover what he had once waited for there. And to have come to her senses, to have started awake and found herself alone again then and there had been terrifying because, No not because of loneliness by itself, she thought, to that she had long before grown numb, or even of his sudden departure, but the terror in recalling, like something one knows but cannot bear to remember, that every presence carries within itself the seed of and is implacably followed by its absence, *All in good time, my pretty,* she cackled mournfully, into the icy air. All this had swept her back to herself, and what was there, she was certain, was only the same wretched nothing that ever was, yes, that evidently, *she* was. She had learned yet again that she was mistaken. Better then to just have a little thrill, a little fun, she decided, to carelessly let that be enough. When one's left with nothing else, let there be self-preservation.

Tell the truth I wouldn't mind getting another taste of that, she said, lifting her empty glass. Well, she thought, nodding thankfully for the refill then guzzling it down much too quickly, if that's how it's going to be, then she wanted to chat, to just jump in there and be one of the gang. After a half-hour of floundering across the oil-stained floor they had gathered around the couch. No, *couches.* Now I know when folks need more than one, she thought. The other two boys, well she couldn't say it was only the boys, got busy with their Fast Moves which they call stealing bases when a girl's not looking. But these gals, they're eyes were wide open, when hers would've shut, she thought, but for a hot second, not proudly. Especially that Frank-Sinatra-looking guy and the redhead child there. His whole long lanky body seemed to twist up tight around hers like a creeper and all her hair had come undone from under that cap, flying around her head. She looked right quick in their direction then quickly looked away but couldn't help but start thinking about those horrible giant snakes, them whatchmacallem, *conscriptors*. His big hands kept roaming around under her oversized jersey, and his mouth glued over hers, tighter than artificial respiration. The other two had wound up beside each other on the other couch, with the boys each leaning in of course from either side, and the redbone girl reaching without looking to hold the other's hand, which she shook off without a sideward glance. Zorro sat like before in the chair next to hers, his arm cradling across her shoulders, which felt real nice without making her feel sick or awful like it would if he were pushing too far. Still she drew back from his touch more slightly than he could notice to return to the safety which she had just recalled she must try to ensure for herself, Yes, at least try. I'm sure grateful for plain old small talk, she thought, at least she didn't have to just sit there and rubberneck at them going at it. Watching it was strange and alarming like something you've never seen anybody do before, you wonder what it is, what it does, why they're doing it, what might happen if, even though you kinda know, even though she should more than kind of know because she'd decided quite some time ago to find out about such grown folks matters for herself and not just have to listen to Pearl Koch boasting about sowing her wild oats and such. That's why she had went on and secretly got herself a P. O. Box for her subscriptions to those little magazines with the stories that told it all, even if they were awfully embarrassing to read sometimes that was easier than to sit there and have these two all up in your face like some kind of peep show, why can't they go on behind his curtains if they want to do all that she thought. And besides, these here project girls, who might have been raised right like she'd been, probably they didn't care to see all that either, but watching their eyes and faces she decided that they probably didn't give a hoot, go figure. But she and them did manage to get a few sensible words in edgewise here and there between the stupid boys trying to turn everything into a dirty joke or asking about this and that *inglés* word when they knew good and well what they meant, But I confuse, teach me how do you say *behine* one time it mean Like we get *behine* in our game sometime *pero* I stand *behine* you an I see your *behine* right? So stupid, she agreed with herself, but felt once again the twinge of an unmentionable shame. The three of them even managed to mention about what they hoped to do with themselves, meaning in the future and whatnot. She was remembering how she had tried to explain to Mother that her so-called dirty magazines, even if the stories were lewd and shocking, they were good for something after all. I saw an ad somewhere for that INTERNATIONAL CORRESPONDENCE SCHOOL, she volunteered, I.C.S. for short, down in Scranton PA. Been down there once, shonuff didn't care for it, the redbone said. Well, you don't have to live on any campus there and you don't have to get stir crazy sittin' up in any classroom, you stay comfortable at home and whistle while you work. I figured, shoot this might be the perfect thing for me, so I tore the page out and filled it in. It said right on top WHAT POSITION DO YOU WANT? and had a big list with all kinds of different jobs under it you're supposed to check off, so I went ahead and marked my Xs for Bookkeeper, Stenographer, and I was curious about Telephone Expert. Now there's one that sure suits you, the redbone girl said to her friend, you expert on that, she said, puttin' everybody's business in the street. Hmph, when it come to that I don't stand a chance to keep up with you, the dark-skinned girl replied. So I need to get my shorthand down, Rain continued, improve at typing and spelling, well as much as I can, and learn accounting —now, figures I can do— then get out and make some money some kind of way, that's all I'm good for, she said, quite sure that this was one matter she had thought over very carefully and could hardly be mistaken about, especially since Mother was even more sure that she couldn't do any better. Straightening up and folding her hands on her crossed knees, the skinny dark one replied, If I have my way someday soon I'll be a stewardess, way up there on TWA. Well, that's exciting and different! Rain said. Don't care if it is, she answered, It's what I want, ever since I seen how them girls be flying off to all kind of different places all over the world on them jets. I know that's the job for me, cause it ain't my style to lay around and spoil in one place too long. You all the time puttin' on airs about it, the redbone girl said, like you been some-where. Anyways, how you plot to be a stewardist when you scared of height just like me, too scared to even climb my back stairs? Any fool be scared to climb them rickety-ass stairs, ain't got a nail left, answered the skinny one. Wait till I put on that uniform and cap, pin on them gold wings and strut down that aisle, she cried, I'll be so high I won't care if I'm a mile off the ground. So you say, said the other, but like I say them jet planes they be crashing every day, and ain't nobody ever lived to tell about it after, so fool when you get up there you go head and stay up there if you want.

Wheeeeee! the scrawny girl suddenly screamed, and they turned to watch her feet flying past their faces as Frank Sinatra whirled her like a rag doll around the room. She better pray them feets don't touch no part of me, redbone said. *Wheeeeee!*, the drunken girl screamed again. Look like she a stewardist already, she said, as they spun past to slip behind the nearest hanging sheet. Out of the silence falling after all soon overheard the sounds of growling, of squealing and gasping, like there were two wild creatures back in there that somebody had forgotten to let out, or which had escaped from the zoo disguised as humans. The project girls were throwing each other sidling looks and grins, but talking quietly with their ballplayers, They're all used to this, she bet, these goings on, but certainly not I. She felt the heat surging, clawing its way out of her, the sweat melting whatever stood in its way. Melting, it moved like the road when, riding in Father's car, she still dared to look out the window as it streamed back and back away from her, its gray blur and everything chained to it relentlessly drawing present then instantly passing away to absence, pulling her back to where she'd just been but could not stay and forward to where she'd never been but could never stop returning. And when that fragile mannequin, that dummy which she longed to call herself melted split and fell away from her face everything which depended upon it began to dissolve, to reveal that it was going down but would soon enough come back up sick, which proved, she was certain, that *she* was. But how to escape from that mad ride to nowhere, she wondered, when he and they're all watching and then they will know, know that she can't go the distance, know that she ought to drop out of the race, know that the cameras actually don't love her after all, know that she is at their mercy, I'll just have to simmer down, she thought. She lifted her glass to her lips to drain its last remnants but found that there was much more left to drink than she had bargained for, that yet again she had been mistaken. The pee-colored drink felt even more than it had at first like hot air blowing up inside her head. It felt like a great big balloon blown up to nearly bursting, it wanted to lift off from the circus ground of her body but was still tied down, so rising up it kept her insides from sinking, but blew up her thoughts as well. They stretched and flattened, grew thin and washed out and weightless and flew every which way like a leaf storm until she could barely recognize them as thoughts she'd had only minutes before, their strange shapes and trajectories reminded her again of how she had looked her first time in the fun house when she finally opened her eyes to see her reflection in the melting mirrors, Who's that? She thought, and unable to stop herself she burst out laughing. Then the worst happened, everybody turned to look at her, faces neither laughing nor speaking nor asking why, faces just deliberately blank and mouths deliberately silent, which could have only been blank, which knew they would have proved themselves to be ridiculous had they broken that silence. She had been the only one who noticed something that stood out from the ordinary, who apparently had noticed the screech of bedsprings beating time behind that curtain ten feet away, a sound which actually she had tried so hard not to hear at all, but had noticed not because it was not ordinary but because she was not ordinary, now she sat there laughing, not at that unseen, commonplace occurrence but in fact only at herself, bursting with laughter and twisted and turned back against herself, caught red-handed in her dizziness, unmasked in all her shameful strangeness. She stared back at them, wanting to shout that enough is enough, wanting to throw in their faces what was clawing its way out from inside her, but she feared that if she were to set it free that she would again be mistaken, that instead of a scream everything in her stomach, the red beans and rice and corn chomped off the cob the pope's nose smothered with hot sauce the piss-water and the missing white worm she was convinced had crawled down her throat, would jump back up the way it had gone down from her lips to spray out like hot air flying from an unpinched balloon all over them and their stupid funhouse of curtains and everywhere.

I need to rush to the little girl's room, she whispered, clutching his shirt sleeve. Ain't no little girls' room here, redbone said, look to me like you got lost somewhere down the line. But she could not stop to listen. She offered up her arm to be led through a warped door in the back, into a cramped compartment, and pulled another dangling string to turn on a bare bulb. He reached over to hand her one of the four dingy towels draped over nails pounded into the bare beams rising to meet the roof. He pressed her hand firmly as he smiled and leaned down to peck her cheek. Thank you, thank you, she said, trembling with gratitude and the demand erupting inside her. But how will, how can I count this, she thought, how could she boast and tell the true story of her first kiss. He sidled out and closed the door, taking her delight along with him too. She hooked the latch behind him. Light and voices and laughter from the room beyond still trickled in through the cracks at the edge. She quickly tugged at the little handle on the inside trying to close it, pulling with all her might to slam it shut, then watching the crack spring open again as soon as she let go. She smelled once again more thickly the stench that had dropped from her nose into the back of her throat before and retched, sicker to her stomach than ever. She gasped, swooning with nausea and tears, knowing that beyond the closed door, even without sight of her, they all knew what was happening to her, knew what she would have to do, knew that she could not find one of her countrified out of the ordinary ways to go about it, to make it different for her from all the others, the boys and girls and fathers and mothers and next-door neighbors who had all done the same thing there, the usual things anyone not given to strangeness knows better than to notice, so many times before. Through the tiny window she saw the backyards stretching into the distance, heard the passing cars, the bored dogs, the sharp, tiny stirrings of scavenging birds, felt the quietness descending everywhere at the end of a warm and lengthening summer's day. But no peace and quiet for me, she thought. She would have to kneel down there if she wanted to keep clean, she thought, and hide the awful sounds she was about to make from the others, To act civilized about it, that's only right, she thought, to be able to walk back out there afterward without flipping out and falling down mortified dead. She retched again, hard, It's coming now, she thought. She bent over to fold the towel on the floor in front of the toilet bowl, trying not to breathe in too much but how could she help it, and at last knelt before the altar. She wound her hand like a mummy with the paper from the reel and held it to lift back the seat. Heaving, she stared down into the pool of still water, but once seeing herself there, an image neither trembling at the edges nor twisted beyond recognition but unmistakably familiar and abhorrent to herself, she shut fast her eyes and let her head sink toward the cool shadows. As the flood rose from her belly and her throat gave way she recalled the too-many times she had been sick to her stomach, how whenever in its heaving midst she had found herself convinced that that time would be the one to end it all, that this time she would manage to upchuck living itself, but thereafter discover that she had been yet again mistaken, that this had not been *it*, no merciful novelty of death, no penultimate purgation, neither better nor worse nor more nor less than puking her guts out, then getting up off her knees to wash her face and then turning back to be born again into yes the same ordinary life, knowing it had made her puke once again because she just couldn't stomach it, knowing that nevertheless she was running back like that fool at the edge of the desert to glut herself on it all, all over again. So, in staring into the implacable sky of washed-out stars from the tangle of her limbs in the snow, she knew very well that all the King's horses and all the King's men would neither overhear nor notice nor prevent nor rescue her from her downfall, in a crashing and crumbling which only she could hear, into smithereens never to be put back together again, into all her drifting snowness.

She got up and, brushing herself off, realized that she'd been so preoccupied with the fact of leaving that shabby little cabin in the dust that she hadn't noticed that she'd reached the edge of the lot, for there she was, not far from the streetlamp, at the crossroads. No looking back now, she would have to hurry, because he would be coming out to track her down before too long, since she hadn't come back like he probably thought she would, and since who else would they come to asking her whereabouts if she really *disappeared*, anyway he ought to come looking after her if he's a real gentleman, Not to flatter myself, she thought. She hobbled into the bright spot at the corner. Well, more like a curve around than a corner, broad and squat like the one kitty-corner from it, on which sat a small place with a simple, steady neon sign over the door, not a fancy jumping thermometer one like the motel's, with a soft amber glow coming out through the windows, a BAR & GRILL like the sign said, with a couple of cars and a pickup truck parked in front. And the other two curves, skinny and pointy, one full of bushes and wild grass and trees, and the other some kind of office-place or house, its windows all dark. Four corners, not squared-off like a cross, she thought, but rather more like an X, neither unyielding nor holy, but shapely, supple, mysterious. Pointing to destinations to which she had never travelled, fruitfully multiplying deeds she had not yet spelled to do, marking the hiding places of secrets she had not yet told herself, itself the vantage point from which she'd noticed the incessant passage of presence and absence she'd never wished to notice, the one thing about which she will never be mistaken. And not a soul around, she thought. No cars coming from any direction. Not that she was so foolish and desperate as to try and hitch a ride, even if there had been one coming. To ask for a ride, To where, she wondered, when where she wanted to go was too far, she feared, to ever reach there. She wanted to ride and ride away in cars and then fly away in a jet plane, yes to some delightful little place by the sea, a place so much further away from everywhere she'd ever been or heard of, from everyone she'd ever known or heard of, from everyone who'd ever known or heard of her and everywhere they'd ever been or heard of, from everyone they'd ever known and everywhere they'd ever been or heard of. So much further away than that rotten old Miami or even than Bali Hai, wherever it is, where after sleeping in scandalously late she could sashay down to the beach and stretch out all afternoon in the sun on a great big blanket like Aunt Barbara and sip fancy drinks through a long elbowed straw or even kick up her heels in the sand for a hot second any time she took a notion, really too far or impossible to get there hitching rides like that, meaning far away to never come back, almost her own secret little place, which, standing there and sighting into the distances of those four directions and upward into the vacant brightness of the sky, she feared might be nowhere. Anyway, she thought, even if she managed to hitch a ride she would surely have the rotten luck to be picked up by the worst monster alive who'd just happen to be out looking for his next *specimen,* which was just what that monster called all them girls he had, No I don't even want to remember, she thought, what she had read about last week in that one story that had scared the dickens out of her even to see that picture of him. A big-eyed, pink-faced man wearing one of them red plaid hunting jackets and caps, who would be so nice at first, stopping and rolling down his window and smiling, asking if she was all right and where she was going, as if neither perplexed by nor cautious of her odd appearance alone in the middle of town after dark. Not saying those things some would sometimes to make you feel like a stranger. Like Remember, there ain't a lot of you, I should say coloreds, out here like there is where you prefer to congregate down in Elmira, make no mistake about that, except for the scarce few that wound up here somehow a long time ago and been living here ever since, till now they're practically no different from the rest of us. While other of you coloreds are still scarcely seen up around these parts, except some jailbird fresh out from Reformatory Hill comes up now and then looking for steady work here, or one of them smart-aleck beatniks passing through on his way up to the Glen or Ithaca, hot to cross the line, or it's a bunch of them half-Negro, yeah I know I ought to call them mulatto, guys we ship in from Banana-Land to play Pony League ball, which is likely all they'll ever be good for, most of em. No, not bothering to tell her any of those un-neighborly things, he would say only kind and helpful things, then smiling he'd reach across the front seat to open the door on the passenger side for her, gesture with a black-gloved hand and say, Come on get in, I'll take you where you need to go. Yeah right, she thought, take me to where I'll never come back anyplace. Then Poor girl, such a shame, they'll shake their heads and say, she must've lost her way. So she decided to scoot right across kitty-corner to that BAR & GRILL and get in out of the cold, and get out of sight of him and maybe both of them before it was too late, and scoot she did, in a limping run that flailed and started, looking wildly as she crossed, in not just both but all four ways on one and three-quarters feet, the narrow waist of that mysterious **X** to that little bar, up the short flight of rock-salted steps, to burst through the door.

Three men, two at the bar and one behind it, all turned to look at once as she entered. The bartender, barrel-chested and balding, stood drying his hands with a towel after washing glasses. An enormous, red-bearded man in grimy coveralls and black rubber boots, sprawling with weariness, sat hunched over an outsize coffee cup, one huge paw scribbling with a pencil nub into a small, frayed notebook held in the other. The second, gray-haired, slight and short, wearing a well-worn flight jacket and gray fedora and nursing a double-shot of bourbon on the rocks, turned just as he pulled a dragged-short cigarette from his lips, puffed smoke with a thin whistle and, without a break in his quizzical stare, neatly snuffed the butt in a plastic ashtray. The farmer glanced in her direction then returned, with a low grumble, to his calculations.

Evening, Miss, said the bartender. How about closing that door behind you?

Turning back, through the window she saw the sudden whirl of headlights across the X, watched the blue Falcon pull away from the front of the cabin to track her path through the snow, cross the intersection, and swerve into the lot, its headlights flashing like a searchlight across the glass. She rushed forward to lean into the door, then whirled back to face them, wide-eyed with panic. The bartender nevertheless calmly asked,

Can I get you something, Miss?

Her eyes fled to two booths, shadowed and empty, beside the pool table in the back, then noted the bartender's solicitous expression. But she'd already decided that she wouldn't ask for a single blessed thing in this place, another shabby old place from the looks of it, not even a glass of water, not even to use any Ladies' Room, that she had had enough of disgusting bathrooms in this disgusting love affair, that instead she would hobble madly to the rear, which she did, hurrying past as all three heads turned, then returned to their respective preoccupations with, she nevertheless noticed, neither word nor glance exchanged between them. Kinda like how Marilyn did in that one picture when she ducked in that bus stop trying to escape from that cowboy trying to what's it called, *abduct* her, she thought, except they kissed and made up and probably got married in the end, even though it almost drove her crazy watching cause it took too much small talk before they just got down to business, even if that was supposed to be funny and whatnot, quite frankly I'd prefer to cut the comedy at the moment. She quickly slid in across a back-facing bench and started to slip under the table, but instead decided that she wouldn't, Whether he comes after me or he doesn't, she thought, I'm through with ducking anything. There where at first she had not wanted to look, she noticed the phone booth, looming over its corner, standing tall like a coffin set on end, dark beyond its open mouth. No way I'm going in there, looks like nobody's been in there for a hundred years, not any time soon, she thought, if she had to call home, she would find some other phone to use for it, if she needed to call, and not until she was good and ready, whenever that would be. Maybe I will have a whatchamacallit, good stiff drink after all while I'm here, make it a quick pit stop, she thought. But all of a sudden she was not so sure that she was ready, or could get ready, even with a lot of strong drinks, to call home, to leap into the floodtide of silence which would swallow up the words Hello, Mother, which she would scarcely dare to utter, which would sweep her over the edge of the world and then they will drag her down after them into the deep, to sink for what seems an eternity before she would answer, asking each damning question with unflappable eloquence, neither angry, nor happy, nor sad, nor surprised, nor comforting, nor any-thing at all, and as she plummets down she will feel the dark crush-ing against her and recall what, at the end of falling, will certainly find

66

what's left of her there. She straightened up primly, folding her hands together on the table, and through a narrow window beside her she noticed, just across the road, that thin patch of straggling bushes, wild grass, and bare trees that had seemed so distant and indistinct before, noticed that everywhere it lay trampled and strewn with thrown out, exhausted, useless things, and thought it certainly a place solitary and uninhabitable because of the presence of those exhausted, now name-less things, visible and invisible, which had been abandoned there, a place much like this shadowed room and others into which she had once foolishly wandered, only to soon hasten away. Nevertheless, this was where she would for now, for however long now had to last, remain, there with her broken shoe and her torn stocking and all the rest that was left of her, like those bushes and grasses and trees and discarded things huddling together there in the snow, neither turning away nor waiting, but like a secret once untold inside herself and now laid to rest, just sitting still there in the dark.

The bartender heard footsteps bounding up the stairs to the door, then saw a lanky figure stop and stand peering in through the glass without entering, as if totally at a loss to know how to go ahead and open the door like anybody else dropping in for a drink, until he had enough of such nonsense and waved him in. He put two and two together quickly and glancing back was relieved to see that this girl had at least enough sense to duck down when she heard the guy coming without making him have to tip his hand, after all he was already stuck in the middle of this crap, the kind of crap he never liked getting stuck in the middle of in the first place, but that's how it is every day, he said to himself again, like he'd been saying damn near every day since birth he figured, there's no escape. The guy stamped his feet hard outside on the landing, opened then closed the front door too politely behind him, then tried to stamp off the few specks of snow still left on his fancy two-tone darkie shoes all over again on the rug, thus making a whole lot of unnecessary racket and already making a nuisance of himself besides, the bartender thought. He stopped halfway to the bar and finally opened his mouth to speak.

Please, maybe you help me Sir, the stranger said. See I looking for a girl, maybe she come in here, he said.

At these words, the enormous man in coveralls and the small man wearing the city-slicker's hat both turned their heads to look and then kept looking.

Afraid I can't help you with that, the bartender answered.

You know, is a black girl, she wear a red coat, Zorro insisted.

Nobody's passed through here lately, except for these two birds, the bartender replied,

with a nod toward the others, who smiled slightly and kept looking, but did not answer.

I think, maybe she get lost around here someplace, she heard him announce, quite loudly.

Easy enough to do, agreed the bartender, it's a big country out there.

I'm sure she walk out, he continued. See, I tell her, wait for me in my place.

So that's where she was, your place? the bartender asked.

First time for winter, I living here, he added promptly, yanking a thumb back over his shoulder. She come there with me, for dinner tonight.

There, for dinner tonight? the bartender asked.

No, we going back in Elmira for dinner, she like that Dixie Barbeque. So I come back quick to get ready. So I say wait a second I'm coming, but she tell me, I step outside. Couple minute I'm ready, I come looking but she gone already. She gone somewhere, I'm looking around, so maybe she come over here I'm thinking, maybe so, he said.

I think maybe I've seen you around here before, the bartender said,

though he knew that this was the lanky molatto fellow he had seen playing shortstop, hitting well but at times fielding erratically, when he'd gone out to see the Pioneers the few times lately he'd had the chance or inclination, since it wasn't like the old days, when practically everybody on the roster was either a local boy or came from somewhere you even knew of or cared where the hell it was, now it's a team half of them strangers coming from God knows where or nowhere, it's just like how it is everywhere else in the country these days, he'd often observe in silence, filling up with strangers, rank strangers who were too much work to get to know, hell and they don't give a damn if you do one way or the other anyway. In fact, he was quite certain that he had seen him one bitterly cold night two weeks before, that just like he had tonight he'd come up the stairs to his front door and stood looking in without entering, fogging up the glass and stirring up the customers, until he had had to come down by the other end of the bar and stare him down till he turned tail and went away. Must be the shy type or some kind of oddball, he had thought, either way, come in or stay the hell out.

You got nice table in here, Zorro said, pinching thumb and fore-finger of his left hand together and pumping the fist made with his right. I see him before back in there.

with a hitch of his head in that direction.

That damn thing? It's broke right now, won't do anything but eat your quarters for lunch, the bartender replied.

She could hear them talking and talking from where she waited, their words spoken senselessly loudly, then softly, then slowly, then quickly, pouring in through her ears to billow up inside her head like a cloud of steam breeding monstrous shapes, but cooling into silence much too quickly for her to name the beasts or catch the drift. It ain't nothing but a whole lot of drift anyhow, going nowhere, she thought, wanting to laugh to herself. Him, all y'all doin' a whole lot of gum-flappin' nobody with a lick of sense would even try to understand, she thought, just to hear yourself flappin' on, when you could be done with it. All of it sounding to her like a broken, uneasy music, or the rumbling of a distant storm creeping into the silence of the sky. Don't care if I never make sense of a mumbling word of it, she thought, all that mush-mouth talk can stay right out there. The three kept watching in silence as Zorro glanced around the room, searching their faces, but not too hard, already knowing there was no point in that. Then peered again into the dark hallway leading to the back.

Maybe you see her coming by the window here, he said, black girl, she got a red coat on.

So you keep saying. But I keep telling you that I've seen no redcoats of any color around here lately, the bartender replied.

Mira, wait, wait, Zorro says. I'm saying is because, first I find *esos*,

extending both hands to delicately creep through the air,

where maybe she come to here, on the snow.

Man, you must be talkin' about Mister Major here, the farmer said, shoving the grimy notebook and pencil nub into his chest pocket. See, he's got them itsy-bitsy cutesy penny loafers on, he added with a grin, before draining his coffee cup.

Well they surely couldn't be your tracks, you big lummox, the old pilot snapped back, as all three laughed.

Maybe she run in here when you no notice, Zorro suggested, pointing to the back room, then you don't see it.

Inside these four walls I notice everything, especially what I
don't see,

the bartender replied, pressing both hands flat on the bar and leaning over it.

Maybe now I go quick back and look, okay? Zorro said, taking
a step forward.

I really think you ought not to try and do that, the bartender
said, as the big farmer turned to stand up tall from his stool.

Why don'tcha try lookin' down the road aways, the farmer
added, I'd head that way quick if I were you, before she gets
away for good.

Then they were quiet. As if all their drifting bluster had at last fallen
to earth to stand by exactly what it all meant, knowing which for her
was already a lost cause, she figured. But one thing she knew was
that that wordless quietness filling up the dark meant that they were
done with talking, that whatever was left to be done between these
men was past talking, and she hoped that he would have enough
sense to not be coming any further after her for now, for however
long she would make now last, and when she felt the cold draft nuzzling in around her legs she knew that he had walked back out the
door and that it would be shut behind him once he was gone. She
heard that beat-up Falcon start, surge and roll away, making that
hollow haunting sound cars make going down a road, the howling
which comes stalking you as they pass you by, and fades into the
distance.

After a while she lifted her head from her arms and wondered if
she really had fallen asleep, or if she had actually lost her mind, had
flown the coop and left herself to join with the silent smoky things
which hovered around her there in the dark, with the exiled things
out in the fallen snow which kept the secret of her escape. And if

I'd lost my mind would I have even noticed? she wondered, as she yawned and stretched herself. Turning back to the table she noticed the glass of water which now stood there atop its white coaster, frosted and glistening in the streetlight washing in from the window, keeping watch over her so patiently that as she looked she did not wonder who had brought it there, but whether it had come to her of its own volition, had bent low in devotion to scoop and fill itself with ice, had run the tap to fill itself, had ridden across thin air atop its coaster like an adventurer on his magic carpet, with its thin slice of lemon nicked to its rim like a feather in his cap, its crimson swizzle-stick his invincible staff vouchsafed by the angels, to come and greet her there when she came back to herself, and how it had known that she was nearly dying of thirst, and how it seemed to carry in its wake the quiet, intermittent voices and laughter now sounding from the bar. She lifted the straw to her lips to drink. As the cool water flowed through her, she suddenly noticed that as cold as it was outside she had been sweating up a storm, Lord knows I must look like the devil, she thought. She daubed her forehead with the water-ringed napkin, then quickly nuzzled against each armpit to smell herself, wrinkling her nose at what she discovered, and decided it was time to freshen up a little, and especially to use the toilet, though she cringed at the thought of what it might be like in there. She leaned around the corner of the booth to look around and saw the door marked LADIES. But somebody up front noticed her right then because a voice calling out said

Don't worry, it's kept clean in there.

She stared out into the mass of soft lights, indistinct figures and shadows at the bar, all seeming at that moment as distant as the planets and stars and guessed that it was probably the bartender who said it, but even him, she wondered, how could he be so sure. Guess I have no choice unless I want to pee my pants, she thought, so she grabbed her purse from where she'd stuck it under the table and went ahead in, promptly thankful that it looked like he was right, and that there was a lock built into the doorknob, which of course she set right away, and turned to look around. Thank the Lord it wasn't in a nasty shambles like that hole back at Mister Mush-Mouth's place. In fact she almost felt comfortable enough to, believe it or not, sit right down on the toilet, and this one you really could call not just an icky old toilet but a proper commode as Mother would call it. But her misgivings of the moment got the better of her and she took the time to cover it instead, carefully arranging the long ribbons of paper along the white horseshoe of the seat. Not that she was one of those shameful types who don't give a hoot about wasting toilet paper, but first she figured even without touching it that this partic-ular throne wasn't likely to be exactly warm and cozy, and second and furthermore, don't we all prefer to put our hands and especially our other parts up against something when we know where it's been and who's been up against it before, shoot, nothing whatchama-callit, *abnormal* about that, she thought gladly. After dealing with that ordeal she glanced into the small round mirror hung above the sink, At least this one's not broke with bad luck, she thought, cupped her hands and washed her face clean of sweat and tears and the traces of dingy snow which had been flung there when she fell. She quickly reached into her purse for her handkerchief, the pre-cious one she always carried with her when she dressed up for the evening, and laid it out across one hand to smooth it out with the other. She was delighted to rediscover at each corner the delicate webs of lacework, narrowing to trace its edges, which grandmother Hannah had embroidered there back when Father was just a boy. It had been precious to her ever since Father had given it to her on her sweet sixteenth, that day she had taken another step, a baby step, Mother said, toward becoming a lady. She was happy now that, Having got all gussied up for that rotten tramp, she recalled, she had it right there with her that night, a snowy winter's night like that one when she wouldn't have expected to even think of using it. Not like in the summer when she went ahead and did sometimes, when she'd feel just a tiny bit overheated and start to break out in a sweat with that tongue-tied or who-am-I-supposed-to-be feeling she'd get up in front of Mother or some of her, what's the word, *clientele*, or other, when she'd draw it from her purse, all in a flutter, to discreetly and gently blot the barely damp spots of her forehead, just like she imagined Granny herself might have done back in them nineteen aught's on them hot Sunday afternoons down in Savannah, all in a flutter, thankful for the instant of relief and quite pleased that its, as Mother says, *exquisite* lacework showed itself off all the while to the Avon Ladies and other such and elicited welcome compliments. And tonight of all nights she was comforted to have, while freshening up in the midst of the dangers which she now singlehandedly confronted, not just another rough paper towel which might dissolve in her hands, but her very own, unsinkable island in the midst of an ocean of ickiness, and her face fell into its softness and lingered there. When she lifted her eyes to the mirror once again it held more than her own reflection. Granny, she whispered, y'know Father always says that you're the one I favor. She folded the kerchief in half and half again, Time to put you back to bed, she said, as if it were a small sleeping creature she could never bear to disturb, which she had woken up only because, at that dire juncture, it couldn't be helped. Like when she'd sneak in after being out late and Cindy would wake up as she crept up the back porch stairs. Sometimes she'd still bark a little, but not like she would when she was a puppy and Rain was just a peanut herself, these days she'd just poke her head out the door of her little red house, quietly conspiring in her rebellion, waiting for her only sister to come back down the stairs and scoot across the backyard to make her bed, Which she gets real cozy in these days, she thought. Now there's hardly a stir in those stiffening legs, those tired sad eyes sparkling in the light of the distant streetlamp, Dear Cat-Chaser, you're getting on now, she'd sigh, and to think we started out in the world together, why'd you have to go on and pass me by? She slipped the kerchief into the pocket of her purse and snapped shut the clasp. She pulled the glass-bead cord to shut the light and stepped through the door. The three guys she'd seen at first were still sitting up front there and they noticed, well that one fancy little man looked back into the dark, smiling and waving. She waved back, but not too much, not to where they'd get the wrong idea. She went over to the table to recover her helpful glass, thankful to have not been abandoned. Mother would approve of her show of proper couth, but remind her that No sensible person expects credit for cleaning up after themselves, All right then, please excuse me for being born, but that's your fault anyway. And by the way, since I'm going back out there, let me check my purse for the extra cash stashed away in there, she thought, because like Pearl says, A girl should never make a date with an empty wallet. Furthermore, she'd advise them in no uncertain terms, I certainly can pay for my own drinks, despite however much each of you gentlemen would love to buy me a round. Yeah right, she thought, peering into her wallet, Five dollars and seven cents. Listen to your silly self, hobbling like a cripple and with no way to get yourself home. Enough to get a nice little drink or two to relax her nerves and help her get up the gumption to call home, which was absolutely what she needed after the terrible ordeal that she'd been through so far that night, and for now she didn't care one bit if these gentlemen or anybody else didn't like it.

Well, here I am, Rain said,

stepping into the light. From the other end of the bar the bartender and the big farmer eyed her without a word, but the slight dapper man quickly stepped up to pull out a stool for her. Even though mother wasn't around to grade her performance, she decided to start out on the correct foot.

Thank you, Sir. Pleased to meet you! I'm Lorraine, but folks in the know call me Rain, she said.

I can't profess to be in the know, the dapper man replied, but I'll accept the liberty, Rain. Those who don't know any better call me Major Tom, he said.

And how're you doing this evening? she continued with a smile.

Still on the right side of the dirt, thank you, Major Tom replied. She wasn't quite sure what to think of the other two: the tall, wiry bartender with that clean-shaven, kind of a Lil Abner handsome face and those long-fingered, extraordinarily pale, delicate hands, or the farmer in his gray coveralls and tall yellow rubber boots, and boy if he ain't got two big old inner tube lips stuck in that long horse face, like a horse in boots, poor thing, it's what the Lord handed him on his way in, she acknowledged, he can't help it. But she would still have to study those two birds a while, have to keep an eye on them, she thought, even though they were nice, well at least it was nice of them to keep quiet and let her hide for a hot second from Crazy Mush-Mouth. On the other hand, maybe she was getting them all wrong, maybe actually they weren't all that nice, no more nice than a lot of folks around here when they see colored folks they don't know, who give you some I-can-take-you-or-leave-you attitude or something plain old worse, which she'd known about long enough of course, she'd been here and seen with her own eyes, that's how it had been forever or as long as she could remember around these parts, the only place on the earth she'd ever lived in to tell the truth so maybe things could be different in other parts, she speculated. Maybe actually they were just waiting for their own chance to drag her into some back room here, or down in the basement if they have one and have their own way with her. Now that Mush-Mouth had hit the road, here in this town where nobody had ever put a name to her face or had ever seen her coming because, just like a foolish girl, every time here she'd hidden herself, so nobody would even wonder if she disappeared for keeps and maybe some of them wouldn't care if she did.

She looked into the slight man's boyish face, with its tidy moustache. Geez, she thought, he looks like a very strange, enchanted boy who woke up one morning with wrinkles and gray hair and tired sad eyes and ever since has been trying to figure out how in the world did he manage to use up his time so fast. Maybe these other two birds, plainly intent on minding their own business despite all the commotion that had just been stirred up in there, they just don't give a hoot one way or the other, she figured, as long as they didn't have to be bothered, which wasn't either nice or gentlemanlike to tell the truth, in the situation which they must have seen that she was in up to her neck. At least this Major gentleman was nice, she concluded, and it's nice for a change to be treated like a lady, like a respectable young lady, to have a nice man serve you a fancy drink, well a glass of water, and to have him jump up and pull out your chair, well a barstool, for you to sit down in or sit up at, it sure felt nice, after the hell on earth she'd been through and lived to tell about already that night. And it suddenly occurred to her, that even the dark clouds that had blotted out the sky tonight had a silver lining, for on this journey she had taken tonight she had gone so much further than just walking out of that rotten place, falling down, and picking herself up and walking on across that parking lot. Really it felt more like ten thousand miles that she'd traveled, like going to Bali Hai and back, or around the world in an hour, she thought, like one of them astronauts getting in one of them itsy bitsy capsules and riding a rocket into outer space and without batting an eyelash, she had come a long way to reach the other side of that X in the road marking the spot. It had definitely not been just a baby step. *Au contraire*, she insisted, it had been a giant step toward that finish line, for at last she too had ventured into the unknown and returned to tell, do tell. And all at once she felt altogether proud of herself, like she was floating just an inch above the floor, with all the surefootedness of an angel walking on the pure air, as careless of falling as a snowflake tossed above the earth in the winter wind.

We figured you might be thirsty after sweating it out for so long, the Major added,

with a smile not seconded in the more or less sober faces of the others, still fixed in silent regard, neither of whom to her surprise offered even one word of remark regarding what had happened there in the last hour or inquired after her intactness after the fact. Just in case you're wondering, gentlemen, if that's what y'all claim to be, she thought, besides a scrape and a broken shoe I'm quite all right. But if y'all don't care to speak to folks when you're looking dead in their face like somebody civilized or if y'all had enough excitement for the night, that's fine with me. I was raised to shun rude folk, and don't exactly crave a piece of your mind anyhow. Furthermore, she thought, I certainly can spell how to sit up here and order myself a drink, I can mind my own bizness and have a fine old time with me, myself, and I.

She emptied the glass with one swallow, hoisted herself onto the barstool, and neatly set it down on a nearby coaster.

Thank you, Sir, I do appreciate your concern, she answered with a nod.

Thank our host while you're at it, he replied, looking across the plank to the bartender who now, back turned, busied himself dusting the bottles on the narrow shelves framing the cash register.

Well I'm surely thankful to all of you gentlemen, Rain said, and decided then and there to prove it by covering a round for the house.

Excuse me she called to the wiry man, who turned back with a perplexed expression, as if he could not imagine what she might ask for.

Set 'em up, Joe, she chimed, waving a hand down the bar, quite proud of herself for having come up with the perfect words along with it, just like them gals in the gangster pictures, she thought.

First off, the name's Delbert, the bartender answered, with an emphatic nod. But Del will do the trick.

Nice to meet you, Del! she piped back cheerily. And how're you doing this evening?

Better than I deserve, he replied. By the way, in view of your generous offer, he added, how about showing me some proof that you weren't born yesterday. A driver's license will do just fine.

If I could drive, I probably wouldn't be here now she answered, despite the fact that driving cars was one of the last things she'd ever want to do. But she was reassured to recall that her pocketbook sheltered yet another precious object. She extracted a small, leather-bound, gilt-edged book and thumbed it open.

But I do have this, she said, handing it across the bar.

The bartender read quickly, turning away from the prying eyes of the Major peering across from his stool, muttering half aloud and half to himself, like one long distrustful of words parsed in silence.

SWEETEST SIXTEENTH, TO MY DEAREST LORRAINE LOVE ALWAYS. PEARL SEPT 4 '55. I'm deeply touched, he replied, handing it back to her, but it's not legal.

Suit yourself then, she answered in a pout.

Suit myself. Yes that's what I'll have to do, he replied, looking into her eyes with, at last, a smile.

I certainly won't stand in your way, she continued. But if you ask me, my little old New Testament here's better proof than any of that legal eagle beagle stuff. Cause who would dare to write beside Scripture and then sign it with their own name if it's not true? she asked, Not me. Besides, everybody knows how they whatchamacallit, proceed in court, and it's shown on Perry Mason and in your movies and such, what they do when they get called up to the box to testify, they lay their left hand on top of that Bible and raise their right hand and word the first they swear to tell the truth and the whole truth and nothing but the truth, she insisted.

I must agree, Your Honor, he replied, nodding thoughtfully, and returned to bottle-dusting. How about a soda pop on the house? I got Seven-Up, Coke, Pepsi, and club soda, what's your pleasure?

Pepsi please, thank you kindly after all. But actually, to tell the truth, I'm in the mood for a chocolate malted. I'm happy to pay my way if you can manage that,

she added, kinda curious indeed about herself, she thought, meaning to hear such words coming out of herself like she'd been hearing lately, and with such a tone. Taking that tone, as Mother would say, as if she were made of wood with not a thought in her head and that someone unseen, someone so tricky and clever that they cannot ever be discovered, were speaking, moving, by way of invisible strings, through her, doing irrevocable deeds, establishing facts on the ground, leading her to that finish-line, that delicate barricade which would snap and flutter to her feet as she pranced through it, into her very own radiant future, I kinda like it, whoever it is, she thought.

A chocolate malted is out of the question, he answered, trading glances with the others as he scooped ice into a fresh glass.

I'm a lot more hungry than I am thirsty anyhow. That sign hanging in your window says GRILL, I hope you've really got one and somebody's cookin' so I can get something well-done on it, she sighed, something worth a piece of my hard-earned pay.

Well just listen to you, she thought.

All I got is fried chicken and dogs, he said.

Dogs? she said.

Hot dogs, whaddya think, Delbert said.

I dine with my share of chicken at home, twice a week, she announced,

but actually it could have been every day of the week, because she loved to sit down with a pile of Mother's chicken wings, fresh from the frying pan, hot and crispy and dusted with salt and pepper and a squeeze of lemon juice. She loved to pick the strands of sweet flesh from between the delicate bones, It's almost like cracking nuts, she thought, except it's better because umph the skin's just as tasty as the meat. But I'm not about to make a fool of myself picking bones or licking fingers behind no chicken wings here in front of these folks, she decided, with two of them looking like the cat got their tongue and this so-called Mister Delbert looking her over like she didn't know what she was about, she knew her share about what makes people tick, she was sure of that. She took a dollar from her purse and tossed it onto the bar like she had a million more where that one came from.

That's for my Pepsi, she said.

Mister Delbert appeared to ignore her gesture, but answered,

Fine. We'll put it on your tab,

smiling in that strange way like before, she thought, wearing, to tell the truth, a smirk on his face that didn't set right one bit with her, as if he were determined to make her out to be some kind of joke. After what I've been through today I surely don't need any more of that, she thought, but this one's determined to try my last nerve.

Then, please put two more on my tab, if you'd be so kind, she quipped, one for the Major, whatever he cares for. And one for your other friend too, she hastily added,

pointing to the big farmer, who perked up in surprise.

You mean, old Mutt here? Trust me, you don't want to get this one liquored up. No telling what he'll do then, Mister Delbert said.

The farmer stretched back in a yawn, like even after all that coffee he was just waking up.

I've been known to whoop and holler along with the jukebox there, is all, he replied. It's hard on folks' ears every once in a while, so they claim.

Trust me, he ain't exactly Hank Williams, Major Tom said.

Since you have to go on and put it that way, he replied, I reckon I will take the young lady up on that, thank you kindly.

You're Mutt? So where's Jeff? she asked,

hoping to get in on the joke which she thought it was.

He's no longer with us, the farmer replied, lifting a freshly poured shot to make a toast, then toss it down the hatch.

So sorry to hear that! cried Rain.

Such a shame about his sad story but I can't keep my mind on it, cause I'm too hungry, she thought, and she knew that when she got entirely too hungry she just couldn't help but get mad at the world. Somebody up in here needs to plate me some kind of food, she thought. Doesn't need to be anything fancy, but some kind of something, she thought, now she was in a pickle.

Don't be, the farmer replied. He run off to Binghamton to play his fiddle, lazy good for nothing.

He means to say the violin, in the orchestra, the Major corrected.

No, I meant to say fiddle just like I did, and they're both the same damn thing to me, the farmer barked.

Geez, it sounds like one of them You say potato, and I say pohtahto things to me! cried Rain,

which neither of them looked very happy to be reminded about. Everybody's entitled to their opinion, she thought. But as far as food was concerned, she would order whatever she could get from Mister Delbert right quick here, not a moment too soon.

I've decided, she announced. May I please get a hot dog?

A hot dog? he asked,

looking at her with that same pokey smirk, like he had figured out that she was one of those whatchamacallit, uncouth gals, one of them Since you insist I'll have a little taste please types who come visiting on Sunday afternoons and proceed to gorge themselves and chew folks out of house and home like it's the most neighborly thing to do in the world, which certainly ain't me, she assured herself, so don't figure so fast Mister, she thought, quite frankly happy to pay for however many dogs or wings her heart desired,

One'll suit me just fine for now, she answered,

even though it annoyed her to have to say it.

Here's for the victuals, she said,

laying another two dollars on the bar.

No hurry, Mister Delbert replied, it's on your tab.

He went back through a swinging door, into a burst of light which turned on, and then off like a spotlight, it looked like to her, when it closed behind him, or like another sun, she imagined, as if he had passed through a portal to another country, where it's daylight now not night, like Bali Hai or places way over on the other side of the earth, as Jimmy Love had reminded her. Or even like a secret place where the sun shines all the time, where the sun shines through your back door every day, where everybody gets lemon chicken wings and french fries for dinner whenever they so desire, Listen to me goin' out of my cotton pickin' mind, she thought. Mister Delbert came back through the door with a hot dog and two slices of pickle, on a plate which said GLEN MOTOR INN in a circle on it, set it down in front of her then reached under the bar for two squeeze bottles, one red and the other yellow, and a few square napkins which he tucked in alongside the plate. She smiled at the steam coming off it, which meant it was really a hot dog, That's comical, she thought, and reached for the yellow one.

Mustard? she asked, holding it up for view.

I hope so, Delbert said.

She squeezed some on, carefully tracing her thin zigzag from one end of the meat to the other, so it looked like the one in the picture on the HoJoMoLo menu, which is very appetizing once you pay attention to it, she recalled. She took a ravenous bite, and that's when he started talking, as if to make sure she couldn't answer back too quickly with her mouth full.

So what brought you out to this neck of the boondocks, and where are you headed for next?

To tell the truth, after what I've been through tonight, I need to recover my bearings, if you know what I mean, she replied, recalling her flight from danger across the empty lot, her falling down to stop and lie still in the snow, her standing up, her determined limping steps to reach the light, to find herself before the great perplexing **X** of the crossroads, but quite certain that, like all the rest, these men (except maybe for that nice, different Major man) did not care to hear about her momentous adventure, did not care to know any more than what they already knew, which was that it was best to watch and wait until the merciful end of whatever this might prove to be, in circumspect silence. To cling, motionless, to each moment as each upwelling surface obliterated that which had welled up from emptiness before, like the face of drifting snow, asking no question any more of a question than this.

Headed for next? I have to figure out the answer to that every day. Funny how you can tell that about me somehow! she cried, suddenly brightening.

Not sure what it is I'm telling, Mister Delbert answered.

Well, since you may have figured me out I must confess. In real life, I'm actually a stewardess.

The men exchanged surprised gestures. Her real heart raced, waiting to hear what words would emerge from their silent faces.

Well I'll be darned, Mister Delbert said.

It's a wonderful way for a girl to see the great big world, said Major Tom.

Yes, it's exactly what I've always wanted to do! she exclaimed, feeling in that instant wonderfully far away from the blurring landscapes which had always entrapped her, as if from the clear sky high above the clouds she could see herself far below, a spineless fidgeting creature running around in circles, now shrinking from sight as she climbed ever higher, to vanish, Yes, once and for all, she hoped, from the face of the earth.

Good for you, Major Tom said.

See, this weekend I'm on break between flights. I'd planned to meet the girls, my colleagues, that is, for a round of martinis tonight, down at that cozy little joint we like there on Market Street, before I ran into my ball-player friend, I should say my former or never was my friend, Mister You Know Who He Is By Now.

Yeah him, Delbert said.

The girls? Major Tom asked.

There's a whole flock of us, and brother do we get around, she replied,

cooly nipping a bit of mustard off the tip of her finger.

So who do you fly with? Mister Delbert asked.

Oh, we fly with all different airlines. Me, I'm working mostly Mohawk, but lately they've asked for me on TWA, too.

TWA, and right here out of Elmira, said Major Tom, how about that!

Oh yes, they do like to keep me busy, go figure! she replied, feeling deliciously scared, almost like when she was seven down in Scranton at Rocky Glen and mean old Sonny Boy tricked her into riding that roller coaster and they reached the tip top and she was sure the train was about to jump clean off the track into thin air and started tingling from the top of her head right down to her feet, except this tingle wasn't horrible, she thought, but whatchamacallit like our Holy Mother says, *luxurious.*

I imagine you must be pretty darn good at it, then, Mister Delbert said.

Don't it ever get to you, bein' way up in the air all the time, with your stomach turned upside down? Mister Mutt asked. Don'tcha get that thought in the back of your mind, *What if?* Reckon it could make you a nervous wreck sometimes.

Well, fortunately I'm not one of those who get indigested that way, and I never have been funny about heights either. Mostly I enjoy every minute of it! And when I hear that word *if,* I just stop listening. But oh yes, I positively do need to relax and enjoy myself for a spell once my feet hit the ground again.

Mister Delbert smiled again as he looked into her eyes but, she could tell, not really at her, which started her down the familiar, usual train of thought. Maybe he's seeing something else that the mere, the very sight of her might have set off in his mind. Maybe that I couldn't be what I'm plotting to be, who cares, but still not at me, who cares, she began, as usual, with that oncoming, familiar twinge of sadness. The mere sight, she went on, like how she'd so often caught so many eyes in so many faces looking when she knew they had found themselves noticing her but then didn't want to keep noticing. The dull twinge like a jerk in her mind, like coming to a sudden stop, to a screeching halt, but with no such screeching, only a dulling silence, as if in that mere sight her very presence had come to a stop and rendered her nothing more than an absence, Or what's left when what's there gets carried away, which, it's plain to see, is, she concluded and started to answer herself, but stopped herself right there. After all, it was only the usual twinge, she was used to all that, after all, it was the freight train coming right on time to carry her away to nowhere, every day. Mere, even though with him maybe it's more, maybe, she stopped herself and started again, This time at least not with a smirk like before, a kinda kind smile she thought, one maybe trying to get away from the landslide of his own sadness behind it trying to knock it down, Don't I know, who knows.

Major Tom lifted his shot glass and looked up, as if through the ceiling and rooftop, beyond the dark clouds, to toast the inviolate, empty sky.

> One day you're up there and *wham*, that wild blue yonder grabs you between the ears and she goes straight to your head. You're drunk with her and you know that she's the one you've always been waiting for, and that you'll never find your way back down again, he said,

seeming not to second her emotion but rather to fly away, through a door opening at his gesture, into a clear day from which he had never wholly returned.

> I think we ought to go on and fix this hardworking young lady the treat she asked for, Delbert said,

glancing behind the bar for the right ingredients.

> Geez, now I feel just fine, Rain cried, and tickled to death to find myself here around such nice welcoming folks like you all. But the one other thing I'd like is . . .

she went on, eyes searching the room, then brightening,

> to play a few tunes on that jukebox.

Before she could reach for her purse again, Mister Delbert reached into the register and turned back to lay two quarters on the bar, both with Father George painted into red-faced embarrassment with fingernail polish.

> Tunes on the house, he said, and returned to his mixing.

No wonder she hadn't noticed it when she'd been rushing to hide before, tucked there against the wall at the end of the bar, glowing faintly among the shadows. Almost portable, like the ones you find at diners in the booths, like an otherworldly creature, keeping on the down low. She looked through the glowing window, round like the side of a big glass, like a crystal ball. She worked the little handles sticking out through the slots on top to make the fans with the songs on them flip around. Ain't a stitch of colored folks' music on here, she noticed. But there was that new song she was really crazy about, that *Stranger on the Shore*, and she dropped in the red quarter and quickly pressed the keys, **A5**, to play it, as if it might be a what-chamacallit, mirage, and disappear before she had the chance. But then it started, the clarinet which sounded its straitened, longing cry, which she knew from the very first time she'd heard it was also her own, the strings which sighed in reply, a sigh from an answering dream conjured up in refuge from loneliness, the melody a fantasy persisting in that quiet desperation, illuminating the room with its own atmosphere. And to listen like this is to pass through a door which Takes you back to a not awful maybe happy day once upon a time, she thought, even if it's only in your mind, even if it's only a couple hot seconds of that day that you can even remember, even a day desperately stitched together from the pieces left of other days that you don't care who says you're forgetful of or stupid because you need so bad to make one whole one from them for yourself, to tell a story telling the truth better than memories which melt as soon as grasped, like a handful of snow. She'd felt good about that song because Mother loved it too, Yes cause the horn's played by that Englishman with one of their funny names, kinda sounds like Crackers and Milk she recalled, and how when Mother was around to hear it she'd laugh about that to herself but not out loud, and of course she and Pearl had figured out the music from the 45 to play a duet, but every time they tried to work on it Mother made sure to remind her that That man's a virtuoso, which you'll never stand a chance of becoming with all that squawking you do on yours. But still she had discovered something, like she did once in a blue moon or so, that a little old song could mark that day, a day now existing only in memory but at every turn ever more lost, like an **X** vainly marking the map of a directionless land of empty roads, on which to travel can only mean to find yourself ever more lost. Oh Lord knows it won't ever be anything important, except that it's Something I love that Mother loves too, which once upon a time would have comforted her, Yes it would have, she thought, once upon a time. Then she looked for her number one sweethearts the Flamingos, but no such luck, like she already knew. The rest of the stuff on there was mostly country music, which would do in a pinch, she admitted, because she'd learned to like some of them Opry numbers she'd hear coming from that radio back in Mister Barney's garage. She'd learned it was better to not think about the folks singing them, not to picture in her mind all of them talking and carrying on the way they do otherwise sometimes, to just listen to the stories they sing like us colored folks sing too, with a simple tune and plain words, like for instance a lot of the ones by that lonesome old cutie Hank Williams. So she pressed **C1** for one of his, then **J7** for one by that Patsy Cline too, of whom she'd already got an earful since forever cause next to Saint Marlene she was Pearl's absolute favorite.

But where's the sound coming from? she asked.

Jeff wired those up for me and didn't charge me a penny, Delbert announced, pointing up to the speakers mounted in the corners of the room.

Quite the clever young man, Major Tom added.

My kid brother, who I still say ain't nothin' but an ingrate to me, Mister Mutt said.

Nearing the end of his handiwork, Delbert set the delicate funnel of the glass down on a fresh white coaster.

And of course, one last touch!

His long fingers parted to release a green olive, skewered precisely through the middle with a toothpick, into the glass. He put on that pinched, dimply smile again, it's almost like one of Father's smiles when he wants to stay mad instead but he just can't help it, she thought, and glanced round at the other gentlemen, each of whom scrutinized and nodded approvingly. This Mister Delbert's quite a nice gentleman after all, she thought.

The Perfect Martini, just for you, Mister Delbert said, flinging his hands open like a magician who'd just pulled a white dove out of thin air. She had come so far to reach this moment, she thought. She imagined that all her forbidden joy to have at last crossed the finish line and found herself at last someone else, all her molting spirits had been distilled into this glass, a liquid jewel veiled in frost, blushing pink.

You're looking at a fine bartender. But we can only hope that his creation meets your exacting standards, Major Tom said.

In other words, down the hatch, Mister Mutt said.

She raised the glass to Mister Delbert and then to her lips. A tiny sip. Such a strange potion, she thought. A small swallow. Right there's another one of them funny words, she thought, small like a bird you can hide in your fist, but when flying, darting, suddenly as trackless as the sky. Or, what's filling up the small pucker pot in the front of my mouth, she noticed, tasting icy-sweet, then tart, then suddenly bitter at the edges of the tongue, here and there then gone, shapeshifting like a ghost, trailing a whiff of roses. She couldn't seem to keep up with it, must be all that whatchamacallit, proof going to my head, she thought, opening her eyes and taking a second sip. Nothing like that nasty worm pee-looking drink, she thought, recalling how it had turned her head to putty. It's quite the nice friendly drink, she decided, kinda sweeps you not off your feet but like into a dance, like when you find yourself left alone at your table, watching your pretty girlfriends who slipped away for a break, from trying too hard to be comforting, to kick up their heels with their boyfriends, until you can't stand it any longer so you roll your eyes upward to watch the balloons and crepe ribbons jostling in the summer night's air, until you look down to find an outstretched hand, a hand requiring not a word of explanation, a hand whose mere gesture lifts your face to meet the face you never noticed before, the hand bewitching you to follow after.

I must say, it's a strong one, she said,
setting down the glass and leaning back with a sigh.

Now is that any way to treat a lady? Mutt asked,

Del, it sounds like you got a little too generous, Major Tom said.

But good, she protested, sipping again.

All of sudden she needed a cigarette. Not to smoke really, but just to hold it. Actually she hated cigarettes, and it had taken her her whole life so far to get used to breathing smoke at home, especially Mother's Pall Malls, she thought, just the smell of one lit up was enough to make her feel like a fly sprayed with gas, to turn her stomach upside down. Why then? On account of all the excitement from sitting up here, she thought, kinda like my very own little old red-carpet moment. After all, here she was, single-handedly commanding the undivided attention of these three gentlemen, even if two of them were probably old enough to be her father. Here's Mister Delbert giving her kind fatherly looks from his Lil' Abner handsome face, and Major Tom beaming enchantment from his wrinkled little boy face, but she couldn't tell yet about Mister Mutt there, and really didn't want to figure out, come to think of it, why he'd kept looking her up and down the whole time she'd been sitting up there, or rather sneaking an eyeful when the other two wouldn't notice, and as though she didn't notice. Don't think for a second I don't notice when folks are looking me over, she thought, but this one keeps looking kinda like he halfway likes what he sees and halfway for that other reason that doesn't care and that isn't about liking it in a nice way but in that other way, which started to make her uncomfortable and wanting to but scared to glare right back, since even if Mother didn't want to admit it, she didn't raise no fool. But still she felt safe sitting up there because of the other two, and now she was sure that a martini was the perfect thing to relax a girl, a hard-working stewardess, back on earth in her home-town after a long hard week up in the air. That's why she needed to get that cigarette, it would go along with the rest of what was going on, and to even try and smoke it. Then the whole shebang would look right, like those movies with that long tall husky-voiced gal whatshername, Lauren McCall, in them. And I know that's what Pearl would do too if she were here, she thought, of course they'd be all over her offering her a light and so on, but soon enough she'd be blowing smoke in their faces and not paying them any mind, she thought, My careless Pearl. At that moment Major Tom just happened to be tapping the end of a fresh one on the side of a thin leather case.

May I borrow one of those from you? she asked.

Of course! the Major answered, but I'm not sure how you plan to give it back to me when you're through.

Yeah what's he get for that, eh? Mister Mutt said,
with a grin that felt to her like a hand that reached inside and tried to squeeze an answer from her, from which she quickly looked away.

He gets nothing, Mister Delbert snapped.
She held the cigarette to her lips and leaned in to catch Major Tom's offered flame. She pulled a puff of hot smoke into her mouth and straightened up with as much broad-shouldered poise as she could

muster, while kind of holding her real breath cause she just couldn't help it. The little boy in the Major's eyes brightened the clouds of his weary face with a sudden thought.

I've always wondered what's it like flying into New York City. LaGuardia's still the top airport there, right? he asked.

Oh my, it's *enormous*, she replied,
pretty sure that was just what she'd read in one of her magazines somewhere.

Must be a real sight to see from the air, Delbert agreed.
She did not know what to tell them, what to dare speak, what misstep might catch her out in her first leading role. She saw herself running down that red carpet, away from the other end that was rolling up on itself like a gigantic snowball getting bigger every second and determined to swallow her whole. But in that moment's sigh she felt that first delirious excitement and vengeful joy still churning to escape from her, Like a fire lighting up a murky sky, yes, she thought, now she would follow to wherever it led her, carelessly, on. Besides, she recalled, she knew very well how the world looked from on high, at least from the highest hill above her town. She remembered when she and Pearl had driven up there early one August night, climbing above the scenic vista of Mister O'Brien's and Father's dining room, above the stone wall of the monastery courtyard, to the woods at the end of the road as the voices of the brother monks, joining in vesper song, sounded faintly across the fields like the waning sunlight above the valley, slipping below the rim of the hills. When she'd got enough of a grip on herself to leave the car, and the only sound left after the evensong had faded was the stir of the crickets. Want to know a secret? Pearl whispered, The sky is everywhere. Even there, where my first Brainless *Wunderbar von* from who knows where split me open *das erste Mal*, she said,

pointing toward the low shadows of a thicket crowding a solitary, twisted tree. Rain remembered how frightened she had felt to be standing there in the twilight, after all the *True Confessions* she'd read about horrible things happening in places just like that. Such a lonely old place, she'd answered, trying to sound super smart and grown up, too. But not lonely when we're here together, Pearl answered, taking her hand, *Also, gehen wir.* So she'd followed after her then, climbing up the rise to the high ledge. Mounting there beside her, she had looked beyond the edge down to the treetops and started backward in terror. But Pearl had held her still in her arms until they lay back together on the stone, still warm from the summer sun. How silly she'd felt ever since to have said, looking up into the moonless night, How about all of them stars twinkling away up there? Oh yes, Pearl said, never making her feel small. But look, it's lovely down there too, she said. She pointed to the fireflies drifting like stardust over the nearby pastures rolling away into the shadows, into the wide dark bowl of the valley filling up with the dark, with the scattered lights of the farmhouses, with the headlights flashing like sparks along the river road, with the distant constellation of dim streetlamps of the town, all impotent against the night and time like a crashed neon sign sputtering at a wide spot in the road. Said that after he'd driven away she just lay there in the weeds, lay there as tiny invisible creatures hopped and crawled over her until she couldn't see the sight of herself in daylight anymore. Until she opened her eyes and all at once, like a gift from heaven, she heard the canticle, heard the crickets chirping like a choir of angels. Then stood herself up and straightened her clothes and gathered her hair and climbed to the top, surefooted across the jagged stones and practiced through the crevices, up toward the the half-moon and stars hanging far above her, to the ledge, flat and empty like the

shadow of a face against the sky. That she'd climbed up not knowing if she would ever come down or come down the same way, that
she bled into the stone and counted the lights above and below her,
everywhere, *Ausgezeichnet*, until she fell asleep. Then Rain remembered how often Mother Superior had counted or rubbed away or
nuzzled the tears from the cheeks of her frail novitiates, scolding
Now now, no leaking, meine Lieben. We must not sink.

Nights I fly over the Big Apple, I see stars everywhere I look.

Specially when you're in the cockpit where them pilots sit,
Mister Mutt suggested.

Talk about a front seat. You look up there's all the normal stars,
and then down and there's the lights in them skyscrapers and
running up and down Broadway and all them avenues, it's like
you could be flying upside down and looking up into heaven.

She took a luxurious drag on the cigarette, breathing it in guiltily,
just a little.

Have to get up there myself one of these days, Mister Delbert
said.

The bombardier now seemed shrunken and twisted around himself, legs crossed, chin stuck upon his hand.

I'll never shake those long nights. The sight of those streets
down there, full of fire, he said,

draining his glass. No more talk of flying, Rain decided, nobody
wants to hear any more of that. Let's try and cheer him up a little,
she thought, while noting that neither Mister Delbert nor Mister
Mutt looked to be concerned about his sudden withdrawal into
silence. She was relieved to change the subject and proud that she
hadn't at all made a fool of herself, that she'd made a good impression, that she'd shown herself capable of holding her liquor, Just a
little tipsy is all, how about that.

The jukebox played her favorite of that big blonde with the smoky voice. She listened as the song brought forth the words she'd been waiting for. Noticing *something sad about the boy*. It scared her more than she'd admit to think he'd uncovered her plot. Probably can't be bothered to say anything to the other guys about it, she figured. They probably don't notice such things like he does, anyway. Plus like they say if you can't say anything good about somebody, why bother, she admitted, which eased her sudden discomfort with herself. Even so, she would try to cheer him up, she would let him know that she understood his disappointment in her. That she was used to almost everybody feeling that way about her and, quite frankly, how often they were right. That she was sorry, very sorry, and hoped that he would understand that she was a spineless fidgeting creature that couldn't help but run around in circles like a chicken with its head cut off. It came like a flash to her, just what to do. That she must be like the one who has discovered him like a sweet surprise, like a gardener discovering a delightful wallflower, one who reaches out her hand without a word of explanation, the hand which lifts its face to meet the first to ever meet its presence, the hand bewitching it to follow after. She looked into that face turned away from the light like a half-moon, and thought she could see, looking out from the open door inside him there, a small face fractured by the dark, floating like leaves fallen on water, Yes, the little one she thought had run away. Now she wanted to call him out, to take his hand and bring him back to join her there, to come back to life again.

She slipped down from the stool and hobbled on her broken heel to where he sat, lost inside himself, as if his scant flesh and bone were a door he had opened and walked through to disappear into a territory beyond pursuit. She raised her glass as if she were lifting a candle to reveal nameless shapes thrusting forth to crowd her pathway through the dark. Drawing near, she felt as if they might fit together like two broken pieces meant for each other, each half-fore-shortened, half-brazen, half-secret, half lie, half-truth, half not yet something, half what she could not bear to think might come to nothing. She set her glass down upon the bar and stood uprightly, primly, hands clasped before her.

Hello Mister. Shall we dance?

No thanks, he answered before she asked, still looking away.

I'll take off these dumb shoes. We'll have ourselves a good old time. Look here sweetie, we must *la rumba*.

I can't take any more Please don't.

Mister Delbert stood across from them on the other side of the bar.

Time to say goodnight, Miss, he said.

No need to worry about me now. When I'm ready, I'll call the girls and they'll come right up to get me

There's no place like home. Call now.

Show me the way to go home. I'm tired and I want to go to bed, crooned Mister Mutt,

looking her over with a spark in his wide, drenched eyes.

You show me, I'll show you, he persisted.

You'll do no such thing, Delbert said quietly,

placing both hands atop the bar. She felt that if she could move even a muscle in that moment she would leap over and stand behind him and cling to him for dear life, until all the rotten tramps and stranglers and monsters living and undead turned tail and fled into the night.

Hell, I'll give the girl a ride all the way home. If she pays the fare.

The hell you will.

After what you hear about them stewardess gals, here's one right here.

Don't make me put you out. Act like a gentleman.

Gentleman. Who's a gentleman any damn how.

One more wisecrack, you've had it.

He opened the register and turned to lay a string of dimes along the bar in front of her, like a row of tiny steppingstones, she thought, then pointed toward the back.

The phone's right where it was when you got here.

The backroom lights came on with a flash, melting her once again. Mister Delbert has the best candle of all, she thought. It looked so different from how it had looked in the dark, when it had been her hiding place. Now it was bright and plain as day all the way there. Now the room and all the forsaken things huddling within it were revealed, in a brightness moving across the dusty booths and the stained scarred green of the pool table, falling into the coffin-dark of the phone booth, sparkling like morning sunlight falling across the water. But it was into that black box that she now had to walk, no longer tipsy but suddenly clear-eyed and with nerves sharpened to a razor's edge, to reach the threshold and throw herself in, like one diving deeply below the waves and wishing never again to surface. Or to let herself stumble in, as if, poised at last on the tip of her blades in the moment of an impossible arabesque, falling through suddenly breaking ice, to struggle in vain against the chill creeping into her limbs until she was breathless and still. Or, as if discovering someone she had never before recognized as herself, to simply enter. Was this the destination, she asked herself, with a retch of desperate unease and sadness, to which she had unknowingly traveled all that night, so perilously through the snow?

Once again she felt the cold draft nuzzling her ankles, and heard a voice sounding sharp and sweet and clear beyond the silence flowing in through the opening door,

Don't forget to wave to me the next time you fly by.

But she did not turn back to watch, or to answer. No time now for long goodbyes, no time for mistaken promises, she thought, smiling to herself, there's just enough time to take this breath of cold, fresh air, just enough. She walked into the phone booth, settled onto the narrow bench, closed the door firmly behind her and turned on the light. She reached for one of the dimes piled in her lap. Won't need any more than one, she reminded herself, lifting the receiver from its cradle, it's a local call. And, sounding beyond the dull buzz at her ear, sounding beyond herself, she heard the screaming engines racing down the runway. Through the glass she watched her big jet plane break away from the snowbound earth and mount to the sky.

Handy Man

Still tingling in bed under her quilt, Rain watched as he worked, amazed by the large, plump hands which nevertheless worked swiftly, precisely, to take things apart, and the parts of them apart, until their indivisible entrails lay in kindred heaps across the spread newspaper. Hands delighted, she could tell, to carry the hidden shapes inside the dark of things into the light of day.

Soon she thought, Even if it's only my air conditioner, this explains something about it, about how and what they had shared through the slow secret hours of that afternoon. That these same hands had for a long time just before been holding her, lingering here and there and there as they rambled over her, lazily, gently, like a pair of merry vagabonds careless of destination, like his eyes wide and glinting in the light spilling in at the edges of the drawn curtains, at peace to remain wherever they found themselves. Poised for her stirring to meet them as they drew near the places she would have wished them to go if she had known where they were, the places which she could not bear to find them approaching because they would find her already there, the places you were when you didn't know or didn't want to know where you were. She thought again, That's right, this preoccupation must explain something about the other, or maybe they both explain each other. The sweet spots, so they say.

Know what? I can see right in through the front of your shorts,
she said,

covering her eyes, to peek through her fingers.

You ain't supposed to be looking for that, Jimmy Love answered.
Nasty boy won't lift a finger to cover up, she thought. Ain't even
summertime yet, his mind's wrapped up in that old box and done
forgot all about fixing me.

It ain't only some old box, Jimmy Love had said while they still
lay entwined together. It's a *deevice*, he'd said, while tracing slow laps
around her nipple with a fingertip. She enjoyed that confident sound
in his voice. Cocky, Sonny-Boy would call it. Enjoyed the way he took
his sweet time with certain fancy words when he spoke about such
things, enjoyed how he sounded so smart, kinda like a teacher or even
a scientist, and it tickled her to death to imagine a mad scientist all
hot and bothered over her, and lo and behold here he's up in my bed,
go figure. She closed her eyes. Mmmm, it felt even better when she
couldn't see what it was he did even though she knew what it was, but
still she didn't get that fancy word he threw in before.

*Dee*vice?
she asked softly, like it was a nasty word she was about to find out
after all this time what thing it meant.

Deevice. Let's see. Means a machine made and known to do
exactly one thing. Like that AC unit there.

The delectable copper finger extended and twirled as he pointed to
the box.

One fan inside pull your hot air from the room here, which cool
off inside against the vaporator coil, then the fan throw it back
out to the room, while the other fan throw the heat off the condenser coil out the window. Might could say it cool your hot to
trot down, and that's all it intended to do.

102

Oh Jimmy Love, cried Rain, cool down your own self. Vaporator, condenser, it all sounds like canned milk to me. It takes me a while to catch on to that gadget stuff, you'll definitely have to come back up here at least a hundred times to help me study on it. At least there's one thing like that I already know about, she says,

rolling over to point right on it.

Least that ain't broke too, he said,

and they laughed a hoot, until they suddenly fell silent.

See, all the different parts of folks, hands arms legs, digestion and whatnot, they just *deevices* too, when you study how all them parts in us set to run together, grabbing walking eating and whatnot, like a regular contraption.

Too complicated for me, Rain complained.

Hold up. Here go an easy one.

he said, taking her hand.

Feel how your heart beat just like a clock? he said,

and she suddenly found herself about to cry like a baby cause of how gently he took her hand and held it against herself. Maybe I'm not a specimen after all, she thought.

Afraid mine ain't keeping good time right now, she whispered. Where your hand's staying.

And the deevice that lives inside us that's what folks be callin' our soul.

First I was scared to think about it, that I might could be a whole deevice myself, same as one of them robots you be seeing now in the movies, like that giant Gort comin' to protect Mister Klaatu when he struggling with hardheaded human folks. Course I know it don't say so in Scripture, and the Lord ain't name us robots back then when he made us. But I reckon if he smarter than anybody could ever be, then he might could have made us like super robots, with a deevice for each part, and a computer like nobody ain't never seen yet and probably couldn't never think of for our brains.

But Mother would call the whole kit and caboodle Plain old devilment, that folks walking around ain't nothing more than contraptions blowing hot air, The very idea. And if the Lord made us, how's that go, *in his image,* and He's only a contraption, well then who made Him, she could hear her now, Stuff and nonsense. Not to mention that other thing he'd go jump off the deep end about right quick, them flying saucers. Not *Mister Klaatu* and his big old *Gort,* but supposed to be real ones that land from outer space, with them critters supposed to be inside who they say can't be human, them so-called UFOs. Mister Professor couldn't help himself, he had to tell all yesterday on her lunch hour down at the Tex Diner, when all she had wanted was to enjoy her extra-bacon BLT. How some of his Air Force folks who fly them big jets and fighters have seen certain things up there they wouldn't ever believe they'd seen till they did with their own eyes. How they've come across certain things off in the mountains someplace that *can't be from here,* that they keep locked up out in the desert in a big old underground freezer, with its own special army to protect it. Most likely we suspect and estimate, he says, that them critters flyin' them spaceships ain't keen to be neighborly. How we see it, he says, they might could take what they please from us and keep on goin', could be every damn thing, how we gonna stop em? Or worse they be doing us just like they showed it on TWILIGHT ZONE. To them we like chickens with shonuff chicken brains, too lazy to crow for day. Therefore and if so they probly ain't got no kind of use for us except, BBQ. But Unbelievably Frightening Object is what Mary Louise VanFleet and her other girlfriends called them when they pretended for a hot second to believe in it, even though Pearl said Little Green Men didn't faze her one bit. But it scared Rain half to death to even think about some three-eyed critters pickin' folks like apples off a tree, and quite frankly being dead would spoil everything right now, so please, girl, don't get him started, she happily decided.

Oh sweetie, she purred,
scratching behind his ear where he liked it,

I can't see how all that could be right. I'll sure have to pick a bone with your whatchmacallit, *wing men* if I get a chance one of these days.

I presuppose you will, Jimmy Love said.

Talk about a hairy man, she thought, Shoot, laying on him's about like laying on a bear rug.

If Mother were to burst in through the door, as she had ninety eleven times before when she'd been too noisy or too quiet for too long or why in the world wasn't she all ears when she called, barge in and catch them all snug and cozy together between the sheets, in whatchamacallit, *fragrántay delicious* or whatever they call it, Oh, she'd be mortified, she thought, chuckling to herself, Lord, every last hair on her head would tighten up like a rug. But Mother, she'd hurry to answer, It's actually, quite frankly, so wonderful. Cause Jimmy and me, we're made for each other, just, just like two parts of a little old deevice, that go together just right, specially with the screw that holds them together. Umph, ain't I got a naughty nasty mind in me these days, she thought. She laughed to herself to find that she could be so clever in her own mind to imagine it happening in a way to keep from being terrified at the thought of it, like what happened at the BAR & GRILL, out in the fallen snow. But they were safe and sound from her, and Father would never know too, both gone off till six o'clock, oh happy day. She had told him so when he showed up at the kitchen door precisely on time, as the bell-jar chimed eleven o'clock, clutching a bunch of pretty stragglers he probably picked from the side of the road, Knock, knock! Who's there? Somebody fixin' to find you, he said. Good morning Captain Henry and Miss Claire, he called brightly, leaning in. Oh, shush, they left already, she said. Oh you told me they was? he asked, not too pointedly. I'm tickled pink to have a man who can put two and two together, she thought, Hand over them flowers and get in here, she cried, taking him by the hand.

She watched him working, intently and quietly, as if he couldn't imagine another place in the whole world he'd rather be, surprised to feel herself at home in that room with the slanting walls where for so very long she'd slept and outgrown and worn out shoes and clothes and learned to put on her makeup up in front of her great big round mirror and sometimes weary of her own reflection and its tormenting thoughts stared out her gabled windows into the oblique patch of sky overhead and the houses and trees and street below without knowing where to begin, but now at home in the stillness of that lazy afternoon in a way which she'd almost never known before. Except maybe sometimes after a good dream from which she woke up early early, when the first light crept into the dark, and upstairs and downstairs even her family of early risers (who enjoyed wishing her Good afternoon when she'd finally drag herself down to the kitchen) were not yet stirring, when in the half-light she closed her eyes again for a little while, just to lie there and pick that happy dream from the roadside of her mind like a wild flower to keep for her basket and stretch herself into the warm dark under the covers and by and by drift into that gentle quietness which unlike the blurring world around her neither turned her away, nor chased after her baying like a hound, nor fractured before her eyes into a forest of walls and dead ends leaving her lost to herself. But it's the *with him* that's the difference, she thought. And feeling herself close to him there, close for the first time to someone there, now she could admit to herself that she had dreamed and prayed that she might live and breathe in such a moment, especially ever since that blessed day her true Jimmy Love first came to town.

But certainly she should say, Showed up, since he must have been Heaven-sent, otherwise chances were he would have never come unless He fixed it so that even he, one so clever and careful about every little thing, took the wrong bus, not the ten-thirty to Binghamton but that ten-thirty to Corning. And she oh yes was certainly the girl he would have never met unless she had come hot-footin' by after work on her way to Cole's to pick up those fresh tripes for Father from the butcher, thinking to hurry past but something caught her eye. Something about the way he stood there in front of Big Bill's bus station window, large and round but standing straight and tall, from the long blue cap perched atop his head to the necktie tucked into the baby blue shirt with the starred stripe on one sleeve which at first she thought to be a curious butterfly to the pressed trousers and shining shoes and the dusty blue sack stretched out at his feet, looking up and down the street and finally up into the four o'clock sky as clear and bright as his suddenly careless smile, glancing everywhere without spelling a direction, as content to be lost as a body could be. Though she started out determined to hurry past, his radiant figure seemed to fill the sidewalk and entire street ahead of her and pranced into her eyes and filled up the windswept space inside her head and seized her insistently, as if captured by some unexpected gravity, as if suddenly she were once again a newborn, still immersed in time, in its still-molten world scarce of boundary or recognition or specious fixity, still adrift in her flitting from moment to moment yet drawn by currents unaccountable to herself to linger and delight in an unexpected presence, sparkling and new.

Turning to glance as she passed, that's what she thought she was doing, but it turned out that she found herself stopping there, standing behind and almost close to him, not sure of what she was waiting for, what to say. He turned, smiled, and tipped his cap. Good afternoon, ma'am, he said. Good afternoon to you, she replied. I've never been called ma'am before, she added, but I do call my mother and a few other folks that. Don't we all, he said. And please pardon me, I don't mean nothing by it no way, cept good manners. Tell the truth I'd rather call you Miss, if you don't mind, he added, smiling again. No I don't mind. But then again, you could call me by my name instead, she said, And what might that be? Most folks around here call me Rain. Like a rainy day, I presuppose? Nope, like a shortcut for Lorraine. Like *Sweet Lorraine*, then, he said, nodding his head like he'd just figured out some kind of fancy mystery, which kinda made her want to laugh. I suppose it could be that notion in somebody or other's mind, she replied. Well, it's shonuff fine weather to find myself here, and that notion suit you just fine too, if you ask me. No need to ask since now I know, thank you kindly, Rain said. But I do apologize, he insisted, since I sound all mixed up about everything, his eyes now slipping off to meet faces in passing cars and pausing to look back surprised to find her here, Like he tried to put on like he wasn't before, she thought. Ain't had nary a scrap to eat since early morning, he said, and the big man inside there advised me that where I'd hoped to arrive at by suppertime, place call Johnson City, This ain't it he says. And you cain't get there on this crate you on neither, so you got to get off and wait here or somewheres around here till four, big man says. Well don't that beat all, I said. So I'm a G.I. just trying to get to where he supposed to be. Mister, I'm very sorry to hear of your troubles, Rain said, holding her hand against her heart, while admiring his delicately plump, handsome brown face, and the delicious gap between his two front teeth. She eyed the butterfly-looking patches on his sleeves and recalled the Army ones Sonny Boy had had on his, and who could keep all them different ones straight, she wondered, Not me. So what kind of G.I. are you? she asked. U.S. Air Force, Airman! he replied proudly, words which flew into her perked up ears like nesting birds and quite frankly stopped her breath. Well, how about that! she cried, in a flutter. That somethin' special for you? he wondered, leaning lower to meet her gaze with his wide bright eyes. I've always wanted to meet one of you fly boys face to face, she almost blurted out, All that up in the air stuff kinda fascinates me. Well, I'm pleased to satisfy your fascination, he replied. Now I know what name this here town called, but I say technically, I still don't know where I am. But I do, she said, wanting to but not reaching to take his hand, Wait and see. About then she got an urge to run over and get a pair of Texas Hots and Oh yes to invite him along, and even to feed him too if he can't afford a dollar fifty right now, after all he says he's hungry, she thought. Quite frankly, it's the Christian thing to do to, she recalled, that's what Papa had always taught her, everybody ought to treat a stranger right, long ways from home. Never can tell who Heaven might send your way, he says, like them guests who drop by in the stories from the Good Book, who never ask to be welcomed, but still some good old folks bring them water to wash they feet with and give them their best food to eat, then come to find out who they were, angels carrying a special message from the Lord. Who knows, this fine gentleman might be some kind of angel, and might have some kind of good news for somebody or other, at least that's how I'm gonna look at it, she thought. Besides, them tripes ain't about to jump up and walk away before I get there, she thought.

The way that blue bag stood up on one end next to him in the booth, it looked like there might even be somebody fastened up in there, she thought. And he wouldn't take Maggie's advice to leave it out back on the deck, If you don't mind ma'am, this here duffel don't never leave my side, he said. Suit yourself, as long as you don't try and feed it I don't care what you do, she answered. In fact, on her lunch hour at Woolworth's when it was nice out like today, Rain liked to come eat out back at that wobbly old table at the top of the iron stairs. Sometimes Maggie would slip her an extra dog or plate of fries on the house or ask for help with her plate when she couldn't find appetite to feed her own skinny bones, or come kick her tired shoes off and have a smoke. They'd sit and watch the freight trains and the ERIE LACKAWANNA local roll past the station-house down on the other side of the alley, stopping even less often, Maggie confirmed, than they used to back when she single-handedly, after her no-good hubby finally did one good thing in his life and kicked the bucket, opened her own now-famous regulation diner, in which she daily took pains with a mute finger to point out to pit-stopping bus riders the sign above the grill and have it understood that THIS CHILI POT'S AT THE END OF THE RAINBOW. Hoo wee, she'd point to the passing cars and croon above the roar, The Atchison, Topeka and the Santa Fe, where my Daddy rode the rails. When I see that short-legged cross rolling by, she said, I start thinkin' about the old folks back home, then stop when I remember that's sure a waste of time. Once, before Rain knew two or three things about her, she'd answered, I'm so sorry you turned out feeling like that, but to me there's no place like home. Maggie flicked her dead butt into thin air, lit up another and said, To me I'm sure glad there ain't.

Rain knew she wouldn't be chatting up a storm with her old chum that day. Not with how tickled to death she was to have happened upon this charming adventure, with how determined she was to do her best to lend a helping hand to another in need, with how especially delicious it tasted to have her usual C dog and jumbo fries and Coke with this Texan so he claimed, who seemed to be as expert as she was about all three, you might as well say had just about fell out the sky, and most of all with how surprised she was to hear what he had just told her, of all things. It's too cute to be true, she cried, nobody could believe it unless they heard it with their own ears, she said. I can prove it, he said, reaching in through his collar under his shirt for a loop of chain, the kind made up of them little beads like a pull chain on a lamp. He pulled on it like he was fishing for what he caught on the other end till, sure enough, out it came, one of them whatchamacallits, she remembered cause Sonny Boy had had one too, Oh your dog collar! she said. He just laughed and slipped it over his head and into one hand. Now look right here what Uncle Sam put down, he said.

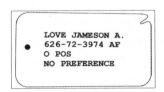

Stop right there! Rain cried, as they fell tinkling into her outstretched palm. She stared past the words graven there in a tongue she scarcely understood, past the unspeakable word she feared, but yearned, to utter. Stared into its brightness until she reached her face beyond it, found its burning eyes turning back from her own, knew that she must follow after, knew at last that it would pass over her lips.. Now how about that for a, whatchamacallit, coincidence, she said, chewing and swallowing air to cool it down. I know I got the right word this time, she thought, because Mother went up one side of me and down the other about it. Coincidence, not that he should have been born a Love of course, but that the actual Mister Love, tender and plump like sweet Cupid himself, shooting his arrows so fast that folks can't get out the way, that he should walk right in, that he should be right here in front of her showing off his dog collar right now, right when she'd been searching everywhere for him. At a time like this, she thought, here I am jabbering with my mouth full. Being named that, she went on, I imagine you must be the type that wears a certain kind of reputation. Aw shucks, he replied, I ain't so bad once you get used to me. I'd prefer to hear that from the ones who got used to you, she said, which was actually the last thing she preferred to hear. Honest I ain't the type who craves the night life, drinking up a whole lot of liquor, running around pesterin' a whole lot of different womens, pitty-pat playin' and crap shootin', I ain't never gone off on no foolishness like that. And why not? she asked, hoping both that it was and wasn't so at the same time. See, ultimately I craves my studies and my calculations, he explained with brightening eyes, to spend my time quiring knowledge. But not trifling knowledge, only of the true and best kind, the scientific kind, to satisfy my soul. He unzipped the long pocket of his duffel and extracted a thick, floppy blue book. Pushing his plate aside he set it down and brushed the dust from its cover. Opening the cover carefully like he let someplace that can't be hid inside him to stand in the light of day. This here's chock full of what I mean by real serious deep knowledge, all built up in systematic style, step-by-step, like stackin' up bricks. She sipped her Coke through the straw and followed his dancing finger down the page. See, this here *my* Scripture, he said. Sure don't look like Scripture to me, she replied. Naw, but I shonuff feel better studyin' this here than strugglin' with all that burning hellfire stuff. All you got to do is be sure you understand what come before in the last chapter, he explained, then you can't go wrong. CHAPTER ONE, WHY ELECTRONICS, FOR THE NAVIGATOR, she read, So why? she asked. See, Navigator need to know to run that radar. That be what I'm shootin' for now, to make First Class, but far as I'm concerned I'm about qualified to fly this minute. So this clever handsome Kewpie Doll's aiming to get his wings, she thought, which got her even more excited over him but all at once downhearted too cause she wished that she too could find something she wanted to tell the world about how much she wanted it, not pretend wings worn to sip pretend martinis but some kind of really real special thing to reach for and get and call her own, be good for it instead of like she kept thinking, like a broken record, she was and had always been, good for nothing. Well, just listen to you! cried Rain. But ain't no plain GI job go even halfway far as the utilizing of true knowledge I got in mind. I got serious plans, luckrative plans, way beyond that, he said. See here, CHAPTER TWO start off with STATIC and MOTION OF ELECTRICITY, then you go ahead into your RESISTANCE. THREE deal with CIRCUITS, how they be running in SERIES or PARALLEL, look out, they tricky at first. FOUR, don't sleep on MAGNETISM now, by thinkin' everybody already know how them little horseshoes work and whatnot. Shoot, I can tell right now how something works, Rain thought, trying to drag me across this table to jump on you. FIVE, he kept on, see here, you run up on DC AND AC current, take your time till they sink in. SIX, here come MOTORS, METERS, now you gettin' somewhere, you gettin' technical, now you in deep. Then number SEVEN, INDUCTORS, CAPACITORS, TRANSFORMERS, that's where I am and what I got to keep all three straight in my mind now, cause I'm fixin' to build some of my own. Certain folks in big business, your tycoon types and such, they come buy up a whole truckload at the same time for whatever use they need em for in they business, see? But why would some big time big shot come buy from little old you? Rain wondered. Good question, Jimmy Love said, but they gonna have to, cause I'll have my patent, just like Mister Edison had on different machines he the first to come up with, for instance the Candescent Bulb and Victrola and such. Which mean mine gonna be made different and work different, better most and generally than the rest. Sounds good! she chimed in. That's why I'll stake my claim with the govermint to get them numbers which prove they my own, my inventions. Let's say, Mister Howard Hughes, You mean that crazy old Spruce Goose Man? she interrupted. Yep I mean him, a man who got nuff sense to build his own aircrafts and get rich off em. If he show up to copy mine like he will, then he got to pay me, and I get my piece of the action, see, it's call royalty. Royalty! Won't be long before you look like the Duke of Earl in them patent leather shoes, she said with a smile. Yep I presuppose that's how unstoppable and great I'll be, he said, grinning back. If that's what you plan to do with that serious deep knowledge, as you call it, she replied, you'll have to be more serious than a whole lot of folks, serious as them whatchamacallit, rocket men down there in Houston. You right, he replied, and I grew up around them parts, I know they serious enough. But they ain't got nothin' on me. I been studying on my own what they could only learn in some fancy school with a teacher, which I don't need since it look like I'm what they call a natural.

Well, Mister Natural Duke of Earl, Rain said, I guess we'll see. We definitely gonna see about that, Jimmy Love said. You'll have to come back here and take me out to lunch when you make your first cool million, so you can show me them papers and prove it to me, she said, pressing the warm fingers of her open hand into his own. I'll be glad to oblige in the event of such eventuality, he replied.

Maybe when he comes back, she thought, not wanting to hear the *ifs* shouted from the back of her mind, even though he says it's not his main thing, when he's finally a typhoon or cocoon or whatever it is he's trying to be like that crazy Mister Hughes he could still take me for a ride in one of his own jet planes. It would be the best patent and proof of all to be so special to somebody that they would come to take her away, Yes even if only for a day, an hour, from that bitter valley standing before her like a wall every which way she turned to run. Somebody like a grateful angel or Superman to take her in his arms and soar instantaneously into the blue, Yes, my pilot to fly me across outer space to another world, if there really was one, where I might be happy, if she had ever really known what happiness was. Shucks, even if I'm not so special to him maybe I could ride as his secretary or some other helpful position, or even a stewardess, if he'd hire me. Oh I need to steer clear of that daydreaming, she reminded herself, since it always left her downhearted like she'd was right then, all over again. And when she could stand to recollect and think about it, she remembered when Mother warned her against telling such fool stories to and about herself. Better to be just who I am, even if that's almost nobody, at least till four o'clock, she thought, and suddenly felt herself falling back to earth, back to that lunch hour which was not really a lunch hour, back to How in the world did I wind up sitting across from this stranger here today and gone tomorrow like all the rest, everywhere you look. Anyhow, besides probably having some kinda reputation, she went on, I bet you got somebody back where you started from waitin' for you to get around to all this patenting and whatnot, she said, blushing to have second-guessed him, to have let on that she might care a whit either way, in the end. He smiled as his eyes lifted to search overhead, as if to glean thoughts from thin air, then dove swiftly to meet her own. And I bet you ain't exactly the kind of girl you like to pretend to be, he answered. But she stood fast before those raptoring words, not taken aback but intrigued that he might already suspect her fragile loyalty to a fugitive one within, poised to bolt without

warning from concealment to lead her, stumbling after, down roads she had never traveled, bent on subverting her timid projects without negotiation or pity, one unashamed of its prancing impudence, running wild. Sorry Mister, she answered, all you get from me is my Name, Rank, and Serial Number, smiling intrepidly in return, just as Dear Mother Pearl had advised them to *Never forget, my chickadees, that as Prisoners of War there are certain questions we must always refuse to answer, certain facts which we must never surrender.* Looks like I do need your number, so once I get rich I can call. And

I presuppose a gal like you got some kind of rank yourself. Oh nothing fancy, she promptly advised, Just call me YOUR HIGHNESS.

By AIR MAIL, it said. By Angel, she thought, laughing to herself. She rolled away from him toward her vanity and reached for the envelope he'd brought to her, Special Personal Delivery, that she'd waited to open as the afternoon's last surprise. Settling onto the sheets against him, she held it up to her nostrils, breathing in behind closed eyes its trace of nameless after-shave, pushing back against curiosity, wanting as they had all afternoon to approach such delectable moments ever more closely for as long as they might, without reaching them too quickly. Her mind moved through each territory where their limbs still twined and pressed together. She sank into the rising and falling of his chest, finding that heartbeat answering her own from the other side of the dark. She let her fingers find their way to the crease where the sealed flap joined the back, she slipped the nail then fingertip between and pushed it along, Surprise! Out comes . . . she thought, eyes opening to what her hands held before her.

Meant to send it before, but I didn't soon enough so I kept it to bring myself, he said.

I simply adore the gardening. Boy, I'd have fun with them flower boxes,

she said, trying hard to sound fancy and particular like Mother would.

I bet your Mama would love it.

He took longer than she expected to answer.

Maybe she would maybe wouldn't, who knows.

You didn't tell her yet?

Maybe I will, maybe not.

And why not?

I'm living my own life she need to live her own too.

But what you gonna do when it's time for her

I can't dwell on all that right now, please.

he groaned, sinking his head to nestle against her belly. Just like the baby man he is, she thought, letting go despite her question, overthrown in that moment, this one she was certain she'd never known before, uncertain that she'd ever know again.

Then she noticed something strange and wonderful in that picture, something which she could make out if only she wanted to, and wanting that sweet moment to stay the more she looked the more she wanted to so the more she did, until at last she leaped in with a sigh.

Well, lo and behold, there I am with my polka-dot pitcher. Sweet-talking my flower boxes, cause they could sure use a drink. But wait, let me get her attention. Yoo hoo! Howdy, neighbor! Yes, I'm what they call a new cucumber here, even though I ain't touched down in the heart of Texas just yet. Pleased to make your acquaintance. Thank you kindly, and likewise! Let me tell you one little old secret, strictly between girlfriends, because that's what we already are. Brace yourself, here goes: I'm you and you're me, but you don't know it yet! Pardon me, you do now. Well if I am, then we're both crazy. Don't bust your brains out over it. We'll get there, all in good time! Couldn't help but notice you showing off all your pretty flowers there, along with your pretty self, exactly as pretty as I'm going to be and as pretty as I know I'm gonna feel. Of course, I flatter myself. Oh I do agree! Mums are perfect for the front ones, I positively adore the whole gang, that's exactly how I'd show them off. I bet you've been working hard all day long, with that pretty bouffant piled up on top of your head. Wait a hot second, it might be a trick of the light but I think I can see a halo! And not a strand out of place to boot. I must admit, you look quite comfortable in your housedress and high heels and pearl necklace, keeping your pretty new house clean and neat as a pin. Ain't you Something Else! But you can't fool me, girlfriend, cause I got your number. You've been watching out that window while you water them flowers. And I happen to know who you're watching for. It's your handsome Jimmy Angel, because he's coming home today. How, you ask? Let's just say, I know a thing or two. Course we both do, girlfriend, we're nobody's fool. You can't hardly wait to see him coming down the street with his dusty blue bag, crossing at the corner, unlatching the front gate, tippin' his way up the walk, lookin' to that same window to find you standing there. Then you'll run and throw open the door and smile and stretch up on your tippy toes to whisper in his ear, Welcome home Angel, and give him a big old kiss. Oh yes, girlfriend, I can see what you have in mind ... And there she goes. Bye-bye! Rain waved back, fluttering her fingertips. Thanks for the girl-talk, see ya later.

One thing I like about you, Jimmy Love said, kissing her ear, lingering there, you plain comical.

She gazed deeply into the bright heart of Texas. The little house crept out from its picture like a vapor, like a light filling the space they had filled together, a light fragrant with secret flowers, drawing near like the face filling her eyes, its every breath taken with her breath, their secret fragrance enveloping them in quietness.

Sure got plenty of windows all round, she said.

Three in the parlor, two in the kitchen, and one by the bed. Once we pick one out.

I must have brass

Brass it shall be, Your Highness.

And a nice big bathtub? she hoped.

I'd guesstimate just big enough for two.

Then just right. I'll wash your back if you pay me off, Mister Duke.

Oh I'll find a way to make it worth your while.

Mother's chiming clock sounded up the stairs and through the door until at last the earth stood still.

You know what you doin' when you do your foot like that? he asked.

Quite frankly, I forget, she said.

Lemme explain it to you one more time.

Cuppa

Rain sat on her hands, on the white sheet draping the examination table. She could not help but hide her face, as she never had done before, from her kind Doctor Schops standing before her. The easiest thing for her was to watch her legs kick back and forth, gone skating without her other half. Whenever she could manage to look into his long sad face and circled around eyes behind his thick glasses, she remembered when her feet had dangled much further from the floor, how he had let her wear that stethoscope *deevice* and listen to her heart, when she laughed and said, *It's mine*. Better to watch them kick, she thought, than to check on Mother, still in her raincoat, still up from last night from a Vestal job, *Engagement*, Mother would correct her, running late.

Claire stood back from the tall office window, beside the tall white cabinet behind whose glass doors he enshrined the jar of Hershey's Kisses, tempting well and ill from behind the glass, but opened only for the good. The good Doctor opened his ears.

You are, as usual, in excellent health, he reported,
standing aside to speak to Mother too. Again Rain quickly hid herself away. Knowing that the Kind Doctor kind since I was born would never pursue her.

I trust that your fellow procreator will be thrilled with the news,
he opined.
Both her hands broke free and fluttered up, fingers crossed.

Prayer has been alleged to be effective as well, he added.

Mother's coat zipper buzzed at last. To pull out a gun, she guessed.

Quite a performance you put on this morning

Claire remarked, looming behind her,

>   Couldn't speak plain English, let alone point a finger toward a
>   living soul. Not even for your own good.

Unlike those who'd never before heard and couldn't help but be surprised, Rain had been wondering forever, whenever Mother cursed
and ramped and raved, if that proved she was nothing more than a
sinner in disguise, or so faithful and righteous that her blasphemies
counted only as accidents. As for herself, she was sure that Getting
Out of Hell Free would never be in the cards.

>   Sorry, Mother. Still not yet, she said,

And at least not wrong yet, she thought, feeling her stockinged toes
curl around the rung of the stool like a perching bird.

>   Schopes still thinks the world of you. If I were him I'd wonder
>   what stripe of a slut you've turned out to be. But how dare I for-
>   get? You're just a poor lamb lost in the woods. Here's further
>   proof that your mind's in a shambles, she sighed,

digging in with the comb at the nape of her neck.

>   I felt terrible last night. Fell out in the bed, brush in my hand

>>   Slouch ass. Sit up straight

she shouted, wrenching the shock of forked hair against her twisting grip. She gasped, bolting erect.

>   Time to prick up your ears.

She reached to pluck her burning-down from the packed ashtray for
a drag. Dragged, coughed hard, kept coughing, stopped to cover her
mouth with her handkerchief. She felt her heaving against her back.

You sound terrible too

Oh you're such a help to make me feel better.

I'm just saying

Don't. Mind your own business, the mess you're in right now.

She rubbed another smear of bergamot into her scalp.

And this one you've handed to me to set straight.

She reached for the hot comb on the stove.

Thank you thank you Mother

She pulled through a patch above one ear, pressing close to the roots. Wisps of smoke rose toward heaven and disappeared, like a dutiful offering. The steely teeth stopped short in mid-stroke, biting their obstruction. Twisting her wrist, she pressed harder, meeting the scalp. She flinched and moaned behind tightly pursed lips, but shortly managed to recover her resigned stillness.

This morning I asked you a simple question. Much as you like to run your mouth. God help you if you don't come up with the answer.

Yes, Ma'am, I promise I will.

Oh you certainly will.

Claire lifted the tangled strands until they gave way and fell into ranks of glistening tufts, vanquished once again. Have to get to those weeds around the *arbor vitae* today, she thought. She set the comb back on the stove and lit another cigarette.

A burn again, she thought. Yep, for now she could do the usual thing, just sit there through the rest of it like a lump on a log and later, behind her own closed door, visit the spot by hand and see if she could check it later in the mirror. Shoot, she recalled, a couple times she'd nearly thrown a crick into her neck trying to find the angle. She could always tell the days when Mother was about to be careless. Careless, mostly on days when she was put out about this and that she'd said or done or been a disappointment about. But not always, like she was saving small stuff up till the heap got big enough to cash in or something. I guess it's only careless, she thought, recalling her studied conclusion, if she doesn't want to do it and it's a real accident, so quite frankly it's not careless if it's not an accident but only pretends and plots to look like an accident. That much she was glad to have figured out sitting through all those times in her whole life Mother had summoned her to get her hair fixed, fixed, finding solace and anodyne afterward in reminding herself that at least she understood, could find a reason to forgive her and forget it each and every night after when she'd kneel and fold her hands beside her bed, while waiting for it to happen again. For a long time mere understanding had helped, but now understanding was starting to sound plain stupid. What kind of person, she asked herself again right then, looking out through the big breakfast room window and across the pasture sprawling beyond the graveyard, to the crowding Holsteins huddling together under the overcast sky, motionless save for their mouths chewing chewing, snorting their fogging breaths into the bracing air, What kinda person keeps tellin' themself stupid things and keeps on sittin' there and afterward sits up in front of a mirror or even two bendin' themself out of shape like some kinda whatchamacallit, *extortionist* in a carnival tryna see what they watched happen while they sat there. Anyway, she wished she could at least get a word in edgewise to explain that she hadn't been trying to hide a single thing, figure the odds. She started thinking about what she had told Mister Delbert and Major Tom about how she stopped listening when she heard the word **if,** and thought it was a joke. But when she started in to thinking about all this she found out that it's actually no joke, Cause it seemed like when my whatchamacallit, *condition,* that's what Doc called it, once it came out of nowhere, now there were so many *ifs* that she couldn't even think straight. First of all she was amazed about the first sign of it, which she'd thought she knew a thing or two about what to expect but come to find out she didn't at all till it happened, but the problem about it happening, when it just stopped, was When did it really happen? OK, if she put it scientific words, in algebra, like Jimmy would, Call that day, *Day X*. Now, go figure. But there you go, there's that **X** comin back to haunt me again, she thought, I'm lost again, in the middle of nowhere. It wasn't like it had gone missing one week when it was supposed to come, like a train rolling into the station on time every time, cause it never was like that anyhow, that's why she hadn't thought much about it at first, It's probably coming back any time now, she'd kept telling herself. Then when it didn't come back after all she worried that something was wrong but instead of putting two and two together she kept on like an idiot trying to figure out what something else it was instead. Like I let myself be stupid and pretend. There's that word again, she winced, pretend like I didn't know most likely what it was even after all that time since her Sweet Sixteenth that she and her girlfriends had sat around with Pearlie laughing at her secret stories and practicing saying all them dirty C P and F words without blushing, carrying on about fornication and adultery and all them other shameful sinful things by way of, what she always calls it, Self-Education. Yes stupid but one thing for sure was that at first she wasn't sad, but quite frankly glad about it. Especially because every time before when it came the only thing she'd want to do was lay up in bed or sit quietly and try not to move even one muscle, just like she wished she could sit still for Mother right then, and even back in school days in class when she was supposed to be paying attention, she'd shut her eyes and cover her face, with all that upset and stuff going on inside that she never could stand to think about, and quite frankly didn't want folks looking into her face to see, Ugh, what she could see was already disgusting enough. So at first she was kinda tickled to wonder What if I don't have to bother any more even though not quite knowing how that could be, until she started really thinking about it, but even then she tried hard to keep happy about it, Hip hip hooray! For instance she had tried hard to believe it probably happened because it had been so cold in her room earlier that winter before Father had come up and packed newspapers in around her new air conditioner, when she'd been shivering even in long johns and Sonny's hunting cap on under two quilts, even with her stuffed Humpty Dumpty from the Fair come down from his shelf to snuggle up beside her. Then she came up with, Maybe I'm sick, awfully sick. Maybe I've caught some kind of blood cancer like what she'd lately heard happened to that poor Ernie Davis, or she whatchamacallit, *contracted* one of them other rare diseases like that one adorable girl did on BEN CASEY, when he looked at her report and he could tell she only had six months left, then tried to find a way to save her while she fell in love with him even though she could already tell that she wasn't much longer for this world, but still happy just to think that maybe he was in love with her too, Oh that was her little old bit of pretend make believe to hold on to, to the very end, *What a world, what a world*, she thought, it just made her bawl her eyes out. But bawling wasn't actually what she felt like doing then, quite frankly sometimes she felt wonderful, just to know that after the awful summer she'd spent behind closed doors in that Heartbreak Hotel with Mister Zero, that Heaven had sent Jimmy Love to her rescue at the bus stop on that blessed day and then, so quickly after it had taken her breath away, those too-short weekends she'd spent down there at his Air Base in New Jersey and finally that he'd promised to soon come back to ask for her hand in I still can't hardly believe it, Holy

Matrimony, as soon as his leave time came around. The best thing she had to keep her mind on was that three by five picture of him in the little frame on her vanity, standing out on the tarmac under the big jets smiling and proud as nobody's business in that handsome uniform, with them sparkly eyes looking out of the picture and that sweet gap-tooth smile beaming just for her. But sure enough, that happy stupid time stopped for good after that, when the sickness came. Cause, something else she had noticed nearly all the days of her life, that getting sick, when it's sick enough, it always makes you wonder what you did to deserve it. Mostly folks think that there's nothing, and that they don't, but she kept in mind how Father says they want to give the Lord a hard time about treating them unfair but if you look real hard at what how you've been living you'll find the thing that just might be what He's been chastising you about and having found it pray for guidance to make it right, he says, as when the Troubled Man looked into the whirlwind to accept the Lord's rebuke and cried out *I have heard of thee by the hearing of the ear but now mine eye seeth thee. Wherefore I abhor myself, and repent in dust and ashes.* And half the time since, locked up in her bedroom door knocked down sick as a dog, she'd been thinking back, even though she could hardly stand it, to all those times with the both of them, the days and hours and places and destinations and big talk which had only yesterday seemed so luxurious, but now seemed a blur of bodies and cloud of gibberish, and before that whirlwind which had swept her up from then and flung her into now she sought repentance, but first to understand, For what. The next Saturday morning someone knocked just how she would. She got up and opened the door. Come in she managed to say, and through her bleary eyes saw a kindly curious face looking back. Hello stranger, the face said, meaning and not meaning it. Lately it seems like you come home from the five-and-dime and don't come out any more, it said. There's no *out*, she replied. Nonetheless, I'm under orders to rescue you from your recently sullen behavior or else, she said, I bet neither of us wants or else, Pearl said. Go away or else I'll might throw up on you, Rain said. But at least Pearl was probably the only person to whom she could explain about the brain-twister she had been going for broke trying to figure out. And boy once she told it Pearl dragged her out the bed and threw some clothes from the heap laying on the floor on her, dragged her downstairs and straight out the front door to her house and up to her room and shut the door behind them. I seek Heavenly Pardon, Rain chanted, playing the charade, if that's what it's been, she wondered, It looks like my indulgences got the best of me, she sighed, hoping to laugh because it might be a way out for a second even if only for a second before it was how not funny it would always be forever after. We'll amuse ourselves later. First I want to show you something, Mother Superior calmly replied. And got her a cup of hot milk and sat her down beside her with that horrible book she had given her last year but that she had hurried to give back. She laid the book in her lap and took one hand and lay it gently upon her back. Why had she decided right then to nuzzle up over her hip and gape at them creepy drawings and diagrams and ugh, *enlargements*, especially some of the pictures she couldn't look at before, pictures of bodies without faces, of this and that different stage or whatchamcallit, *activity* in what somebody had decided to call the Cycle of Life? Because it was like riding in a fast car with somebody who didn't make fun of her difficulties and sickness but helped her out of the goodness of their hearts, at last not looking alone. Especially when she turned to the worst one where it looked like some poor girl had been, Lord have mercy Rain cried, covering her eyes. Look it's called a *cadaver,*

Pearl said. But to her it sure looked like somebody had cut Miss Abra Cadabra or whowhomever it was clean through the middle wide open and there in the picture you could see the whole awful insides and where what they say, Pearl pointed at it, That's where the baby starts, she said. *Baby*, Rain repeated, like it wasn't even a word to her only a sound that had just dropped, fell out her mouth. Here's what it says, Pearl said. She read it out loud but just like somebody talking, taking shortcuts, picking out just the words to read from among the pictures or simply telling on herself. And even so Rain got so embarrassed and scared that she shushed her as if all the neighbors could hear, Forget about hear, they'll see soon enough, Pearl said, making her listen to the part of the story of life that had sounded so sickening that she had wanted to cover her ears, when she clenched her fists and shouted back I know, I know, you must think I'm stupid, then curled up very small until morning.

I'm not stupid she shouted into her shut mouth so loud that Mother leaned over to look at her with eyes wide with fake perplexity. Muttering again, eh? she growled, For what? For what? the *Ifs* shouted back from the back row of her mind, Fool you know very well for what, Shonuff I know it's for my sins cause I'm a sinner she cried, Like every poor sinner born to die I commit all different kind of awful sins then I crawl back and ask forgiveness and when I get it I feel better and that gets me feeling good again but I want to keep on feeling good so I go and sin again, and then I come back again over and over again. And she thought a hot second to think it and be done with it that maybe even if she wasn't asking for it hose so many of those times long ago, maybe now the Lord was just giving her a taste of that destiny guaranteed to the hard of heart, *Where their worm dieth not and the fire is not quenched, for every one shall be salted with fire.* But listen y'all, what I really want, she stood up in front of her mind to testify, Quite frankly I want to be blessed and walk up them red carpets even though I'm a sinner like all the rotten folks do, and I'm not even hurting anybody except maybe myself, but still I need one of them special deals, I'm gonna find out where to sign up and mark my **X** and pray *Please Please Please* like James Brown to get one of them handy GET OUT OF HELL FREE cards in my wallet like everybody else. Just like them Brothers up on that hill who Pearlie says whip their own behinds with them whatchamacallit, cat-o-nines, I can keep gettin burned up and cry three tears in my bucket, if then it's all fixed and I can enjoy life for a hot second. For she had always been so careful to keep in mind every caution and preparation required for HOLY SELF-INDULGENCE prescribed for them all in blushing detail, careful and she felt she had to cause particularly that Zorro could get all worked up, hot blooded and bothered right quick like Mother had warned her men of his tribe tended to do and in a hurry, and sometimes she'd had to stop him in his tracks a hot second Wait this ain't stealing third base let me check and hold him off long enough to take a quick peek down there all up in through around underneath between themselves all tangled up in each other just before, Shoot, there I was bendin myself out of shape all over again, how bout that. Because she could always just tell by that brainless look in his eyes he'd get that he could be the kind of tramp, who would forget if he could get away with it, especially if she had turned lightheaded or got carried away too from all that rub-a-dubby so-called dancing or some of them drinks he'd make for them that should've had smoke bubblin from the top like them whatchamacallit *potions* in them monster movies, and so on, too many times to remember especially when she might wind up ashamed to remember what how this and that had happened, more ashamed than she already was. And then when she started to get tired of his mess especially after that wonderful day she met Jimmy and then when he came all the way from New Jersey for just an afternoon for his Top Secret repair of her air conditioner she had thought for a while like that it was exciting and luxurious to have herself a time with both of them and that all she'd have to always make sure of was SELF-PRESERVATION, which she had thought was so easy with him cause he's always so scientific about it, explaining everything, as if he was a girl once and it had all happened to him, she had found that sweet that he would try to show off like he really knows. Always, always every little thing, but what if it wasn't always and quite frankly it wasn't. Burn again.

Nodding to herself as she smoked, Claire concluded that the girl's collapse that morning into tongue-tied confusion, had at last delivered the verdict. That, in keeping with the wreck she had managed to make of her life in just a handful of recent weeks, Lorraine had acquired nothing in all those years during which *she* had struggled, against all odds and to the point of exhaustion, to prune her detriments and guide her toward dignity. That she would likely have been better off had she never wasted her time on her, that time in which, evidently, she had learned only contempt. Better to be that than to have taken the wrong turn she had taken and now drag down all those who had gone out of their way to treat her kindly, into her perpetual misery. Better raised up, as they once used to say or so she had heard, green as a cucumber. The bitter taste of this moment was, mercifully, diluted by her resignation to an unexpected sense of relief. That she would be free at last from the false hope that she might inspire her to discover her own sense of what was worth living for, and perhaps turn out to be that ally she had never known in her own journey through the wide world. Then and there, wishing it to be the last time, Claire recalled and confronted the illusion of that happiness, the image of that daughter she had longed for in vain. A partner and confidante who would have stood beside her in shared progress toward security and prosperity, until the day came for her to carry their work forward without her. A fellow-traveler through that progress which every soul must make through its dispensations, from innocence to conscience, to dreams and responsibilities, through all manner of suffering and punishment inflicted upon rebellion and foolishness, and through that suffering and punishment to discover humility, forgiveness, and grace. That road which, despite appearances, she was certain she had always traveled alone. She recalled the end of her own girlish days of magnificent transgression, when with all the stamina of her newfound faith she had learned to pray for a steadfast companion in the midst of a life which even though granted grace, remained one never quite lived in the midst of others, but in another territory altogether, all her own. For long thereafter, by faith, she thereby denied her distinction and calling. *Tried to be what all folks should, forgetting the bad and doing good,* until she had run the gauntlets of misunderstanding and betrayal, *But no matter how I tried, my troubles always multiplied.* This, the tale that might at last make sense of me for someone, but one that I can never tell, she recited to herself, with no one to be trusted to hear, what was truly her own, a hidden mystery. When at last she surrendered to the fact that this story, this mystery, concealed, was her own, she understood that there was nothing left to be done but walk alone through that shadowed valley alone, sheltering her lamp against each ill wind, letting so many pass by without expectation, without clinging, without being duped. Looking into the thicket of disaster below her, she braced herself against a sudden reflex of pity welling up from somewhere within that she would now leave behind her, against a daughter still that, but a child no longer. She, too, could put away childish things.

It should be just right about now, she thought. She took the hot comb from the burner and, holding the sectioned strands caught with the cold comb in the other hand, slowly sank through to lift from the roots once again. The girl twisted and bit her lip in a vain effort to stifle her cries, her hands gripped the edge of the stool. Her unvanquished whining was promptly checked by the hand clenching the scruff of her neck.

You never sit still.

But aren't I sitting still now? Rain sobbed.

Hideous that you've let it come to this. You've got no one to blame but yourself.

Yes Mother it's nobody's I don't blame anybody else she wailed, although trying hard to speak clearly and quietly without mistakes which might set her off again, but having to stop to catch her racing breath, which frightened her and made her flinch and talk loud and wrong anyhow.

Cause I'm so lucky I mean fortunate for all the ways and knowledge you've tried to teach me to bring me up right and stuff

I've failed miserably

Oh no you haven't Mother. Cause you've helped me all my life even though it's been so hard cause it takes me too long to get everything, I get tangled up cause I'm not a brain like you. But I am really so thankful that's why I am so thankful to be your child.

You're a regular damsel in distress. Head up she shouted, twisting and pulling back hard, dragging the girl's head backward until her features were inverted, the mouth with its gnawed bleeding lip above, the upstaring weeping eyes below. She stared down into that face and recalled that once it had been a face which she had delighted in despite herself, recalled how she had pinched the dimples in tiny round cheeks, when those raisin-brown eyes had sparkled with mischief, when the baby-toothed mouth had churned with the laughter which once cured her lonely weariness. A face now turned upside down, opposite itself and all it had once been, flung into a strangeness beyond recognition.

Miserable today. But fine weather expected tomorrow, Claire recalled. She would be up early, to sprawl beside the shady bed beneath the window and meet the first primroses, to dote upon their motley faces, to inhale their musky tang of impending spring. The thawing earth drawing the soreness from her hips, the dead house and graveyard standing still at her back beneath the hemlocks across the winding road, the pastures rolling over the hills beyond, the houses and streets, their silence empty of questions which she can never answer, empty of all to whom she can never say that for them she never will be and they for her will never be enough, sprawling into these merciful hours of refuge from the irreparably broken world, inevitably cut short as petals wither and fall and drift far afoot, but not before telling their truth, speaking of a destination once lived for but long since forsaken, a distant morning recalled in a fragrance lingering into bitterness, another day lost.

Rain woke to the sound of the rain falling against her crooked walls, against the windows. Not only the sound, it seemed to her as if the rain itself was coming through the walls to fall over her, as though the roof and walls and inside and outside had disappeared, and she was in both or everywhere at once, or nowhere at all. Rain falling not just like it sounded outside, lightly like a whisper, rising and falling with the bursts of late winter wind, but feeling like a stormy downpour running over her in a torrent. Behind closed eyes she ran her hands over her arms and legs and chest under the covers trying to unravel that drenched-ness, and even after lifting them up and opening her eyes finding nothing the feeling remained and she suddenly understood that it could not be unraveled, that the torrent was welling up from within her, that the hours from which she'd fled in exhausted sleep were rushing back to fill up her senses almost like a dream, and she shook her head, wishing it were. But no, she could still hear Mother's voice over her shoulder as she worked, buzzing faintly like a mosquito next to her ear that she couldn't shoo away, that would stop sometimes, awaiting reply, like the critter expected her to jump up and talk bug-talk too, well she went on and just grunted or buzzed or said her usual Yes, ma'am. The swift hands braiding her pressed hair tightly, so tightly that the sting of burned flesh was stretched into numbness, so tightly that the cabling locks had often seemed to her like ropes tying her down, to keep her from her short-circuited tics, from hop-skipping for a stretch here and there as she walked through the streets of the town running errands for Mother or headed to work, from throwing her outstretched arms back gracefully and just so like Her Highness stepping down to earth from her Cadillac Convertible cloud to make room for hips and behind and all the rest to shimmy and shake to the beat of her latest favorite song playing on repeat in her mind, from smiling and waving or poking both pinky fingers into the corners of her mouth to whistle piercingly and perfectly like Father had taught her as she hurried down Broad Street to the shopgirls and passers and drivers by who smiled and waved back politely, just enough to let her forget that she knew how little they cared to notice her. Tied down at last to sit still and forget trying and forget about everything, to surrender.

When she'd finished she came around front and looked her over a minute while she smoked, like she often did when Rain would expect it, and worse, when she least expected it. She'd sat slumped over on the stool, eyes staring down to the floor, praying not to be a living creature anymore but instead be a lump, a dummy like that funny looking JERRY MAHONEY, with that big old mouth that looks like a scar across his face, a dummy with somebody's words tricked into that mouth. And of course Mother was right on cue to help things along. *Now you resemble a human bean,* she said with a grin, like she was supposed to take that as some kind of joke, or like she was kindly helping her feel better about how she'd mix up words sometimes, or like it was so clever that she should laugh every time she said it, which was all she ever said, especially after a bad day, never Oh it turned out so nice or You look halfway pretty or look like anything worth looking at, not on your life. Shoot, ain't no surprise, she had got over all that ages ago. She would look at her the way she would at some weed to tear up from one of her flowerbeds, or how she looked at something she was frying up like chicken legs or a piece of liver. But actually, No, she thought. Actually more like one of them critters you whatchamacallit, oh what's that word they used in her horrible Biology class, whenever she heard it she knew what was coming, it meant another trip to the so-called laboratory, which she couldn't stand for even half a second. Ugh, then she remembered how skinny old Mister Meeker Skeleton Man had reached with a pair of them long tweezers like Doc Schopes kept on his shelf into one of them jars he kept back in that nasty old closet and pulled one of them poor frogs out and they'd all crowded around to watch him pin it down on a board by its hands and feet like a tiny Jesus and cut its chubby little white belly open with one of them cute scalper knives that it was a shame as far as she was concerned to use them for that since they sure would be the talk of any buffet they were set on for dinner. Then he pulled apart all the insides and told them the fancy names for each different kind of organ, all the while making his joyful noises about Natural Election of the Fittest and whatnot and of course the boys couldn't get enough of that, and even if she could've stood to watch that far, ugh when that pickle juice started to run out from everywhere she just had to cover her eyes and heard them all bust out laughing. Then lifting a bony finger he announced, Now each one of you will work with your own Whatchamacallit, that creepy word whenever I hear it it's always about something or somebody creepy, *specimens*, to whatchamacallit, *bisect* it, no wait that was in another class, *dissect* it, he said. It, it, it. And that was her cue to skin on out of the laboratory and head for the *lavatory* and stay in there, even though she knew that meant she might get sent to the principal's office for another so-called good talking-to. But *dissected*, she realized, that's the perfect fancy word for how she felt when Mother was or when she caught her snooping on her, plain as day. Why, because it always felt like somebody cutting into her, not that she knew any more about how that really hurt than she imagined sometimes from those awful stories they write about how they find some girls *took apart*, please don't tell us one more word about the rest. Funny thing, she thought, it wasn't every time she turned around, but sometimes she would turn around in the middle of whatever she was doing (or doing nothing much which, Lord knows, is a first-degree crime), and there she was, giving her the eye. She was quite certain it was an eye or two she was getting, probably not really one of them Evil Eyes or anything really bad like that, but still it gave her the creeps sometimes, like she was spying on her in a way she couldn't figure out, she couldn't figure out what it was that she was finding so interesting, couldn't figure out what facts about herself that she didn't even realize were facts or were secrets which she didn't realize she was giving away and couldn't stop giving away to save her life.

Nevertheless she was surprised to find that she'd come back from dead to the world much improved, not lumpy and noisy but soft and quiet like those empty porches, front yards and streets she'd seen all her life from her windows on such midafternoons, now looking not quite real, more like one of them movie towns where nobody really lives waiting for the stars and extras to come so its scenes can be played. But certainly not on this rain-check day, this her sick-day from Woolworth's which she'd felt scared to ask for, but now was so happy she did, to fall out and rest a spell after waking up day after day half-asleep with a troubled mind was such a nice surprise, she thought, almost too good to be true. Or maybe it wasn't, maybe it was just that she had finally managed to die and it had been the kind of dying she'd always wished for, first not hurting and second coming in the blink of an eye, like Father reminded them sometimes about how *the Lord will come as a thief in the night,* on that day and hour unknown by men and angels, to carry away his own, catching lots of folks right in the middle of some kind of business they have to mind, *the one shall be taken, and the other left,* and we'll be swept up like Elijah to meet the Lord in the sky and *Poof!* disappear from this rotten old world to live forever in the new, or how when falling asleep nobody knows when they slip beneath the surface, beneath the drenching torrent of the day, into the deep, which could be kinda like what she read once about how the sea really was, far beyond the horizon, how it goes on and on and on and on, till there's not a sandy beach or boat in sight, only *water, water, everywhere* in all directions, and down to the very heart of it, miles deep and darker than darkest night, a land forever dreaming. If that's what happened, how folks just slipped away, then she really did know that it doesn't have to hurt to die, she thought, except unless she had died from having her hair pressed, she thought. She pushed aside the blanket, rose and stepped into her furry slippers, stretched herself and yawned. Then I just might be a dead girl walking, she thought, but I'm sure hungry enough to be alive. She sat up, rolled out of bed and darted to the window to check the cars in the driveway, a method she'd long practiced to divine the state of the family weather. Of course she's still here, what in the world was she thinking, she thought, down there getting everything ready and just so. One thing we all know about Mother, she's always on time. She turned back to her closet, certain before opening the door that she would wear, wrinkles notwithstanding, the same skirt and blouse she'd worn the week before.

Rain descended the stairs as the bell jar clock, atop its white doily on the television set, chimed four. And heard those waves of keener sounds, coming from the kitchen. Cupboard doors, drawers, pots, porcelain, crystal and silver. And that voice which had always seemed to her the cry of a stranger, forever hidden from the other, never known.

Love, careless love,
You fly through my head like wine.

The cracking voice rafted down the stream of her practiced movements, of the ringing collision of things she brought to completion and rest in their appointed places. The girl crept across the living room and stood aside in the hallway, lingering to watch in fascination and puzzlement as she had so often before, trying in vain to discover that one whose voice she had never believed could come out of one such as this other before her eyes. Already SATURDAY TEA-TIME again, she thought, recalling Mother's lessons, in happier days, before her fall from grace, (Traditionally denoted 'Low' by the well-born, she noted, and mind you, the term refers to the height of the table where tea is taken, not the social caliber of its takers, and to tea taken prior to their Hyde Park Promenade or Constitutional, she'd explained, and likewise advised shamefully uninformed customers during her engagements), it comes around so fast. And knew that what she would find when she stepped into the kitchen would be the same thing she'd found there every Saturday, same as it ever was. But today, she if nothing else would *not* be the same, she decided, and trying out the tightrope, put on a drowsy shuffle as she turned the corner into the kitchen, passing the stool which had been the throne of her torment a few hours before. Noting the amber pill bottle on the counter next to the radio, not yet tucked away, only one of the two tall glasses of water usually standing side by side there each morning, and already half empty. She's usually more careful than that, she thought. Got herself all worked up this morning, she figured, couldn't wait on me.

Claire washed, dried and anointed her hands, untied her apron and hung it on its reserved hook alongside the kitchen sink.

Do you object to picking up your feet when you walk?
she asked, glancing back, water pitcher in hand, then promptly delivered her usual up-and-down look and shake of her head.

That's the best you can do after all the time I spent rescuing your appearance?

My feet hurt. I didn't want to be late
Rain replied, surveying as she stood before the breakfast room, as if from a great height, the Saturday tableau, centered on the spotless tablecloth. The Spode tea service, pot and cream pitcher, cups saucers spoons, and, to her surprise, the silver tray of fresh-baked scones glowing in the light from the picture window.

Here we are!

cried Claire, smoothing her dress, adjusting her rhinestones. Casting a lingering glance out the window, as if departed souls or cattle or incurably nosy neighbors had posted themselves at hidden vantage points. There go her eyes, Rain thought, twinkle twinkling like it's all some kind of special treat just dropped down from the moon. Her teatime face, whose expression neither inquired nor welcomed, fixed in a mask of solemn serenity, which she had long before learned never to mistake for gentleness. She cupped her elbow and led her to the table. She sat still, hands fallen into her lap, perplexed to see Claire set the trayed sweets down in front of her.

So now we're back to goodies?

For you, not for me, Claire replied.

But she was not inclined to button her lip and perish her next question.

So no more Pixies for me?

Use your head if you can find it. Whatever you supposedly don't know or really do know right now, you should be concerned about your *appearance*

With practiced quickness, she picked up the antique spatula and switched a scone from the tray to her plate. She sidestepped her sudden irritation by considering Mother's point of view, scientifically, historically. Recalling bodies like her own she'd seen all the days of her life, swelling wondrously, unmanageably. Fair enough, I get it. That what looks the same as it ever was, what never shows, never has to be hidden. After all this time starving, now to fatten up for the whatsthatword, slaughter.

But I don't have much of an appetite right now.

You'll start to go back to your bad habits soon enough. I'd think you'd be happy about that.

Jeepers creepers, Rain thought, those pixie eyes. Looking like they might start flashing like a neon sign any second.

At least now you won't have to wait on me

Ha! I'm thrilled to give up on it.

The kettle whistled behind them. She recalled watching the cupcakes and scones, then the finger sandwiches, then bread, jam and butter disappear from Saturdays' fare, as the amber bottle refilled ever more frequently, as weeknights running the pass and weekend catering distended Claire's twelve-hour confinements to one kitchen or another into sleepless months. And they were together but then the fire burned the bridge and then they weren't partners anymore and then this happened to me. The irresistible memories filled her eyes, the words dropped from her mouth, which she had that very morning sworn to forget.

Mother, you've been running yourself ragged these days. I remember when you used to try and get more rest. Back when I was helping out

But helpful you weren't. Let's not revisit the disasters you created for me whenever I tried to put you to work.

Even after Mother fired her she was still proud to have such a popular, Shoot, even just about famous mother, thought so well of by folks for her fine cooking, her knowledge of etiquette and of how things need to be arranged just so for this and that function, and proudest above all of her use of fine words and perfect whatchamacallit, *diction* which she could turn on and off whenever she wanted. How often she had first talked on the phone with a new client say up in Corning or Owego who had never seen her, and then later when arriving on the job at their homes and so on they'd creep over and smile and tell her By gosh Claire I had such a different picture of you in my mind before today, and some would

142

even get downright flattering, as Auntie Barbara had mentioned many times, they'd come right out and stop being bashful about it, talking about Don't take this the wrong way Claire but you don't sound like you don't talk like or even think or act like one of I don't know how to say it the normal run of colored people is that how I should say it? they'd ask. To see or hear tell of it always tickled her to death. But Rain was especially proud because she knew all that meant that Mother was somebody special. Even if once upon a time she had been maybe an eensy weensy bit jealous or even more than an eensy over it herself, and made fun of it all in her mind. So she talks like them, well whoop tee doo. Maybe I do talk like Father, but folks just love him to death too because they can tell he talks and thinks and acts like himself not like somebody else he's pretending to be, and couldn't care one whit about showing off to folks like he's so refined and high and mighty, plus he was so sweet to her most of the time, and not only when other folks were watching. But over the years she had learned a hard lesson, had learned to admit that quite frankly she *was* jealous. Probably cause I'm one of them ignorant and short-circuited types, she could admit it, even if I don't know how else to describe it, I must have some wires broke loose, like Jimmy says, in the *deevice* of my brain, like maybe the run of us colored folks are cause of how everything happened way back in the old days, not that I'd ever say about Father that he's a short-circuited type too, only about myself. Now she could happily admit it, so happy that it brought her to tears sometimes to admit it, so very happy for and proud of her mother for being such a special gifted person, who had to maintain a good impression which of course was expected of her, as Mother said herself, a kind of person she had finally learned to admit that she would, could never ever be.

Cuppa, cuppa!

Claire chimed merrily, tabling the brewed pot.

Here they come, Rain thought, even without the pill. Her insides twitched and churned into panic. Mischievous sprites stirred up the mud at the bottom of her mind, dredged up the threadbare confidences of their former conspiracies. Just like in the movies, she thought, when they have them whatchamacallit, *flash-backs* to show what happened in days gone by. CUT, TO: daffodils leaning from crystal vases, sugar-dusted tidbits, glittering drageés, irresistible lashings of clotted cream flashed before her like neon lights in the dark. Mother presiding in aproned housedress and pearls, and she the eager apprentice at her back and call, all eyes and ears and up-turned nose, in anklets and kitten heels, fervently hope-ful to pass muster as a Proper Young Lady. Oh, I can mix the bat-ter! Keep it out of your hair this time, Mother says. Watch through the oven window as the lumps turn into treats, Who asked you to carry on like a banshee there? she says. Carve out the peaks to make Tinkerbelle wings, Look, you've made devil's horns instead. Knife goes in first, then hot water, then pour it off, God help you if you ever crack it. Three tablespoons to the pot. *And who am I, short and stout, here with my handle and my spout, words steeped in piety and dread, pouring out.* Serve the guest of honor first, Which appar-ently is I. Lid off the sugar bowl on the doily, not upside down. First the tea then the milk, and no stir, stir, bang bang. Clutch the chair tightly, to straighten up and fly right, and not tumble into the sky. Napkin across your lap thusly, opening to let you peek in. Cup to mouth, not vice-versa, and we do not believe in flying saucers. Blow over your first sip, and contritely take it all back, but too late, You'll be written off as a hayseed. Pinky held clear of the cup, she says, rescues from clumsiness. And God cannot forgive slurping from a saucer. Break the scone thusly, she says, don't maul it into crumbs. Aht aht ah! there's dunking, but never dipping. Hold the sandwich with two fingers thusly, she says, and no wolfing, lest you murder by embarrassment. How she'd followed her across the kitchen floor, staring devotedly upward into that severe, pockmarked, powdered face, those rouged lips pouting in perpetual dissatisfaction, those relentless eyes darting from object to object at hand in each deftly executed task and sometimes turning down to meet her own.

I must say, I miss making our Fairy Cakes
cried Rain, not at all having to say so, not really missing them anymore but saying so nevertheless, as if saying itself helped her to forget.

Claire poured their cups, then placed the lumps and tongs well within her reach.

As I recall that the sugar I dumped into all those treats I baked was never enough for you.

Yes, Mother. I remember not.

Especially not for you.

Sometimes you get so tired of it starts sounding funny, she thought.

But thank you, Mother, cause you protected me from myself. If it wasn't for you I would've probably gone clean out of my cotton pickin mind and blown up big as a house.

Funny, how all at once it all makes sense. Ain't like I don't even know two or three things about myself, ain't like she don't know herself too. And we both know what's really and quite frankly happening on this last stroll down, what's the song, MEMORY LANE. She looked dead into that worn-out face straight across the table, looked past that dumb old look she kept stuck there that's supposed to fool somebody she's some fancy somebody else, and found the same old keeping on, the same old sickening swelling up behind her jiggling electrified eyeballs like a flood. And why, because it's *who's there,* and it don't matter whether you keep on or keep away, there BEFORE and AFTER, in both of them same old pictures supposed to fool somebody into swearing to God that just like it's guaranteed, it works. Shoot, both of us born blown up already, blown up or not.

Boom, boom!

she whispered, throwing up her arms, throwing open her eyes as if at the sight of fire lighting up the sky. Claire reached for a cigarette.

You really are nuts. Positively shocking.

I like when you laugh at me, Rain said, then at least you're laughing.

You better thank God I am.

Now maybe they could keep on having fun, Rain thought, maybe she could coax some more fun out of her if she worked at it. Kinda like the old time cowboys and Injuns way out on them wild frontiers when they made little piles of all different kind of dry leaves and grass and scraps of bark and twigs too if they could find them, then they grated that whatchamacallit, *flint* against that piece of iron to throw a spark in it then they blow and watch, but not blow too hard, and not study it too long and study wrong like Sonny says, they work at it without trying too hard to work at it, nursing the tiny flame into its own keeping on, into its own relentless devouring. That would be so much better than the silence which had slowly filled up the space between them as the years passed, until flooding over into an inescapable dullness, where it was blank and silent like dark water, where you could never know what might jump up from nowhere and snatch you down, and when it was blank and silent she did not want to know how she was seeing and what she was thinking of her then, she wanted to keep all her seeing and thinking secret to herself, wanted to just keep on without blowing up, impossible.

Animal, Mineral, Vegetable

Rain descended the stairs, letting her steps fall carelessly upon each knotted board, sounding its alarm. Putting my foot down, she thought. Not trying to get by her, just next to her, long enough to throw in my two cents. Touched down in the living room which Mother, always the last to bed and first to wake, had inspected corrected and ushered into the dark before prayers, leaving neither cushion nor slipcover nor coaster, nor rug-edge nor knick-knack nor ashtray out of place, each particular still frozen at twilight, save for the carousel globes of the anniversary clock whirling soundlessly under the bell jar. She crossed to the window to peer out from the curtain's edge, sighting beyond the porch to the rosebush tops swaying in the morning air, as if searching a mirror for symptoms of herself, for the other body, for someone and not someone else.

As the early hour struck under glass she gathered grandmother Hannah's velvet robe around her, tied it tightly at the waist and stepped out the door, onto the front porch. Here comes the electric chair again, she thought. She skirted the gray milk box, stalled at the steps, already bracing herself to hear the usual words which would intercept even her most painstaking thoughts and cut her down to size, smaller than even the quaker's bonnets crowding at Mother's knees, down to nobody. The damp grass lapped at her ankles as she crossed the front yard to stand behind her, growing all the more unsettled to sense her quiet steadiness as she worked, lifting each

seedling from its peat pot to tuck into its furrow, never once looking back.

Good morning Mother

she ventured, finding herself promptly impatient.

What dragged you out of bed so early?

Too much thinking, couldn't sleep.

Too much is not good, especially for you.

Here I go again, about to waste my breath, she suspected.

And what's been on your mind, Mother?

You ask like you don't know. Everything which shouldn't be on
my mind. Things which I shouldn't have to be concerned with,
she answered, speaking almost too softly to be heard, as if to insist
that the whole world stop to hear.

These are whom I should be concerned with. *Primula vulgaris!*
Claire gazed fondly upon her seedlings, nestled in their rows like
newborns in their beds, regretting that her own children had been
nothing so lovely in her sight as these.

After breakfast I'll fix your hair

I've got good news, Mother. It's already done.

she said, reaching back to the nape of her neck to untie the draw-
string and lift the net from her hair and turn her head for her to see
in the gathering brightness, as she had long practiced to do so well.

Jenny pressed it for me last night.

I can see what all Miss Good Hair knows about that.

Didn't burn me even once. Now you won't have to bother.

When Madame Jenny tires of catering to your whims and your
head gets tight as Buckwheat the Pickininny, don't come running back to me.

Claire turned to face her and reared back

What in the world have you thrown on?

I'm wearing Granny's things, which fit me just fine. To dress up fine like she did on Sundays.

Forget about looking like her, a Georgia Peach.

Yeah, I already did.

Yeah this nope that. You sound like a common tramp raised in the street. And worse every day.

It's for my special occasion

Rain insisted, finding it hard to catch her breath as the current crackled through her limbs. Nowhere to run back to now, only a place to gather up what she will carry away. As she had for the first time the night before. Pushing back the hanging coats and dresses to reach the attic door, pulling it open and stepping through. Standing with closed eyes in the dark, that dark upon dark where she would always come to her to keep her company, knowing what had been and what was and what was to come but patiently listening. She waved through the dark to find the string to pull the light. She crouched over to settle onto the trunk in the middle of the splintered floor, sinking into the quietness with the abandoned heaped up things gathering near, stopping to set a spell. She stood on tiptoe to nudge the shoebox from the shelf. She unhooked the dress bag from where it hung at the apex of the ceiling, the crisp silk twitching out through its unbuttoned mouth like ready wings leaping from a cocoon. She reached into pockets to roll the cool mothballs against her palm, pressed the brittle corsage to her face, felt its withered rose against her cheek. Yes, the one you made for me, before I was.

Special for you, trouble for me. No telling what you might say or do.

I'm still troubled too. I can't help it

Claire stabbed her spade into the dirt and, rearing up, threw her hands onto her hips.

Let's go through the whole shit show one more time. You

CAN'T HELP IT and you run your big stupid mouth. First, we drag that two-timing guttersnipe back to town, to trade notes with your new playmate, none of which are likely to be flattering to you. Next, we watch them both run for the hills. And for the Grand Finale, wind up stuck with a bastard we can neither afford nor get rid of nor ask either of those dimwits to support, and have every living ass in this town minding our business. Sounds like no help for you.

Maybe I don't need to stay in this town

she replied. A modest proposal, erupting forth from the hidden thoughts of another, undiscovered but now stumbled over, someone she had never been before.

You wouldn't last a week.

But I could start like anybody else, somewhere. Father would understand

Yes he never admits that you don't give a damn about the rest of us.

I should tell him too,

They say a hard head makes a soft diasticutis. Don't think for a second that he'll save you from what's in store for you then. You'll wish I set your hair on fire instead.

Words which seized her and lifted her up like an enormous hand poised to fling her back to earth.

Rain took him by the hand. They pushed through the bus stop doors, crossed the sidewalk to the curb. Stately behind the wheel of his Deuce and a Quarter, Henry rolled to a stop alongside them. She opened the back door. Jimmy tossed his duffle bag across the seat. The driver's side window descended with a whir.

Good afternoon, soldier!

The boy straightened up to answer.

Good afternoon, Captain.

Henry looked up beyond the rooftops, to the tattered clouds glowing under the sun.

Lord seen fit to send the breath of springtime.

Yes, Sir. A blessed day

And all things He send us we ought to cherish.

Yes indeed, Sir.

Like that pretty gal next to you, she all the world to me.

And also to me

Jimmy insisted, speaking with calm certainty. My sweet mad scientist, like it's one plus one is two, Rain thought happily, holding fast to every word.

Don't look like you lost now, like you was the first time.

No, Sir. Managed to take the right bus ever since.

She leaned in against the fender, smiling uneasily.

Please tell Mother we'll get back soon.

Henry smiled in return, but answered the boy.

Reckon you do need to shake a leg some after all that sittin.

I do feel some earthquickens about now. But both my feet on the ground. And I know how to put one in front of the other.

Henry answered wearily, like an angel looking backward, into the long days of winter.

Just make sure my Rainie look both ways when she cross the street. She watch for where she goin, but not for how she gettin there.

Off with my overcoat, off with my gloves

she sang to herself, tenderly hanging the antique duster from the coat tree,

My springtime is here.

Well, take a look at you, cried Maggie,
darting from behind her crowded counter to their table.

Pearl says I'm a regular clothes horse,
she announced, lifting a hand to steady the ostrich-plumed hat,
Maybe not like Jenny
who would sew her own, who would never wind up in a mess like this
but I've got my own druthers for sure
she added, as the fingers of the other pinched the hanging strand of
pearls as if it were counting a rosary.

Your name on them yet? asked Jimmy Love,
pointing, then drawing the beaded chain of his dog tags from the
neck of his winged blue shirt.

Got news for you Mister. They've been *mine* since I was born.

Granny and me, we're both in this dress together
she said, knowing it was both here and there, and now and then, at
that very instant. That she had crossed eternity to stand beside her
and hear her plea for her pinched instep, Please help me walk in
these hard old shoes today.

You a regular séance, Jimmy said.

Oh they use that extra special kind of electricity on the other
side.

Give us a twirl! cried Maggie.
Turning she looked into the light still falling from those extinguished days. How it must have shored up even Hannah's invincible
spirits to step into that cool waterfall of ivory linen, its taut pocket
holding her kerchief and fan close at hand as she darted through the
Sunday afternoon air, keeping her crowding suitors at bay.

Nick Pallas, impresario of egg creams, curator of *karaméla,* architect
of *rizogalo,* pawnbroker of instantaneous happiness, sole owner and

proprietor of the Sugar Bowl Fountain and Sweet Shop and one-man show, hustled up and down his crowded marble counter, endlessly reflected in sparkling front windows, chrome spouts, crystal parfait glasses, long-necked silver spoons, and everywhere in his celebrated temple of mirrors. Old Nick with his bald dome, crooked nose, cauliflower ear and wandering eye, his feinting sticking jabbing heart forever searching, like that kindred heart he'd known since its baby-toothed days, for the right words to say. He stopped to lean in where they worked on a hot fudge sundae together, putting on Rain's pouting face.

What, I'm not making em good no more?
With a listless smile, she shaved a scoop. Dreading to devour and numb herself in that icy hot sweetness. Longing to run away with the pixies and backslide into delectable sabotage, to keep cooking herself down at teatimes until the mountain of brute fact was all that was left of her, just as she told herself she wanted it to be. And not feel anything more at all when he'd take off with his big blue sack and never look back and Mother would say, Told you so.

She lifted her downcast eyes to find Jimmy's cherub face shining down like a harvest moon.

Ain't this your favorite?

Course it is. It's just
Crashing head-on into myself then, she figured, no surprise. That special electricity seized her once again on an all-too-familiar frequency, with a transmission still pulsing across the years. Of a trip downstairs, taken half asleep. Walking the line through the living room to the kitchen, the cool linoleum curling her bare feet. Dragging the hot-combing stool to the icebox to climb to the upper door. The spilling light routing the graveyard shadows from the dark, her small hands reaching in to seize the frosted carton. Twisting the

spoon to mine the treasure, serving that hunger goading her from dreams, ravenous for what it can never find to eat. Waking in the burst of light revealing the great bird hovering overhead, screeching in discovery, pronouncing its verdict, carrying out its sentence. The brain freeze spiking behind her eyes with each swallow and the swipe of the knotted cord when she let go the spoon, Pick it up, the bird shrieked, striking again, pick it up. The retch pounding like a fist against her breath until she emptied herself into her lap.

What Kind of Fool Am I.

She dug in for a mouthful, excavating a cherry-topped heap.

That a girl, he said.

Perfect punishment for a flim-flam like me, she thought, awaiting the enduring chill.

The town clock tolled one. In Chevys and Fords, pickup trucks and sedans, double parking up and down the block, the boyfriends and girlfriends rolled into town in search of Saturday's glory. Pouring from driver's seats and backseats, rushing in to claim their territories and pack the booths, rebounding to crowd the soda bar and jukebox. Huddling, sidling, dodging, blowing smoke signals for dear life.

Rain watched anxiously as Jimmy's eyes roamed the hall, fearing that they would pursue fresh faces passing by, tempted by their curious glances, astounded to find their perpetual wallflower in the company of a handsome soldier boy.

Bet you ain't never seen so many pretty gals in one place before Her Highness ventured, with fear and trembling.

I reckon they all right, long as they don't get no bad ideas.

You can forget about that.

I see a lot of chaps up in here too. They had the good sense to chase after you yet?

Never

she now happily confessed.

An oncoming engine roared, the street cleared quickly, a car hurtled by.

That's Butch, the gravedigger's son, our neighbor. Pearl said that old hearse is the fastest thing in town.

Wait till you see the hot rods them crackers run down in Galveston. I know the mechanics of course, but they ain't my main thing no more. Once I get my Coupe de Ville I'll be satisfied.

But will you take me for a ride? Even if I have to sit in the middle in the back?

Back, front, around the world, Cuddly. All around.

She remembered waiting, but hoping, for no good reason, for a ride one winter night not so long before, Or was it ages ago. Standing at a crossroads under a streetlamp in a bright spot in the fallen snow. Heading for the next light, a neon sign over the door of a small place across the road, not a jumping thermometer too hot to cool down but a steadfast glow. A light that might mark a spot where a girl running for her life in a broken shoe could rest easy for a hot second. Where she might even run into a kind lady or gentleman whom she might trust to give her a ride to somewhere or away from everywhere, who would let her lay down across the backseat out of sight from the dizzying windows, who wouldn't try to fill up the silence with cheap talk but could just let it be, who could let the unrolling miles rock her to sleep, someone like this absentminded angel who had dropped down from the sky into her world of troubles. Now she stood at another crossroads, this time not alone but, as she supposed and longed to confess, as a great pretender, keeping quiet as a mouse, in the back, in the dark.

She let go his hand to run, like she used to run at first sight from Father, to the shining display cases. Looking down through the glass she spelled a notion to contemplate Whitman's Samplers, brown and white Easter bunnies, peanut butter eggs, plump peeps, red purple black and blue jellybeans, to crowd out what offers no rest, all in vain. He followed behind, uncomprehending, bringing only another tidbit of mere sweetness, the only thing which his logical omnipotence imagined to be sufficient, to bear.

SUGAR BOWL. This joint got the right name
he said, arms drawing her near, kissing the thicket of her hair.

Two faces approached from the crowd. The unsinkable smirk of a big-boned redhead in a too-small sweater, the thin-lipped glare of a gangling boy with a sky-high ducktail.

Well look what the cat drug in, said the redhead.
Rain turned and stepped up for the standoff.

And what brings us to your attention, Loretta?

Gosh I really wish I knew
the other replied. The boy eyed the uniform up and down as if it were on the wrong body. Jimmy wavered, then recovered, in the presence of mystery.

See, they know not what they do, Rain said.

Call it curiosity if you care to, no offense intended. We don't get many zoomies up in these parts, the redhead crooned.

You down at McGuire? asked the boy.

That's it. The 26th, DC-01.

Spec?

54230. Radar, Navigation.
The redhead skewered her companion with a grin.

He's just an Apprentice, like my brother Ned.

He's a top Airman, cried Rain, flying the big jets.

Their faces registered dull surprise, then amusement.

Well ain't them some stripes for that, the boy replied.

I bet he don't fly nothing but a kite, adds the redhead.

Rain took in Jimmy's silent face at a glance and answered without hesitation.

He's special

Ain't nobody special in the military, drawled the boy. Least of all a

A what? Jimmy said,

then she stepped to one side to block him.

A plain old grunt, answered the redhead.

It's a top secret his work, what do y'all know anyways

Gee whiz, a regular spy.

The redhead said. They looked to each other and laughed.

Retta, you'd best get up away from me before I have to show you how one more time.

Uppity with a man on your arm, ain'tcha?

said the redhead, turning away.

Now run and tell all, Mouth Almighty

she cried to their retreating backs, returning to the herd.

Ah Cuddly. If I

If I, if I. A pleading bell, tolling across the years of all God's dangers and the turning world, ringing up the curtain of the soap box and piping organ of the afternoon show. An unwitting lightness surged within her. So I'm not the only pretender, she decided. *To resemble a human being*

Shoot. Lemme play a tune for us once or twice.

Once again, she found herself at a jukebox, its glowing buttons and whirling disks looming before her like the dashboard of an other-worldly spacecraft. She dropped a quarter into the slot, pressed the keys, and in that instant of anticipation recalled the loneliness of the intergalactic messenger, forever setting course for another fallen world, bearing auguries of doom. She still felt his eyes glowing darkly from the screen like the void of outer space, heard his last words to the prodigal sons of earth, *You have been warned.* She stepped out of her velvet pincers, threaded her belt through their straps and tied them around her waist. Her stockinged feet settled and fixed her where she stood. She turned back to face the enormous room, to find him now standing apart from her among the rest, at a distance she found herself unworthy to ask him to cross. The music rose behind her. She heard the long whistle above the clicking metronome, then the voices entering in song, the one clearest and most delicate testifying from the center like a raft drifting downstream on its companions' chanted reply. *Hello, Darling,* it said, coming to call. Yes, she thought, another canticle sent from heaven to *drive the shadows away,* but not mine.

The floor cleared around her. The boy, dreading to wonder if that was what he still was, stopped short on the arc rippling away from her like water from a fallen stone, no longer fit to play the kind stranger stopping to offer a ride to anywhere, but yet another who suddenly finds himself the drifter, *sans* vehicle and destination, thumbing a ride on the frayed shoulder of a highway. *Ven acá.* She opened her arms to him, affirming, despite her wretchedness, that he had been chosen and, she hoped, had chosen her in return, recalling other arms, other words, other bewitchments now returning to mind from an incomprehensible distance. One last time he searched the crowd, then stepped, No need to throw yourself, she thought, from the edge, to join her at the center. The song played on. The chanting voice crested above the answering wave. *A world completely new,* it proclaimed. Not turning out to be the same old one like the rest, she hoped, and wondered if she could ever get there.

She laid hands on his starched shoulders, nudging him from side to side. Then pressed a finger to his lips, nipping his reluctance in the bud.

I'll show *you* how, she said.

She felt the upwelling memory of another bright afternoon, of her first pirouette at the schoolyard rink, when she suddenly could but not knowing how, stepping from the blade's edge into thin air.

Simon says, do this.

Side by side, they trod the overthrown sidewalks. I've missed you, she said but just to herself, scarcely moving her lips, watching the cracks flirt with her footsteps. How easy it would be, moving together step by step, she thought, to finally break her back. But then what. After all, I've missed you she said inside her head again, like words she had no right to speak. Missed you like the missing piece with a funny odd shape all around, fitting in just one empty place, that you could kick yourself for taking so long to notice where it was. She thought how sweet it is to walk together after so long walking most times alone. Not running like she had to keep up with Daddy Long Legs rushing as if stealing bases to get back home, had kept hanging on, chasing after, dragged along.

One more thing you should keep in mind. I've been mad at the world since the day I was born.

I believe it.

Why? I ain't been mad with you, not yet.

Not particularly

Particularly what?

What a mouthful, she thought. Here comes the world.

No. But I can see when you and Miss Claire

There you go again. Just say My Mother and get it over with.

Your Mother. When you two about to murder each other.

That'd be a trick, put each other out of our misery.

I admit sometime she give you a hard way to go. But she just care for you to be a good gal, like every man want.

So Mister Every Man, that's what you want?

Yep. And that's what I got.

Long as I'm bad when you want me to be though.

Now that kind of bad is good.

She tried to smile along with him but the frown stuck.

Why you so sure she's so wonderful herself?

Your folks come up here an settle in the midst of all these hard white folks, an ain't but a few of us. Even so they ain't ask nobody for nothin, went on and got they own. In my distinct idea she an admirable woman.

Right then a funny thing, at least she thought it was for some reason even though she wasn't quite sure why, popped, poof, onto the diving board in her head and belly-flopped straight into her mouth.

Sounds like you like her more than you like me

she said, not quite knowing where it came from but quite frankly not wanting to take it back. He stopped in the middle of the street.

Ain't so. It's a few certain things about her I like

She tugged his coat sleeve to spur him across. Let me count the ways, she thought.

I can see y'all meant for each other.

Ain't no met for each other, it's just practical miration. We cain't deny she know how to take care of business.

Who's *we*?

Including you.

We ought to skip this subject.

Fine. No point in me talkin to myself

Then before she could say boo he jumped up away from her and ran off into Judge Burton's great big yard, spread out like an oceanic moat between the street and their practically a mansion behind it, and knelt down in the grass under that big oak tree smack dab in the middle like a sinner come down to the altar. Oh thanks now I'm plain mortified, she thought, because at first she figured that he'd just run off in a fit over her scolding him about you-know-what. Here I'm dressed up to the nines like the world's never seen just to have this crazy man turn it into an awful day. Cause all her life walking up and down this side of Loder Street she'd never done anything but steer clear from that lawn, not even so much as stepped too close to the edge of it, because You never know if folks might decide you're up to something suspicious, which she would have and even tried to tell him before he took off and got too far away to yell after, tell him that traipsing out there in that yard is the worst place in town to get on the wrong side of the law, cause the Law Himself lives right on the other side of that lawn. Cause folks said that lawn had always been mowed and trimmed so perfect, some folks who worked there claim the Judge make his son get down with barber shears all around the stones and even worse. Right then she remembered one day when she was little, hot as the dickens when Sonny Boy, after Mother had got that job for him, he quit halfway through. Come home talkin bout how Your Honor wasn't nothin but a crook asking for all kind of extra work from sunup to sundown then after he don't pay for it. Oh man Mother heard that and then got after him on the spot, cause everybody knew she and Aunt Barb had forever been doin Miss Mayflower Liza Standish Burton's fancy whatchamacallit garden parties, till he forgot like he always did who he was talkin back to and she knocked him down the porch steps, And don't come back till you finish she said. Cause I'd never dare to even think of, forgive us our, *trespassing* like that in the first place anywhere because it's their own private property and Mother always says Now when you all want to run around in somebody's grass remember we got plenty we paid for right here. Cause who knows what might happen if they look out and see me lolly gagging in broad daylight with this G.I. fella crawling around their front yard like a dog fixing to dig a hole in the ground, she imagined, leaving her mortified down to her last nerve, Even more than just before when he was talking like a whatchamacallit, turncoat but shoot who and what am I to knock somebody, quite frankly if he's digging a hole I hope it's deep enough for me to crawl out in China on the other end, or jump in and please just go ahead and bury me alive.

He stood, turning slowly, shifting his hands to keep what they held out of sight behind him. Returned step by pacing step from that incidental distance, not distant far away but distant ago. To the girl watching him come back he looked small, small but resistant to vanishing, maybe like when he'd first figured out how to get away, a solitary child left to watch over himself, rambling everywhere and to anyone who might take the place and time of those too long absent, keen to show and tell of whatever wonders and miracles he had discovered, certain that should they stop to look to listen he might at last prove that he is more than nothing and at last see himself and never again disappear.

They stood face to face. One arm drifted forward from hiding, its upturned palm bearing its weightless burden.

—

Empty, in this case

he said, as if reporting the merest experimental fact, such as reading a thermometer, as if once again taking matters in hand. As if he had found what she had lost or forgotten or never wished to keep. It would be so easy, she thought, to just say it now, to confirm such uncanny cleverness. What's missing in the puzzle? It's this, it's, she'd begin,

Ain't that sweet?

she said, instead.

Allow me

he begged, reaching above her head to lower it into the nook of her ostrich-plumed hat. He smiled, delighted to have once again proved, beyond a shadow of a doubt, that he was.

God save the Queen, he said.

She had always loved to wind up there after running all over creation. In that sheltering room belonging to neither the town nor the valley, but at once to everywhere and to nowhere in particular. Loved how the sunlight fell in through the high, tall windows, how high-heeled clicks and thudding rubber stamps and tearing open envelopes and leaning in to whispering echoed from the ceiling to the polished floor, sounded through the open hollows of the mailboxes lining the back wall, to create an infinitesimal roar in the postman's room across the counter, mailboxes which she had come to know, without wanting to know, were more untenanted, more empty, than her own, one faithfully visited the last Saturday of each month by a flat oblong package in a plain brown wrapper, And there it is. She turned the key.

Knew you'd show up today, come hell or high water!
cried the Postmaster, leaning over the counter to peer beyond the
window.

An who dat? Jimmy asked, with a frown.

Just Elmus. My favorite lunchtime partner.

Partner?

Don't worry. There'd never be any of that between us. He's a
regular hoot. I'll introduce you

No need for all that.

He hovered over her shoulder.

Trixie La Rue? Who?

A poor cousin of mine.

Live here in town?

Oh no. Way out in the boondocks.

Maybe she live up in your attic. What's in the mystery envelope?

No mystery here
she tweeted, and unveiled the merchandise,
holding up the cover against her coat for any to see.

—

He narrowed his eyes.

What I see is a man talkin bout how he change hisself to a woman.

Right. That's just what she had to do.

He she ain't done no such thing. It's impossible, like making 1+1=3. No thoughtful person would read that smut.

It ain't smut to Cousin Trixie. She gets a whole lot out of it.

Such as what?

That true knowledge she's looking for, just like you.

The Postmaster merrily rang his bell.

Closing time, please leave and let me go home.

Rain hurried to the counter.

Didn't mean to neglect you before, she said.

Dig that hip doodad up top.

Why thank you, Elmus. Soon it will be all the rage.

He searched the distance in all directions, as he did the first time she laid eyes on him, glancing everywhere, but intently now, taking inventory. From the bridge spanning Dry Brook where Moore Street turns into country road, to the houses recoiling from the grey walls and greensward of the dead house, winding uphill along the narrow road for the black car, to the grove of hemlocks and the ranks of gravestones standing fast at their feet, to the pasture rolling its half-mile between barbed wire from the hilltop down to the ponds still ringed with ice, to the next-door neighbor girlfriend's house and the brother and daughter-in-law's place above their garage, whose names he now uneasily failed to recall, to the red roofs of the white house from which they had started out at noon, to the bare rosebushes and porch windows poised to betray their presence as they passed.

We finally back at home base.

Oh that's what this is?

We could make a pit stop, say hello to folks.

She lifted her arms to stretch herself into the light spilling from the clouds and delicately resettled her crown upon her head and turned around and around in the middle of the street.

They can wait on us for a hot second, she replied.

One last chance now, she thought.

Past the bridge they veered onto the narrow lane running past the stripped tennis courts and cold fireplaces and the kiddie pool gathering fallen leaves, into the heart of the glen. He climbed to the top of the ridge and kept abreast high above her, meandering through the stands of bare trees. Not just up there, off somewhere, she suspected, on the verge of disappearance, all at once again the restless boy grown tired of the familiar hide and seek and marching off to find another playmate, or something better. Off and running to where she could expect to find or not find him thereafter, or I'm already getting what's coming to me.

Passing the vacant tin-roofed pavilion enroute to her future, her thoughts returned to summer, to her first glorious straying to him, from her rotten tramp. In those midsummer days when they'd slipped from the kitchen out the back door and run like hell bent for election through the backyard, up along the hearse road past the gravedigger's shack, across the upstream bridge into the Glen, out of sight.

He came down the pathways other boyish men had discovered while climbing and falling, quickly now to stand beside her.

Here we are all over again, she said.

It was in the hot spell days of August when they had lay there together in the lacy shadows of the elm trees. When the day campers riding the big slide arching overhead flocked and chirped and fluttered indifferently going up and coming down around them. The tired sand clung to their dirty feet and she lay her tired head against his shoulder, but *nonetheless,* recalled the melody which had long bewitched her, *Here am I, come to me,* and exclaimed to herself, lips nearly still like leaves in the summer air, I have arrived. Like at the first moment of her first rumba with the one who would now remain nameless, and the melody which had carried her away to walk out alone as the singer had walked along that beach, and the meaning of the verses he had whispered into her ear as they danced, *I would lie to say I could forget you today for another.* Words whose days are numbered, at remove from secrets lying forgotten in the keeping until remembered, then emptied of sense. Forgetful heart, still broken. Arriving nowhere, mouth full of nothing, instead of what she could not say.

What's wrong now?

She looked above them, into the bare trees. He took her hand.

Come on. I need to see that froze waterfall while it's still light, he said.

He scrambled across the rocks to the foot of the falls. She stood waiting, huddled in her greatcoat against the piercing chill, discovering the red winterberries scattered under the pines among the fallen leaves and patches of snow and her crowned reflection in the oval of the pool, still shallower then than in early spring when it churned and writhed over itself as it rushed down to the crick, *uneasy lies the head* she recalled hearing somewhere when she wasn't quite listening. She shut her eyes to just and only hear the crick still running off the ridge to fall down beneath the hanging sheets and stalactites of ice, full of a sound like falling rain, or falling as if raining only there in some imprisoned spirit-shape, that hidden place within this hidden place like the place where she kept what she kept to herself.

    Clouds flyin by so fast in the sky. And consider this froze waterfall here,

he cried, reaching up to lay a hand upon the ice. Maybe everybody acts strange sometimes, she decided.

    Look what's happening right now. Suppose we ask, Why it melt?

    Why ask? she asked. Springtime coming.

    I mean the real reason why.

    What's the real reason for any old thing?

He extended a single pointing finger into the void.

    Heat be *the motion of molecules.*

    I remember that cules word. Itsy-bitsy teeny-weeny pieces of everything, like H_2O.

    And how fast these here H_2Os go, that's *temperature. These here,* them two little words' actually the important thang to keep in mind. Now molecules, here there's hot ones be flyin around knockin into the others, which knock into others, and so on, a perpetual mix up, an eternal accident. But strictly speakin that ain't *heat.* Cause if you look in the dictionary first thing it say heat ain't nothing but human feeling.

    No accident, no feeling, she contended.

    What feel cold to us might feel hot to them flying saucer folk.

    At least then they won't ask to borrow my sweater.

    It be called heat but it ain't nothing but motion. Hold on to your hat now, we gon throw out the dictionary and get truly physical

    I can't wait.

Now when a body *hot*

Thought you just said there really ain't no such thing as hot.

When a body called hot that really means it be mixed up. All them molecules in it be jumping round every which way. But when a body cold

Like the ones they find and take to the morgue?

Any body, it could be animal, mineral, vegetable. Girl you got a one track mind

And how about you?

Me, I say, when a body cold it ain't moving inside hardly atall. It ain't mixing it up.

Now you got me mixed up.

Think about our deesert today. All that heat in that big old room full of folks got in our ice cream and it melted

Now I've got to dwell on how *they* melted my ice cream

and the whole room around it cooled down, cept most and generally we don't notice that.

It got real hot in there though when we started everybody dancing right?

The room got less mixed up than before and the ice cream got more mixed up than before. If we left that ice cream sit there before too long it would get to the same temperature as the room, and vice versa, each one just as mixed up as the other. And furthermore, the ice cream with the room together be more mixed up than before.

And you got my koodies cause you ate off my spoon. Ain't it just about romantic?

He flung down his hands, kicked a stone into the water. The falling melt and the trickling of the stream filled up the sudden silence between them.

Can we move along now?

Oh am I still on the bus?

As he turned back she found once again, like the shape of an hour marking the face of a clock, that face like the face of a man standing at the edge of highway, which she'd first seen when he'd stopped at the edge of the circle, wavering at the edge where he might have still turned away and held fast to that complete consistent and sufficient life of one who rambles on alone, never embracing the one who can never be trusted to stay. But who am I that he should come to me?

All them itsy bitsy pieces of the world be like cards in a deck, they always stay mixed up cause tain't likely in the shuffle they all go back to where they started cause there ain't nothin to make em fall back in line like that. Like when we play pitty pat. You get the luck of the draw one hand then most and generally you don't get lucky let alone get the very same hand the next.

Except I kept on winning and got you down to your birthday suit, remember?

Everybody need to understand that everything bound to stay as mixed up as it can be. Most and generally anything got so many more ways of being mixed up than it got of being set right. That's the way of the world.

But sometimes we could have a perfect day like today

she offered, as a sudden downdraft from the ridge struck her face like a chastening hand, lashed like a branch across her open eyes, swept a withered petal from her corsage into the stream.

One day. But perfect, it can't never last.

Of course never, she said,

watching herself hanging on all over again. He stood at the foot of the frozen cascade, staring upward as if awaiting a heavenly portent.

That's why this here gonna melt and won't never jump back to be froze up identical to as we see it now even if it do freeze again. And why none them china folk you so-called accidentally knocked down and broke gonna stick back together and jump back up on the shelf

Thanks for reminding me

And why time don't run backwards like when Mister Henry run his movies backwards so we can see folks and our ownselfs act the fool one more time. Why everything that happen must be what happened once it happen. Why the whole world bound to cool down and kick the bucket and die. Cause even if it take a gigantic long time sooner or later anything anywhere be as mixed up as anything anywhere else. Every thing be just as cold or hot as everything else and there won't be nothing left to make some other thing move anything no more so ain't nothing gon work, not any deevice not even us so anything living have to die then too. And therefore nothing that work to live can live forever. And if the world been around forever before now, how come it ain't dead yet.

Glad you're happy to see me for a change,

she cried, looking back and back to porcelain faces irretrievably lost, the merciless teeth of iron combs never broken, to all that which having happened now must forever be how it was and felt the leak coming but held on to pose her question, one to which she hoped she did not already know the answer.

So even you and me, we'll disappear?

He replied without turning back, calling to mind another.

Into cosmic dust, leaving no trace.

No trace, two little words. I get it,

she answered, and walked away. Mister Great Pretender. Shoot, ain't no news to me, she thought, what I've always known. But turn around and here come folks tellin me Shut your mouth and listen, all I get is the same old story. Shut off can't even crack a joke about it. It's too hard every which way. On our own, she confided to her unseen companion, Just us two. Least then I can eat my own troubles in peace.

The lengthening shadows crossed the road before her. Then she heard him coming, Took him long enough, she thought, and picked up the pace. Granny we're the Three Mouseketeers, thankful for our plumed hat now a birdhouse, our pocketed linen dress, our lace trimmed kerchief, these stout shoes making their way through the dust. Mournful to imagine her follower as one who pursued at an unhurried pace, having already calculated and taken for granted that he would soon enough overtake her by sheer dint of stride, that she has nowhere left to run or to hide. Taking his time, aroused by her fearful cries, waiting for her exhaustion, for the hole to wrench her ankle, for the unsettling stone to throw her down to deliver her, helpless, at his feet. He ran to catch up now, shouting

What happened?

Go on. I ain't waiting on you

His footsteps fell at her heels. She stopped short as his arms reached from behind to close around her. She spoke for the stillness which was all that was left her.

Quite frankly, I realized something today.

That you're crazy about me right?

No. That I kinda really don't want you.

Say what? Oh yes you do.

Cause you don't really want me. What good am I really to you?

Some kinda stuffed cuddly thing that's all. Teddy Girl.

That sound like Elvis, not me.

She pushed with all the dwindling strength within her to keep the right words coming out, right enough, she hoped.

    Yeah, not you. Too busy zoomin and planet-hoppin to even take me out to the picture show.

    Look, I'm right here. And I ain't goin nowhere.

He held on, waiting for her answer.

    Here, now. I might give you that much.

    But I got a certain superpower he shonuff don't. Which I always keep secret till just the right time.

    Do tell. Such as leap tall buildings in a single bound?

    Naw. Even better. I can summon odds and ends from the four corners of the earth, in the twinkling of an eye.

Above them the last passages of sunlight crept over the ridge. She shook her head, wondering, longing to keep saying No.

    Odds and ends. Now I've heard everything. Show me.

    Cept you can't watch how I do, it's CLASSIFIED. You gonna have to close your eyes.

Too late now, she thought, in the sudden dark. He reached between her plumes to raise the crown.

    Hurry, open them now.

—

Up in the sky she found neither bird nor plane, nor angel nor devil, only the condemning clouds driven, without destiny, by the wind. Go on, fool, she thought, surrender to your own fool self. Like all the rest who soon thereafter grow cold and disappear, reduced to smudged lines of print across coarse pages packed in plain brown wrappers delivered to nameless mailboxes, Yes, anybody knows why. Go head on.

Your Highness, now you know my real identity. Will you promise to keep my secret till death do us part?

What secret? she answered, instead.

Miss Abracadabra

Pearl flew her '55 Chevy by sheer lack of faith, both when gazing intently down the road ahead and when looking back. Rain, riding beside her, kept her eyes clear of the passing blur of the river road, eyeing the ashtray, waiting for a chance to steal a drag to which Dear Mother Superior would pretend to object.

She pulled over beside the wide crescent of the riverbank. Rain leaned into the windshield to look downstream across the ice-fringed water, meandering through the stubbled fields. So this is that summer place, she thought. Out there, in and under those bushes, it happened. Memories, secrets told and never told, carried on until lost and forgotten. They got out and leaned against the fender.

This was our secret garden. Where we first pretended to know
what we were doing, like the Big Fairytale says.
She booted a stone into the weeds.
All that wouldn't do for a proper young lady like me.
Until I corrupted you with growing up absurd.
Holy Mother, I confess to have spoiled myself, thank you.
Rain knew why she had brought her to the place from which she had warned them all to keep away.
Picture this. First, Diaper Man—I've mentioned him before
Which term Mother Superior had quite frankly nearly copied from her, How about that! Rain crowed to herself.

Yep. He's the one who you

Right. He tells me how his Daddy Your Honor and Registered Mommy sat him down to explain what was best for us. Well ain't we fortunate I said. They weren't calm at all he says. No way should I waste my life in orbit around an unfortunate mistake, they said. Giving handouts to her tribe of Holy Rollers, we'll be utterly shunned. Unthinkable that your future should be sabotaged by this trailer trash. This must be fixed, they said. I ask him, Why are you even telling me this creepy stuff? Oh I told them Don't talk about her that way, he says, I want you to know that. I say Please, at least spare me that. You're just making sure I get the message, like you were told. Then he starts with that whining, which you know I can't stand.

They laughed as long as it lasted.

I was the first one to tell. But when Your Honor called, Barney went ballistic. Mutti helped more than usual, she jumped on to cover me when he started kicking me. Then he kept me babbling on my knees, all night long.

Who'd ever think

Forget thinking. The Holy Ghost flew down to sit on his head and it hatched. He grabbed my face. You'll lie in the bed you've made for yourself, he said. And by God you'll come out from among them. Among them? They wouldn't give me the time of day.

Sounds like Mother, Rain said.

Next Attraction was the Fireside Chat at Mommy and Daddy's highball hour. Barney and Mutti dressed for church and smiled without stopping. Thankfully we're in agreement, Daddy said, happier than a pig in shit. Amen, Barney said. Mutti nodded, not a peep. Thank God, Mommy said, dying for us to drop dead. Diaper Man's scared to death. Clink go the glasses. We all see what must be done, Barney said. What must be done for *her,* Mutti said. Pardon me, I said, I'm right here. Old Barney Fife didn't dare slap me around in front of them, not even with Jesus backing him up. God grant us the serenity, he said. To accept what we cannot change Mutti says. With all due respect to the faith which we share and admire, Daddy said, we're glad that you too see this as an *exceptional instance.*

Instance?

Yeah, just add water. Hold on, it gets even better. As we've agreed, it's best to nip the prospect in the bud, Daddy says. And avoid matters which might end unpleasantly for all concerned.

Where's Perry Mason when you need him?

Sehr schnell, Big Shot paid to get my twisted mind straightened out for keeps. Your hero Barney wouldn't have any further part of it. Too busy being everybody's friend but ours.

I remember folks said you disappeared to Towanda.

Yeah, that threw them all off the track. Meanwhile Mutti snuck me into the big city from Elmira, on the bus. To see her old friend from back in Tiergarten.

For what you told me about before?

For what spared me the worst, but not the rest. But what a laugh, after all the crap I'd heard from them all my life.

It's not funny to me

Obey the Supreme Commandment, *Render unto Big Shot.* I finally realized it's got to be a joke, it's really Amazing Grace, at last! I rolled back the stone and crawled out of the bunker where they hide from life, where they'd kept me locked up all of mine. And my first sight of daylight on earth was pure salvation.

Her doll arms reached in supplication toward Heaven.

Behold, I'm born again. Washed white as snow. Get a load of my halo, Amen.

Thank you thank you,
Rain whispered, grateful for Pearl's fingers digging up her bones. Before her shut eyes she recalled her first hour on 8th Avenue, how she'd looked way up till her head wouldn't go back any further, as they'd walked to their hotel, right up the street from the Authorities. To think of that great big **M** they'd stuck way up there on the very top! Big as nobody's business, like a great big copy of one of them sugar toppers Mother puts on birthday cakes, she thought. And that big lobby full of folks walking and talking so fast or lined up  at the long counters, scads more folks that one day than had hit the bus station back home in a hundred years. And the room, **1919**, some number to remember, she thought, was just about perfect for them, quite frankly. In fact, she'd been so surprised when Mother had agreed to them skedaddling as soon as they brought it up, and even helped them by looking up a place in her indispensable GREEN BOOK. *A real lifesaver,* she noted. Then lo and behold, even paid for their hotel for the weekend, one where they wouldn't have any *color* issues, one practically next door to the Great White Way, a place that saved them, she said, from winding up in Who knows what kind of place uptown. I guess she's not half bad, Rain admitted, every so often. And she'd gotten such a kick out of helping them to choose things to see and do. The night before at the dinner table, she had given them their going-away surprise, called Worthwhile Entertainment. She'd set the

manila envelope down beside Pearl's plate. I've called in your res-
ervations, she said, they'll have your tickets at the box office. Pearl
opened the envelope and excitedly thumbed through the playbill.
I'm such a sap for Rex Harrison! she sighed. He's simply magnificent, Mother agreed. Now they'll hand it to me like I'm some kinda
ignoramus who's never heard of a show even the milkman knows
about, Rain lamented, but Believe It or Not y'all, I *do* know a couple
things about it, Rain added, it's actually one of them old time stories, but this is how they tell it now. A plain old flower girl meets this
so-called Professor who teaches her how to speak and act so-called
proper, and overnight she turns into a so-called princess, then Her
Proper Highness throws his slippers at him cause he still treats her
like the maid. I read up on it some time ago in one of my little old
zines which I keep hearing nobody should bother to read, Rain said.
And they shouldn't, Mother answered, giving her that old down-
turned look in the face. You should be the safekeeper! cried Pearl,
jumping in with a smile to hand her the tickets. Nonetheless, I hope
you watch the show carefully, it might do you some good. Such
as? Rain asked. Such as, remind you of things you'd rather forget.
Make sense? Thank you, that's just what I need to hear, I must be
getting too happy and Lord knows that don't ever make sense. But
she really was a tiny bit happy and quite surprised that Mother had
thought so well of the idea. Turns out you've got a touch of romance
in you after all, she'd said, waving Bon Voyage as they boarded the
high noon Greyhound, racing to the Big Apple between the devil
and the deep blue sea.

I can feel the heighth down in my feet,
cried Rain, looking down from nineteen stories up, quite surprised,
despite her vertigo, to find that even at nightfall she could still make

180

out each of the itsy bitsy folks in the crowds crawling along the sidewalks, hear each tiny car and bus and truck horn-beeping rattling and rolling along to its somewhere along the glowing river of the street, people shrunk down to scurrying ants, sounds welling up like the sound of the ocean in a big seashell. All right, she confessed to herself, that at the Bar & Grill, even though I whatchamacallit, *mispresented* myself, still it's just how I pictured it to Mister Delbert and the Major, she thought, how the city lights heap up like a starry sky fallen to earth. She eagerly studied the shadowed skylines in the distance, wondering where it was they'd be headed in the morning.

Show me where we're going

Over across that river

I wish I could find it now

It's out of sight, a long cab ride away. We'll cross that bridge down there,

Pearl said, pointing from behind her.

Wherever it is. Please stay with me

Rain said, covering the hand upon her shoulder.

Everything's going to turn out just fine with our manicures.

Gosh I almost forgot about that part.

Remember, we scrimped and saved to treat ourselves to a manicure by *La Divina Signora Scioscia*. Well of course we are. Since as everyone's read in the latest fashion rags, she's renowned as a genius of the art. Plus we're feeling rambunctious and want to look especially glamorous for our night out on the town, and since she kindly fit us nonentities in on such short notice, we'll give in and splurge a little, though it's positively a steal for the quality. See for yourself

she cried, holding forth her hand to play the part, casting wary glances into the dim corners of the room.

I'm afraid we've garnered rather more than our share of positively envious looks here at the BROADHURST, not that we've
flaunted our appendages. So we'll keep our little alibi in mind.
Because who would forget having had such a perfect day?
she said, wriggling under the covers of her bed, closing her Dorothy
Parker and turning out the lamp.

Unforgettable, that's what you are, cried Rain to all which lay
before her eyes. Yes, she was certain that she would always remember everything bound to happen in those next three days, always
remember even if she tried to forget, bound to happen even though
she did not know what was coming next. She crossed to her bed,
kicked off her furry slippers, threw open the covers and lay down. At
first she twitched and shivered but soon warmed up under the tight
sheets and blanket, felt wrapped up like one of them, Oh what's
that Indian word, she thought, *papooses,* that's it. Oh and didn't that
know-it-all Jean McBride make sure she told the whole crew how
babies actually like being wrapped up like that. It's a good thing
nobody's up in the middle of my business now, she thought happily, Running my life and trying my last nerve, noticing how strange
the words *my business* sounded to her, as if she'd never before had
the slightest notion what her business might be. Day after day from
the beginning, Whenever that was, while I was laying around,
Mother, apparently doing nothing, she had gathered her own drifting thoughts into a great big snowball or the start of a snow woman
in her mind. Now it's here, that daydream, in the dark, or what folks
here must call the dark, she noticed, looking into the dull glow pouring in through the windows rattling within the vast groan of disqui-
etude rising from the street through the steel and concrete, from the
rooms below and above and beside them, muttering through the
walls and floors. Lying very still there, she gathered her snowflakes

together, making them out to be the figure of a few things about her, *bone of my bones, flesh of my flesh*. But the blizzard caught up to her just as it had every day before. Soon she couldn't go any further and fumbled it from her numbed hands and it broke away and hit the ground rolling into an avalanche burying the valley under a mountain of snow. At the moment of her last breath she knew that it was too late, that the wind would erase any trace of her presence, of the flesh and bones of her gathered thoughts, of her struggle against disappearance, all would be swept away without a trace. Buried alive, she reflected, just like how that sickly gal wound up in that horrible story of that Falling House. Who could find me now?

Then Pearl came and stayed. They sat together and skated together and walked and rode around talking through things together for a merciful time and figured out some things and figured out for the rest to let the mystery be. She even felt bright moments again every now and then. For instance they had figured about when it would come, if she let it. So even if she still couldn't say for sure how or where or when or by whom, she knew what was bound to happen *if*, that is, what happens every time. More than I used to know, she whispered once to her as they lay face to face together on her double bed, That is, nothing. And they agreed, without even a trace of the willies, that it, *It* sounds terrible but it's better, Pearl insisted, it wouldn't even be grown past a fishy thing yet. Wish I could swallow a message tied to a stone, she thought, to hit bottom where they could find it. She shut her eyes and laid her hand on her stomach. She could still see back in her mind the pictures in that Time Life True Body book and them other books about what happens every time. How from Picture **1** to **23** it looks most times like every other thing besides a human person. And she'd kept seeing them in her mind ever since, just like she'd kept on staring at them at first cause she could hardly believe it. She imagined once again as she had so many times since then which picture it probably looked like right then at that moment. By now it must've got past **12**, they figured that by now it's probably more like **13**, that it hadn't made it to **14** yet, and she thought so too, even though she still wasn't sure when **1** had arrived in the first place, which reminded her what a fool she'd been all that time, how she should straighten out her own twisted mind once and for all too. Even if I'm a fool I'm pretty sure it's bigger than any of them tiny critters you can't hardly see with your bare, naked eye she thought, maybe already big as one of them tadpoles you see in ponds or in Mister Meeker's big jars, since it's got those fish things like flowers, um, gills, she finally recalled, which anybody could believe only after they saw that picture with their own eyes then scratched their head a while over it. Or maybe looking something like one of them alien critters Jimmy likes to scare me half to death about, sneaking around in their flying hub caps, she thought, old Klaatu's poor cousins or whatever, who like human parts for a midnight snack. Um um, she insisted, stop right there, I may be confused, but not that confused. Cause by now, she suspected, it could look more like one of them tiny fishes circling around one of them whatchamacallits, *coral wreaths* piled up in all different colors and shapes like a rock-candy garden, the ones that dart and flash in the light sparkling down through the water. But then again it's not really like the seashore down there, it's dark down there, she thought, pressing against herself, searching for the trace of what it was she felt inside, for what she did not know about what it was, for what she did not know she wanted to know about what it was. Wondering what it must be like to be what it was, to be there. It's too deep, too dark inside to be like that, she suspected. More like the bottom of the sea, like that picture she saw of it in one of his SCIENTIFIC AMERICAN books. *Seven miles down*, it said,

showing in that spot of light only a patch of dirt, bare except for a creepy bug-looking critter and some starfish with long snaky arms. And close at hand, the vast cold dark into which light has never penetrated, into which none have ever ventured. Which being down there could be like those times back when we're still a **9** or **10** or even an **11** probably too, times which nobody can remember, she conjectured, too scary to remember.

But she reminded herself how she'd already been all up in through over around underneath it in her mind, how she had lain awake alone nights waiting until it was quiet everywhere around and inside her, and then calling or whispering or murmuring Hello, Hello, and listening for an answer but never hearing a sound, not word the first, not a peep. Not like it would answer plainly but still, she thought, it should give her a sign. She had yearned only for a sign, in the sun or the moon or the stars or upon the earth, she had kept watch and waited but found her watching eyes and pressing hand still unanswered. She had decided that that itself tells the tale, or something, doesn't it, didn't it. And agreed to or decided to or wound up coming all this way to this place which might as well be the middle of nowhere, this place she'd once put on like she'd been here before, to this big old Apple, not to take a bite but to spit one out, to correct her big mistake. Just a mistake, Pearl kindly said, one like any girl could make, the one that she herself had made. DEAR **13**, she'd write, I'm sorry, but you won't get to be somebody because you won't get to be here, not this time. So sorry, unless you holler up quick before morning it's Please accept my apology. There you go again girl, talking to seven miles down, she noticed, just like when she first found out she was like this and couldn't stop figuring it out, trying to be sure about it whenever she took a notion to do something, or nothing, but wound up exhausted.

If Father could see me now, she thought, frozen stiff. She dutifully indicted each inert limb but found no damning devices there, the requisite levers and ratchets had slipped from their pins, the mainsprings had fallen slack and unwound, denying their mechanism to the world. If he were here, she thought, he'd climb the stairs, knock then open the door just enough to look in, that's how he'd sometimes come to see about her after she and Mother had walked away from each other to see about her, after he stood up for Mother against her. *Backsliding, backsliding,* he'd cry mournfully, to see her not take even the slightest notion to rouse herself from the blankets nor to kneel at her bedside nor to fold her hands nor to close her eyes nor to bow her head. Then remind her that *wherein thou judgest another, thou condemnest thyself,* standing there only long enough to say that all that is ever left us is to kneel and offer up our sins and sorrows to heaven. But what would he remind her of now, she wondered, If we Told All on our secret plot, *Well that's your Mother* would he say again like he always said, she conjectured, at the verge of laughter, *Now get a load of this one,* she'd answer. But he's not here or not wherever like always before and I get to live through this the same way I always have by myself so then why should I, now we're even. She felt her face wet and heard herself carrying on so she covered her mouth.

Can't sleep?
Pearl whispered.

I

she answered, not finding words for the rest. She lay still as a stone but churned up inside at the same time all over again. Because by this time tomorrow there'll be nothing left inside me there to become somebody, and having perfect nails won't make one bit of difference, how about that, she thought, rubbing, scratching, while her insides kept fussing every which way to keep her wide awake.

Come on over

Pearl said into the dark. Rain felt herself rising, a body with a mind of its own, pushing aside the blanket to meet the cool air unflinchingly. Her feet met the floor between the beds and pressed into the rug only to support the single short step across to where Pearl lay opening the covers, wide eyes closing again as Rain slipped down beside her, as the covers fell over her like a returning wave.

The yellow cab swung from the avenue onto the street, entering its post-rush-hour silence. She turned up her wrist. Ten-thirty, Timex said. Here's the green house, she noticed, the hitching-post at the curb, the porch swing, the big tree, just like Pearl had said. But seeing that post at the curb right then she wished they could've rolled up here in a horse and carriage instead, just like back in the old-fashioned days.

Here we are,

Pearl told the driver, opening her purse. Rain offered the dollar bills she clutched in hand.

Treat me to a malted sometime, Pearl said.

She led her up the driveway to the side door and rang the bell twice.

Won't be long, she said. She comes quickly, like Jesus.

The door opened on its chain. A face looked out through the gap. It must be her, Alice, Rain guessed. Or could be her whatchamacallit, receptionist. Then she remembered what Pearl had told her, She's not a doctor, not anymore. Her eyes widened at the sight of her, opening the door, standing silently, waiting. And not a big talker, Pearl had said. Long, lean, greying, wiry in her high-water pants and shirt, buttoned up to the neck. Clear blue eyes giving nothing away, looking straight through, saying what mouths would not, what she had always watched them saying, once they had fixed on her: *A black girl.*

Do come in, she said.

She'll remember me but won't let on, Pearl had said that too the night before. She felt her sharp fingers against her back, pressing her through the door. The same way she'd pushed her into so many other things before, things she'd been standing still in front of, like trying reverse figure eights at midnight on Archie's Pond. Things she had let her push her into, or if not let her then what, not taking the blame cause I was blameless. Here I am again in front of, what, looking in as she had once looked down to the ice meeting the skate's edge, to the lantern shadow turning and twisting across its still face.

Turning back, Rain saw that Pearl's eyes had opened wide and started to leak a little, though she knew that she would never let on even if it was so. Rain had seen this same expression on her face before, this same far-off way she'd get when you least expected it, when she reminded them of where she was while thought to be elsewhere. Now she felt like she understood what's working on somebody drifting far away like that. About her own troubles now, about how a body can get worked up sometimes, how she'd gotten herself lately and couldn't shake it, how she'd wound up, before she knew it, right in the middle of everything. Then she stepped through the door behind her and took her hand like she had promised the night before she would, and the shakes Rain got wouldn't let her keep her secret any longer, that even though she'd been practicing all morning pretending to come for the manicure, she was still scared and certain that however it turned out it would still be horrible and unforgiven.

They followed her down the long hallway, past rooms which seemed to turn away from the street. Rooms sunk in shadow save for what light leaked in at the edges of the draperies veiling the tall windows, sifting against the walls, falling extinguished to bury anything that stood. Quiet as a mouse church in there, Pearl said, talking in her sleep, and she too noticed, except for the ticking of the clock. They mounted the turning staircase, two stories, brightening. They reached the top, she turned to point the way through an open door. It's the round room, in the tower, she said. The bed, the chair, the nightstand, the pitcher, the bowl, the white towel folded beside. Where it happens. They stepped into the room. I can sit on the bed? Pearl turned behind her to close the door. Up there away from the street and the shut-in rooms below, with daylight pouring through every window in the bright flood of morning. She took a few steps across the floor with lowered eyes, not wanting to look anywhere. It would be better downstairs, from where they'd hurried to get up here, she thought. Downstairs in the dark, where you could slip away into a corner and disappear and not have to talk, not have to explain, just follow each step, put one foot in front of the other. Instead of with the daylight knocked into you with no place to hide. Tall Alice leaned in to say,

Going to put on the kettle.

Rain

Pearl was close beside her now. Speaking softly,

It won't be long now,

taking her bag, unbuttoning her overcoat, untying her cap.

Let's kick off those shoes. One. And, two. Good girl. Now let's get those buttons in the back.

Funny. Already she really couldn't remember about the cab and how everything had hit her all at once the second they got there. But she did remember the horse, which wasn't there but was in her mind then. How she watched him throw back his head in the air and shake his shaggy mane as he trotted to a stop. Quite aware of the bit which twisted and shut off his words before they had a chance to be spoken, telling now about the reins which imprisoned him to the ones who think they're so nice and good to horses and know all about them, about how that whip can drive you right out your mind if you think too much about it, yeah, go figure. That's what she remembered. But had already forgot about getting out and Pearl pulling her up the driveway to the side door like a child not coming along quick enough to suit her mother, right into the sight of that house dead up in her face. How right then it had swallowed her up like she'd fell down into a pit or fell up through the clouds into an empty blue sky and kept on falling forever, like how she'd been dreaming of it lately.

Prompting hands turned her through the four directions. Her eyes filled up with distances: windows, rooftops, brownstones and tenements, treetops, steeples, smokestacks, bridges, a whirlpool pouring into her head, offering no escape. Now I'm going every which way like somebody up there dropped my strings, she thought, letting her head sink to one side, hoping that the crick which had crept into her neck during the night would fall out quick like they will sometimes if you catch them just right, she thought. But no, it was worse now than when she woke up. Must have got out the car wrong. Too slow or too much in a hurry. Too clumsy, losing track of her bloated up self. Or too ladylike, which sure can

throw a whammy into you if you get caught putting on airs and signifying. When a body doesn't know what it's doing and bam, you
thought you were being polite and had couth and all that stuff and
here comes that cracker crumb flying out your mouth across the
table to land dead in somebody's plate. Or using some ten-dollar
word cause you think it's the right whatchamacallit and it will make
you sound so smart but it's the wrong one and you sound like a
plain old idiot. Or out someplace in front of the whole public you
trip and sprawl out when you think you're carrying yourself so nice
and proper. Or here it comes, bam, a crick in the neck to knock you
into the middle of next week. Her arms slipped from the sleeves of
her blouse and dropped down to her sides like two sticks joined to
her shoulders that she'd never noticed before. But there they are,
she thought, all mine. Stick figure, that's me.

She looked up into Pearl's sad face, eyes at once attentive and
looking from far away. She covered the hands busy at the straps of
her slip.

I'm cold

If you keep it on it might get mucky.

She stepped out of it and sank onto the bed. Pearl covered her with
a blanket, heavy but itchy. Can't touch the floor, she thought, pressing beyond sight with both feet, rolling her head against the cramp.
Pearl sat down beside her and rubbed her hands together to warm
them up then reached across her back to gently knead the nape of
her neck. Could be I'm just shrinking, she thought. Maybe it goes
along with it, you shrink one which way and stick out the other.
Guess I did my share of tossing and turning last night. Maybe that's
when I got it, or brought it on myself, she thought. All that tossing
and turning I committed, heard the milkman at the door all right,
she remembered. Because it was almost light when she had finally

shut her eyes and had tried to shut her ears too, to Pearl's chatter and worst of all snoring. Girl more gorgeous than Carol the Baby Doll, sawing wood to beat the band and wake the dead, it don't fit, what a blip, she thought. But now there was neither tossing nor turning, just this old crick chasing after her every which way she moved. She slackened in surrender to the wiry fingers finding the hard spot and tried to keep still, to drift neither up nor down nor to the right nor to the left, without even the slightest twitch of her head or twist of her shoulders. For instance how your squirrel or rabbit or other small critter type gets when it's looking out the corner of its eye at you to fool you into thinking it's not there, she thought, for instance, to fool the one that's got her eye on me. And all at once that stillness came to her and, finding herself at last in one place at one time, she heard the watching one asking, How did I get here? She answered without waiting to find the words, Not by moving. Only moved, she thought, amazed to hear such an obvious explanation, one which had never occurred to her before. Not moving only moved, taken and moved by another, a mere device. That's right, she thought, knowing at last that she could not stand for it any longer. Even if she did nothing else forever after she resolved to give way that very morning to the caged one who had for so long shadowed her, pacing within all she had done in search of a way out, glaring back through the bars.

Pearl stood there, holding out her purse.

Time to pay, she said.

Look in there.

This is it? Where's the rest?

I paid for that pizza. And that box of chocolates.

You could've told me last night

Pearl sighed, counting.

I can't think straight. Or even crooked.

Neither can I, Pearl said,

closing the door behind her.

Good morning, Granny. I'm someplace in whatchamacallit *Flat Bush* and in my mind also in that place where everybody comes from, on my *Sea Hunt,* like Mike Nelson. Diving
seven miles down to the desert. Asking around regarding their
whereabouts. Telling all the different kinds of creatures I meet
even the blind ones their description, that they might look like
a walking cucumber or jellyfish or ghost shrimp or starfish or
a transparent catfish or one of them with a secret name that
Adam never told. Diving everywhere across the sea, still coming up empty handed. But I keep coming back, wondering if
they've watching me from more close by than I know, or from
the dark out of sight,

drifting above the dunes, scarcely beyond stillness, refusing to
answer. She wondered if they might be shadowing her every step,
every fidgeting of limbs, every turning toward and turning away and
standing up and sitting down, every hand clenching or opening to
grasp or cast away, every head scratching to understand, but in that
instant understanding nothing except the words of a voice from
another room, hovering just above a whisper. With a velocity which
suited her purposes,

You said you'd wait to hear from me once we got back to the
room.

We paid. She's starting soon.

When she's comfortable.

Scared like I was.

That's the time it's going to take.

A velocity which as well suited the other, listening to one side of the conversation but knowing well the other, one much used to weighing words spoken and left unspoken in the always the same and never the same days of such mornings, neither asking for nor giving names, working deliberately but never too quickly, gently but not tenderly, mindful of arrangements, wary of long goodbyes.

Time it's going to take, Rain thought, sounds like time just how it used to be. When Mother would drag her up the hill to Connolly's kitchen at still dark in the morning to help with her weekend matinees. In her glory, and who could keep up with her or could stand her? The ones who kept diving in were the same ones so ready to comfort her that she wasn't quite like Mother, That's right, she'd promptly agree, Not me. But she came to do her best to earn her allowance anyway, jumping around like a pinball between the stoves and the ovens and counter, fumbling through the motions of this and that chore knowing only halfway what she wants cause she never asks for help and I'm half asleep too, get in the way till she'd yell Get on the ball with that English downturn look. Wake up watch that gravy don't boil it to death if you had half a brain you'd see you've got the gas way too high, too lazy to learn how to cook. You always run me out of the kitchen. You'd rather run your mouth than do a lick of work so make yourself useful, call that drunkard Ricky let it ring till you wake him up, make sure his feet have found the floor and warn him we're leaving by eleven. He'd better have put gas in that truck and loaded the buffet and tables, except for that kneecapped one. Tell him first he'd best neither forget nor break a blessed thing, this time I will dock him full retail repair or replacement price on all damaged equipment. Second, drive carefully, if he wrecks my truck he should just go ahead and leave town change his name and get a new life. She couldn't help that itch to snatch a biscuit just out of the oven and not get caught, couldn't help but hurry over to look when Mother opened the stove to check the ham studded with cloves pineapple rings with fresh cherries in the middle, took her baster and drizzled them drippings Father loves to sip from a spoon all over it and glared back with the sweat running down her face, Get on with the coffee. Couldn't help that she hated to stand in a backroom in the dead in-between times waiting on unpredictable guests, after playing dumber so she looked smarter, and meanwhile sight her reaching for the bottle in her apron pocket, to count her hurried trips to the ladies room to cough her guts out, and after yet another notable success drag herself back home and through the front door to fall into bed dead to the world or worse, poor crazy lady, never like me. Thank you Jesus whose Father in his mercy and wisdom saith Every other Saturday at still-dark thirty let there be famous bacon pork chops and brown gravy ham and home fries scrambled eggs and buttermilk biscuits, positively a steal for the price, ready to be tucked in the hotbox when the truck came to carry them off to Welcome Wagon Rotary Kiwanis Lions Loyal Odor of Moose Country Club Boosters Harris Hill Aviators Finger Lakes Bridge League Bradford County Sheriffs P.T.A. Marching Dimes Methodist Mothers Daughters of Evolution Chamber of Commerce or whatever other gang she could never belong to even if she was a member. So I could almost can't help but wonder if I'm, she thought, the latest whatsitsname, *pièce de résistance*, the specimen plucked cleaned spiced up trussed and cooked to death, stuck in a box and carted here to arrive right on time, ready to be served.

The sunlight escaped a patch of cloud and poured into the room beyond her closed eyes, warming her face and crossed arms and shut-tight legs and the mound of her belly from which she turned away as nothing more or less than her own and she felt herself melting, like the crick mixed up by the fallen petal, the frozen-still creature darting at last from the brightness. She opened her eyes wide, I'm turning again, keeping it only a thought, to keep quiet. The windows glowed against the hanging lace and captured a figure like and unlike herself, faint and shifting, mingling at its edges with all that lay in the distance. It too wandered with her through distant windows into their empty rooms, jumping rooftops, running up smokestacks, tight-roping over bridges. How about *my* super-powers? she thought.

Rain turned to look back down the enormous staircase she'd just climbed to reach the platform and, sighting no pursuit, turned to rush through the opening doors of the car with the onboarding crowd. She reached for a spot on the pole and held on tightly, swept into the tidal wave of mysterious people places and things pouring through the doors and windows as the train stopped and started, lurching forward above streets stretching into the distance in all directions below. More fun than a roller coaster ride, she soon decided, feeling better than she had all morning especially from when she'd been practically lost inside that house, Where I'm definitely not now. Must be easy to disappear in this town if you want, she figured again. So many stops, so many folks everywhere. Nothing like that parking lot way back at the Thermometer Motel, which she had thought of before today as being positively gigantic, where that night she'd felt like the only living person in the whole world. Shoot. Here I'm just another *Mysterian* and don't mind if I am.

She was startled by a tap on her shoulder. She turned to find a lifted hand offering a card. Her eyes traveled upward from its slender fingers to the dark eyes staring downward from the narrow face. A poker face bewitching her to take a look then moving on, the wrists of its spindly arms poking from the sleeves of a long green jacket,

the ball of a striped stocking cap dangling below a head of black hair chasing
after its back. One of them poor handicap girls, she thought, glancing across
the rows of pictures now pinched
between her thumb and forefinger, let-
ters each naming its figuring hand and
feeling her own hand wanting to try out
the funny shapes. She understood a few
things about folks like that, folks born
that way or left that way by some kind

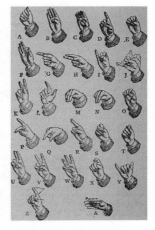

of awful congenial sickness. One of them that, like Mother says,
children are born with, and why lies beyond our poor understanding, within God's plan, as Mother says, she recalled, and folks also
say it happens because of what the mother ate or some pills or dope
or whatever she took while she was in the family way, it's like in that
Miracle Worker when the mother looks down at Helen in her crib,
The wonders of modern medicine she says then while she's laughing
she sees something's wrong and snaps her fingers and calls her name
and waves her hand right in front of her face, and then she knows
what she doesn't want to know. Awful, terrible. But her mother and
father go plain crazy right then and she'd whispered to Jimmy Sure
looks phony, that ain't how folks would whatchamacallit, *react*, and
that supposed-to-be awful scene had made her laugh out loud right
there in the theater and then she'd felt embarrassed, cause after that
she couldn't keep from crying her eyes out, especially when Miss
Annie pumps the water and it runs into her hand and she says *water*
for the first time, and especially knowing it's a true story, so terrible
and wonderful. But at least this girl can see, she was glad of that for
her sake. Her own short stoutness came to mind, so she was a little

envious of her statuesque stature, which never cowed to a hunch as she moved from rider to rider, enduring each scowl or sidelong glance, each posture of indifference. She could hear Papa singing his sinful old railroad songs to himself when Mother wasn't listening, *Got me a woman long and tall, When she sleepin in the kitchen find her feets in the hall.*

She watched her head tilt one way then the other, back and forth, with her mouth kind of stuck out, she thought, like Don't ask me to talk, as she worked her way down the bench, placing a card in each space between where folks were sitting, moving quickly down one side of the car then up the other, not stopping to exchange glances except to cut her eyes away like, Don't bother looking too hard, and kept on going. Then turned around right quick and went down one side and up the other again, lifting and shaking the cup tied to the belt around her waist, getting one or two folks to drop in some change (including her fifty cents), taking cards back from folks who thought they'd keep one like one of them whatchama-callits, souvenirs, without paying for it, and reaching to gather the ones left untouched in between, all before the train slowed to the next stop, how about that. Except for this one last man next to her who just had to try and prove she was some kind of phony. Who after looking her up and down all the while had the nerve when she reached down for a card to clap his hands real loud right behind her, and when she turned around to ask for his he wouldn't let it go, so she finally had to snatch it out of his hand so hard that she fell back right against her, and when Rain reached to catch her from falling she twisted back and pushed away like, Get off me. Suit yourself, she thought, fall and bust your behind next time she thought, but then on second thought, That's not nice to wish on anybody, especially a handicap girl, she admitted to herself. The girl whirled away, losing a red mitten from her coat pocket then rushed to the very end, into the unexpected roar and blast, out into the tunnel.

Yes please Miss, snatch it back out my hand like I picked your pocket. Plain to see you're mad at the world, Rain thought, even though she knew a few things herself about that too. Look at you, twisted up in a knot. Staring down into that cup, sipping and looking hard like you're spelling somebody's fortune in there. Mad at the world, she thought again, sitting down next to her anyway on the small corner seat, But dis here diasticutis due to drop right dere whether you like it or not. Guess I don't faze her one bit, she thought, noting no reaction, no huffy scrunching over like I've got some kind of disease, no jumping up to get away, only more sipping, looking, sipping. And here I'm putting on airs like she should pay attention to me, like I'm some kind of nice girl. Go figure. She sighed and settled back against the seat, happy to take a load off her feet. To drift into the world rushing by just beyond the window, as the surging and rocking of the train shook all that had seemed to make sense out of her, all the fancy tough talk she had talked about who knows what, the plotting which had amounted to nothing. All out but the wandering behind her eyes, still craving no destination. I'm worn to a frazzle, she thought, and then it occurred to her that this girl might be worn out more.

The girl hiked her eyebrows and pointed to her sweater. Rain lifted a hand to pull and tucked her chin to find, sure enough, the tag up front.

You know my type Rain said. Don't know if I'm coming or going.

She looked to the left, to where she did not know she was headed, and back to the right, from where she had not wanted to be, wondering who around them was listening. Then wondered if she'd already given the girl another reason to think she was stupid, talking out loud to somebody who can't hear word the first. Or maybe she's reading my lips. The girl patched on a smile, raised a finger and twirled it around and pointed to her own head. So we're both plum crazy. To find ourselves here. Guess that's about right. I must look thirsty, she thought, because all at once the girl drained her cup and poured another which she offered, her long brown face softening with concern. Her koodies can't be any worse than what I've got, she thought, taking the cup, taking a sip. Sweet tea, sweet and strong, like Father likes it, how he says they serve it down home in Georgia. Except she don't look quite like she's from down in them parts, she thought.

The girl turned on the bench to face her and handed her a card. She pressed a finger firmly against her chest and made her other hand into a shape.

L,

Rain said, pointing to the letter. The girl made another.

A.

The shapeshifting hand moved again, then the hand of the other,

N.

And once more,

A.

The girl poked herself again, then crossed her windmill arms with satisfaction.

Jimmy would sure love that word, and this place too, Rain thought, watching folks streaming in from the street, picking plates from the little boxes which they then ate much too quickly, and streaming out. It's got that echo from the noise and voices, and all them tiny windows in the walls, just like our Post Office, she thought, leaning in to look at one. And a slot for a quarter like a jukebox, by the handle. Quite the *deevice!* she decided. All different stations. SANDWICHES, HOT DISHES, DESSERTS, DRINKS & COFFEE, full of windows for each one. Both he and Mother would approve, she thought, of a good device making good for itself in the call of duty. Miss Lana *Turner* (which she'd found out when the girl spelled out the rest) took her arm and led her to a corner in the back. With the sunlight streaming in through the windows it was warm at their table, so right away they took off their coats. Lana held out her hand and rubbed her fingers together. *Hand over the dough,* like she's some critter from another world controlling my mind, one who has no need to talk to reach her thoughts, so troubled now, and impossible to hide. Rain put three dollars and forty-seven cents from her purse on the table. Then just like with the mitten Lana went on with her business there, sorting the change by pennies, nickels, dimes, and quarters, adding hers in from her coat pocket. Put all the bills from lowest to highest in a pile which she folded in half and stuck in her shirt pocket. Slipped the change into her pants pocket, and took off for the SANDWICH wall. Rain wasn't sure why she didn't take a notion to jump up and run after her to ask, What about what I want? She just got herself a glass of water from the station and drank it down and filled it again and went back to the table, happy because she hadn't realized she was so thirsty, and watched the girl go to work. HOT PLATES, she thought, seeing her stop there, sounds hopeful, she was hungry too. Then she stepped up to the counter, holding up a plate, trying to ask for an extra one, how she tried so hard to tell them, head-shaking nodding and charading to the guy who kept pretending he didn't understand her, and it troubled her to see how awfully skinny she'd turned out to be. Practically a scarecrow, nothing but a whole bunch of that long curlicue hair on top of her dressed-up bones. Nothing like how the real Lana Turner looked or her perfect figure, and of course not even in the face, Is it her real name or a whatchamcallit, *alias*? she wondered, and who knows why she calls herself that, even though it's kind of a wonderful gumption that she would. Funny, right then she wasn't quite sure in her own mind which one of them Lana Turners was real or alias, or if any of all she'd seen since morning was real, anyway. And here I didn't even go up to try and pitch in with words even a dummy like me could've said, she thought. So maybe I'm not myself either, or maybe I'm really myself now, she wondered, or maybe I'm just nobody. And a helpless cry suddenly erupted from her, *How can I ever go back home?*

She brought back one hot dog on the plate, and one paper dish full of fries. She started in with a knife to cut the hot dog in half. Shoot, half will still suit me just fine, till I go back to the, Rain thought. But when she reached for hers the girl promptly smacked her hand. Well ain't that peculiar. The girl took the other half with a few of the fries, wrapped it up in a napkin, and sunk it down in another one of them coat pockets of hers. And with no kind of shame, she wanted to think, but, *Let he who is without sin cast the first stone.* And quite frankly, she was not raring to argue and scuffle with her, she decided further, what if she goes plumb crazy and ready to do who dares to find out what. She split the half and they shared it between them, with the girl smiling and nodding as if apologizing, giving her most of the fries. Turned out to hit the spot, she thought, even if they weren't famous like Miss Maggie's back home, still quite enjoyable. Except it was spoiled a little, she was sorry she couldn't help but notice, by the smell that. Kept coming off the girl, whew, most other times that would be enough to. But on second thought she admitted Guess I ain't exactly sweet as a rose right now myself. Meanwhile, Lana Turner, just as dainty as you please, nibbled at hers from one end, put it back on the plate and looked at it a second, then picked it up and nibbled from the other, taking itsy-bitsy bites and chewing each one a long time, probably to have a reason to stick around in that nut house a while, Rain guessed, or to set it in her mind and taste it too for a long time so she could keep the memory for the next time she got hungry, turning it side to side till the last tiny bite, which she popped into her mouth so politely that Rain was embarrassed at how she had bolted hers down then licked her fingers clean besides. Right then she wished that she could take this poor girl back home to the Valley with her, because she could see that even though she was handicapped she had real ladylike potential, or what some grown folks call natural class. She would take a few dollars out of her savings account, take her up to ISZARD'S and get her a few nice girlie things she could enjoy, such as bubble bath and a great big bottle of JEAN NATE along with some fancy skin lotion, make up and cold cream and lipsticks and nail polishes and such, to give herself a good old time with and feel luxurious after riding them dirty old trains all day. She'd take her up to the girl's floor, walk right in that Bridal Shop and show her all them fancy white gowns on the dummies and tell that snooty old Miss Carlson, Oh she's my girlfriend visiting from New York City. Lana Turner, you heard the name right, I didn't stutter.

She took out the change and stacked it in two identical piles, one nickel, then one penny, and the dime on top. After glancing all around right quick she poured them another round from the NAUTILUS. Rain lifted the cup to her lips, straightening her idle pinky like a periscope breaking the waves, threw back her head and swallowed, narrowing her eyes in delectation. Mother said Somebody way back when said Watch what we can make people do. Still sweet, warm. Full of koodies and germs from another world, far away. Or could she get there, or was it right here, or had she already caught the fever. As she brought the back of her hand up to her forehead, she went back to wondering what she had been wondering about this Lana Turner for a while now. Even if she's from another world she's still a human, she must have some kind of folks, peoples, kin or relations or whatnot, she thought. After puzzling a moment she dug through her bag for the latest number of JET, which with her Pocket Gospels she always kept close at hand, for salvational reference, and flipped open to a featured photograph of Nat King Cole, the true man of her dreams, posing with wife and daughters by the swimming pool of their wonderful home. First, she pointed to mother Maria, putting on a questioning face. Then to herself, then back to Natalie, standing in the shallows with big sister Carole in their swimsuits and prim white caps. Her favorite. The baby of the bunch like herself, the one who like in so many other pictures taken looked neither toward the camera, nor toward her father's grinning face, nor to his fingers cradling the box bearing his latest surprise, but gazed ahead with narrowed eyes and faithfully played her part, delighted, Rain was certain, to be captured at precisely such a moment in such a perfect picture, delighted to reveal her then-unshakable faith that their life together would persist as indelibly as its image, despite his ever-more-frequent absence, despite stalking thuggery and thievery and burning crosses, despite all future tribulation and danger, just as it had persisted all the days of her still-new life until that morning, and would forevermore.

The girl took a stubby pencil from her coat pocket, hunched over to sketch quickly on her napkin, then shoved it between them.

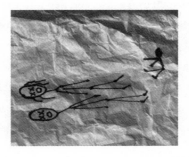

Nearly running to keep up, Rain followed her past the stone lions through the gate, into a vast table of yellowed grass patched with fallen snow, ringed by bare trees and bordered at its distant edge by the bowl of a silenced fountain. Gray, empty, like that place where she had once wandered lost, frightened to wonder if it stretched on forever, or a place that chased you and caught you when you tried to run and dragged you back. Nearby, two ragged men huddled against a stone wall, sharing a bottle between them. A woman sitting on a bench, wrapped in a quilted blanket, looked over her shoulder as they drew near. Her lined face brightened as she nodded, then promptly turned back to keep an eye on the one out there, chasing the birds, rambling alone. Even from far away, Rain thought, that small body seemed to exhaust space and make time its own. Darting between the snow patches, then slowing to creep forward in approach, until pouncing at the verge of its quarry, its thin arms reaching upward and flailing with abandon as the pigeons and sparrows fled into the air. Its rag-doll parts and Lana face and Lana eyes looking everywhere like looking into a well.

She was on her way to him by then. Not hurrying now, patient, following first this way, then that as he kept away, in sudden flurries of his rubber-booted feet. She cornered him at the lawn's edge, along the withered flower-beds. He shouted, snarled, in a cry which she too could not spell into sense, and fled into the unkempt brush. The girl drew nearer. Stood unflinching as a thrown stone struck her head and fell at her feet. She stood still until her head sank low and she turned away. Now he crept out, to follow after. No longer larger than all that surrounded him, Rain thought. Now, smallest of all things before her eyes, he came near in haphazard, halting steps, fearing both to escape from and to disappear within the advancing shadows.

He run around, don't eat, the watcher woman said.

One of the men came and offered the girl a drink, which she refused. She reached into her coat pocket and handed him a few loose cigarettes, which he accepted gratefully, stooping unsteadily to kiss her hand. Rain moved over to make room beside her, hoping to give her a hug and cheer her up a little, she thought. But the girl didn't look once in her direction as she passed, to sit at the end of the bench, by herself. The boy swerved to draw near. The girl reached into her big coat pocket, which now she could not deny was like a magician's that holds the whole entire world. She took out a paper napkin and spread it across the seat. A carton of milk an elbow straw and that hot dog and set them on it. Once he noticed the milk he came more quickly.

When he reached her she pulled him up into her lap. He coughed and sniffled, she wiped his nose with a tissue while he held it up. He touched the bruise on her forehead, but she pushed his hand away, buttoned his coat and straightened his hat. She poked open the hole in the side of the carton and pushed in the straw. She coaxed a thumb out of his mouth and held the straw up to his lips. As he drank his fluttering legs grew still and his cheeks worked in delicate twitchings, his eyes renounced their vigilance and sparkled, sleepy and soft and wide.

Rain fastened her collar against the chill and looked beyond the park, into the wilderness of lights. Strangeness, and all her strangeness, had returned to haunt her. While her back was turned the wide world had dwindled into a box, holding only this scene played beneath a solitary streetlight, and beyond lay only the streets, into which she was frightened to venture alone. She wondered if what lay before her eyes might persist like a common territory, a bridge or passage between here and where she could and ought to be, and she by crossing here, reach there. Throwing one foot before the other again and again, in uncertain watch over herself, Yes, the only kind of moving I've ever known, she thought, going about her thankless business like all the rest she had encountered that day. Flying high above the streets and under the earth, voyaging out and back and out again through dark passages rumbling everywhere underfoot, the shape of a five-thousand-limbed creature creeping through the ever-falling dust. She would tell a story about herself just like the papers taped up on the walls in the stations, she would take her time to make it very neat handwriting, it would say, Once she gave the whatchamacallit, *reference* they said give us the deposit by Friday, after work is fine, knock downstairs by the way first I must meet your husband and any children, Please don't ask like I'm stupid, that's how she trains everybody to recognize me, I will keep hating my guts no matter what happens, so please go head and be happy for that, please can I just imagine for a hot second that I could disappear and begin again. She would go about her thankless business like all the rest, sitting waiting to get someplace then go on as if deaf and blind, to stand fast among yet apart from those who too would confess themselves *strangers and exiles on the earth*.

The girl took the hot dog from the roll and held it up to his mouth, the child took a bite. She took a french fry and dangled it over his open mouth and dropped it in. He chewed with his mouth open and laughed at her glowering gestures. He coughed, she laid a hand on his chest and he kept on laughing. Her fingertips crept up and tightened around his throat, pretending to choke him a little, he kept on laughing, she pressed her face into his shoulder and growled, and he gasped with a short, sharp cry, that stopped and he kept still, and sat looking out there, eyes wide opening into the gathering dark, and put the bread she handed him a piece of back into her coat. He will give it to the birds tomorrow, she thought. If they are still here tomorrow, or wherever he will be or need to be waiting for her, but also for them like in her three figures she drew on the receipt in the Automat, which is what she is already trying to tell him, to explain, what to remember.

Rain did not wonder why she herself stood up and went to them, with outstretched hands. Nor why the watcher rose as she passed, nor why the child shrank from her approach into the girl's arms and her opening eyes answered, as she knew that they would. She reached into her purse for the envelope of tickets and dropped it into the shaking-cup on the undone belt beside her, deciding that Mother's primroses were better off left in her basket.

The girl's hands moved quickly, making shapes which rose from her very flesh and in passing away returned there, not meant for her comprehension but whose sense was unmistakable even before the watcher turned to take her hands in her own. Like how when she sat and ate her sandwich with her elbow on the table and a single extended finger made circles in the indeterminate air as she nibbled guiltily, and she knew it was Lana Turner. Then Rain knew that it was time to hide herself away again.

Lana Turner say, Nice girl go home now, not run away.

The girl signed to the watcher once again. Who then called sharply, with strange words she had never heard before, to one of the men now half-asleep, waking him up. He came to them quickly, then she could see that underneath his long hair tied back with a cloth and his unshaven face he was not a man at all but just an overgrown boy. The woman smiled and spoke slowly.

Where, home? she asked.

Manhattan Hotel, Rain answered,

mistaken but not mistaken, remembering but still not wanting to remember or to find some way, home, not home, somewhere, nowhere. The woman spoke to him once again and, looking far off, pointed the way. He walked a few steps along and then he turned back.

Miss, please come on, the big boy said.

She hesitated, thinking that he might be clumsy with drunkenness, but when she followed he took her hand firmly but gently like some bashful admirer who had just worked up the gumption to come and ask her to dance and she followed his sure-footed steps across the stones under the trees. She looked back one last time from the gate. The girl held the child close to her. Humming a melody she could not hear but which flowed from everywhere within her, into the small body listening, already asleep.

The policeman leaned forward to listen as Pearl spoke, too far away to be heard from where Rain watched, at the foot of the staircase, hidden behind the rubber tree plant. And lucky her, sitting up there drinking too, a martini of course, the one she loved the best, a perfect one, of course. Talking in outbursts, starting and stopping, one hand tracing explanatory shapes in the air, the other stuck with a cigarette as usual. Funny how it looks almost like how Lana Turner talks, she thought, but only almost. Especially only almost today, she decided, because even though it looked like Pearl was finding the words she wanted, answering in her perfectly bewitching or hardboiled or in between way like nobody else could answer, as usual, she could tell that she was trying hard to keep a grip on herself, that she was quite in a flutter. Not quite like Lana Turner, after all, someone who she could never imagine fluttering or scared of anything. But what's it all about? she asked herself, trying to open her ears to hear better, while noting how right then Pearl was holding her hand stretched out flat at just about eye level, nodding like she was showing him how tall somebody was, then nudging in a little, which she probably did to tell him somebody was on the chubby side too. So she's talking about somebody, some girl supposed to be gone missing, who's supposed to be me, she figured, who else could she be going on about.

As Pearl kept talking he kept staring, but she could tell he was trying to be kind and helpful, to actually listen, not ask any more questions, not ask her to repeat answers she'd already given, her account of the day's events like they do in the pictures. Probably trying to make head or tail of what she's saying and still doesn't quite get it, she thought, no surprise there. She lifted her glass to her lips, then pressed one clenched index finger against them, shaking her head, then took another drag and puffed the menthol smoke, then looked away toward the revolving doors turning, turning. He kept his hands folded over his kneecaps, his arms and legs and black brogans sticking out from the rung on the stool, into the distance between them. His head nodded and shook in the tight collar of his uniform with that big shiny badge on it, he studied her tearstained face like a cat watching a bird. When he did ask whatever and was looking down pretending to think hard about something and write it in his little black notebook, he couldn't help but peek down at her crossed legs descending from the sheath of her dress. But even without being able to hear she could tell that there was no tough-guy stuff coming from Pearl like there usually was by now if she were talking to a man. Only answering the questions asked once again, only the fluttering, or smoke blowing, or the sipping that was now gulping, or the flitting of her hands in thin air, or drying her eyes. Not the usual Pearl, not at all, she thought, not even eating her olives, how about that. Right then she felt so thankful that Lana Turner had helped her to practice watching how folks tick, even when they didn't talk, all day long.

Rain figured that even though the policeman may have been taking notes he hadn't been listening very carefully, since he walked right past her like she wasn't even there, out the door. Had to finally hightail it out of there, she figured, before somebody wondered if he was gonna buy her a drink, and while on duty, which would be a No-No, even she knew that. After all he's just one of them what-chamacallit, flatfoots, on the beat, not one of them lean Hungry Bogart types who gets next to the rich girl to pump her for the evidence she's hiding because she's scared or cause she's actually in on the crime, but keeping it strictly business, trying not to fall too hard for her. That's at least her third glass already, she guessed, that's why now the bartender's looking at her and then around, like, Who are you with? But he's probably seen this type of girl before, she imagined, the type who keeps reminding folks that they don't need anybody, she thought, so they say, they can stand up on their own two feets, don't need your crutch. Till they fall off their stool. Right then she felt like she was finally good and ready to stop being a pushover herself, In my own way, she thought. And just about took a notion to jump out from behind that rubber tree plant and traipse across the carpet right over to her and say, smiling and happy to see her and saying easy as you please, Why, fancy meeting you here.

Pearl asked for one more for the road but the bartender refused her, shaking his head, speaking softly with words which she leaned in unsteadily, too late to hear. She sank back onto the stool as if taken by surprise or overcome by what she could no longer keep at bay. Hands clasped before him, he spoke once more, beyond hearing, as her head sank low, as her hand relinquished the stem of the glass, joining the other to cover her face. His bespectacled eyes lifted to check the wall clock then returned to their watch, as each regarded the other in silence.

Looks like it's not helping, he said,
so clearly that Rain felt as if he were standing beside her.

Nothing ever helps, Pearl said,
rubbing out her cigarette. She wished that she could get the gumption to jump up out from behind that plant. To rush over there and throw her arms around her like she did so many times when she was angry and drunk and tired, hold tight and whisper, Girl you need to give that mind of yours a rest before you drive yourself crazy. Can't run and do that now, she thought, only run and hide from that. Cause for crying shame, she accused herself, sure looks to me like you ran scared today. Not cause I was scared, but cause I wouldn't, she answered. Ha! Wouldn't. Yes, not wouldn't that, wouldn't the other. Sure kept bragging all them times before that you would. Don't care if I did. Then running all over town playing the tramp. Figured you'd make a fool of yourself, ruin everything from the get-go, Ain't ruined nothing. Scared of your own black shadow with your retarded lying self, can't keep a single word straight. At least I can spell my name, Not a lick of spine,

And make my own shape, I know how. Then let me see you do it, Miss Don't Need Nobody. Here it comes, she thought, dragging me back down again. Certain, to be mistaken. Turning up, overlooked. Speaking, unheard. Dreaming, unremembered. Searching, lost. What to live for, out of reach. Stuck in that half-broke chair peeking between the leaves like what else to do, hiding without a hiding place.

Pearl headed straight for sight of her. She darted around the corner into the elevator bay and pushed through the crowd to the window of the gift shop, ringing the bell as she stepped through the door. She watched through the glass as she passed beyond the bodies and baggage crowding in and coming off the cars, lingering once, and again, to search the swarm of faces moving past, now visible, now obscured, now fragmented and interrupted, like faces in the water falling to tatters in the wind.

At the counter, a short thick woman topped with a red beehive do poked the keys on the register as she pawed through a wire basket heaped with souvenirs. The thin man waiting to pay pulled a king-size back scratcher from a larger heap of junk dumped inside a cardboard box. Reaching back, he pushed the clawed hand down behind his collar. Rain was surprised to see how far he bent his body out of shape to get it there. He sighed, grunted and twitched with pleasure as his arm pumped diligently. The woman stopped to laugh at his contortions.

Ain't you a regular money-maker, she said.
While scratching and hip-twisting, he lost hold of the handle. Red-faced, he groped back, fumbling to free his shirttails from his pants.

Now you see it, now you don't, she said,
laughing again, too loudly. When he turned around to unfasten his

belt he noticed Rain watching and looked her up and down with a frown. He recovered the gadget, flung it back into the box, and paid for his heap. Disgusting, I feel sorry for whoever gets that one, Rain thought. The doorbell tinkled brightly as he left.

The woman's grin collapsed into a glare as she hurried down the aisle to stand between Rain and the crowded shelves. Pointing a finger, she snarled

How many times do I haveta tell youse, keep your bizness out in the street.

The thick red fingernail hovered before her face, nearly poking her eyes. Rain drew back to look down her nose, but before she knew it she had opened her mouth to snap at it with her strong white teeth, One nasty mouthful, she thought. The woman leaped back, rattling the merchandise on the racks behind her, and at that sound, leaped again.

We came here cause we thought you folks were nice and act civilized. Room 1929, she said,

dangling the key,

Let's go to the front desk and check me out, she added,

wondering why she was even giving her the chance.

Well why didn't you say so? the thick woman growled.

You jumped all over me before I could

Maybe I did. But

Excuse me, you definitely did.

The woman shut her baggy eyes, raised both swollen hands, slowly shook her head on her drooping neck.

I don't need this, she said,

and turned away to drag herself back to the counter. Shoot, she don't need it. No I'm sorry, or nothing, she thought. But she was used to no sorry or nothing, she recalled.

She had been ready to skin out of there, but now she felt like looking around.

I should get one of these here, right?

she cried, waving a Yankee ball cap overhead without looking back.

My hubby's from down South, but he sure loves to watch them on TV,

she added, recalling how that rotten tramp Zorro had wanted to be a *Yanqui* too.

You're hitched? Don't see no ice on your finger. Not that I'm surprised, especially workin in this joint.

Since you must know, Miss Nosey. I'll soon be happily married!

Then he ain't your hubby yet, kiddo. My advice is, take your sweet time and get your lingo straight.

I do take my time. To give him all the time I can,

she replied, trying to talk in a slow sultry voice just like Miss Gloria Grahame would, to show off how she most certainly knew about all that love-making stuff, even though she wasn't in that other business this one had the nerve to think she was.

Now the thick woman was shuffling back to her in her sequined slippers, looking down to fuss with some skimpy something hung over her arm,

Now if you wanna bring him a really nice present,

a skimpy slinky see-through thing trimmed with lace,

nightie night. How about this? she said,

tracing between the stringy shoulder straps,

Verrry volupchus. See that neck line, like the Brooklyn Bridge.

I own one myself, of course.

Wondering whether to believe her, she pressed it against her face. Ouch at the lacey part, she thought, cheap she could tell, not delicate like the border of Granny's handkerchief which lay in her purse at that very moment. But the parts you could see through, the parts she would have to hide the whole thing from Mother for, the parts that Jimmy would do delectable things to her for when she put it on, those parts were soft, unexpectedly soft. With a softness which comforted her as she looked around, wanting to leave, but also wanting to stay, because quite frankly she didn't want to be bothered with figuring out where to go if she left. Holding its softness against her face she felt the wary, circling nearness of this thick, brassy woman, who had not asked if she liked it or wanted to try it on, who had already slipped away to tidy the shelves and racks on her way back to hunch over the counter, who might even live behind there down in some dark cabinet underneath, who looked like she might fall over any second, who like Mother probably smoked too much all the time, who put on much too much nail polish, who probably thought she was already old even though she was trying hard to keep feeling alive. But she still felt thankful that she had shown her the nightie, and for the little hints she'd dropped along with it. Even though she probably tried to sell one to every girl who wandered in, she figured, even though she probably didn't want to even give her the time of day really. Even though she still felt like she could snatch her baldheaded if she said one more mean thing to her.

She draped the lingerie over her shoulder and paced the aisles from rack to shelf to rack, not wanting to get sick from starting what was bound to happen if she stepped out that door, wondering at the ten thousand things crowded in waiting before her. Souvenirs. *Mementos*, Mother calls them. Poised and conscripted to go forth alone, to be seized and carried off to a land where no strangers appear, save for themselves. To revive in their captors, by way of that selfless strangeness, the wonders of their brief adventures, to disguise and divert their attention from the fact that their time too is short and their days few, that they too will be forgotten along with them, but more quickly. Before today, she thought, she would have been charmed by their offer of themselves for the taking, careless of destination, of danger, and at one fell swoop, forget where she was.

At the back of a wide shelf she spied an idol of the silver screen who had once visited her dreams, now looking lost like Pearl had, waiting for the elevator.

Great to finally meet you, Miss Liat, this time I think I'm awake. Sorry you're here all by your lonesome. You must get tired of signing autographs.

Don't I wish. I'm the Display Unit, the last remnant of my troupe. Day by day, my hundred thirty-six sisters and eight brothers were swept into the unknown. I've been stranded on this plywood plane ever since, left to live inside my gig, being slowly dismembered by my audience.

Folks with their hot little hands, including mine.

Nobody left to display for. Till the dame up front noticed and moved me to the back of the shelf.

Who or what, Rain wondered, had called or led or dragged her six thousand miles from home to dance and sing on the streets and in the parks, and once in a blue moon after hours at the joint around the corner, wherever, out alone. *Ti-leaves* whirling in the dance, or stilled while she sang her requiem.

So sad to hear about your Mister Cable. Now everything must feel so different.

After that there was nothing I wanted there. It was time to go.

She stepped from her pedestal onto Rain's outstretched hand and stood sure-footed as she rose to eye level. Rain leaned in, to speak in confidence.

You can jump into my coat pocket and bust out of here if you want.

I can't stop thinking that maybe he's still alive but something happened and he can't remember. They won't send me back, there's no place for me to go back to anyhow. I figure my best bet is to stay here, where the whole world might pass by. Maybe one day he'll remember. He'll turn around and I'll be there.

Nobody will notice you if you're back under behind everything like before.

Rain parted the ranks of jacks in their boxes and took out her handkerchief and dusted off a place for her and set her on the ledge, front and center. She wondered how and why to cry for help from her sisters welcoming sea-sick sailors, in the same boat. And she looked everywhere around her like the one night with Pearl when they had looked down into the valley and wondered What about the rest of it? Useless, the Matchbox taxicabs buses trains stopped still in streets empty of travelers. Useless, wristwatches losing time, star-spangled fountain pens bleeding ink, transistor radios impossible to keep tuned, sunglasses too narrow to ride her nose, postcard pictures of places she had never been, which she would never mean to send.

But not far away she found something she had not noticed before. A reason to stay there a while longer. A snow globe perched at the top of a pyramid of boxes, each holding one of the rest. Looking into it she wondered if this was how the earth looked to creatures visiting from foreign planets. A drowned world, she thought, hold-ing it up to the light. Not the first. Punished, like that legendary island swallowed up by the sea to hide its shame from the light of day. Where there must have been another harbor, another Mother of Exiles facing the night with torch and scriptures, guid-ing those who crossed the waters to refuge, to ruined tenements sprawling far beneath the cathedral spires tolling each day's allotted burden. Until the rain came and filled the dome of heaven and high and low alike were swept away. Now she understood how Mister Klaatu felt after he'd turned off all the devices on earth, when he was a dead man walk-ing. So it's really what you'd call a memento mori, she concluded, Which must not be confused with the other, Mother says. So maybe not useless.

That's why it's the snow that counts, she thought, shaking to stir the flecks into the water. She reached underneath the pedestal to turn the key, not tightly. The blizzard surged and fell in drifts. The cathedral bells sounded the melody in the frigid air.

I want to be a part of it, she sang,

as she descended into its atmosphere, darting like a seahorse through the empty streets. She wished that all the drowned and dis-appeared folks could come back and join her there. Maybe they'd show her around, offer neighborly advice. Or would they sound the alarm against this stranger who had searched this heap of things made only to be broken and found nothing, neither postcard picture nor doll nor stuffed creature, nor jack springing from its box, nor face, nor frame, nor voice, nor gesture which resembled her, who found none to companion her in her monstrosity, except there in that bubble world where no troubled girl was ever welcome. They would cry to their King for rescue and he would send his swarming air force and his army and battleships to fire their guns and rockets at me until I'm full of holes and crash down to earth. I don't blame them, good riddance.

At the counter Rain arranged the nightgown on the hanger, partly to save her the trouble.

I'll come back for it with my hubby, when he is.

He'll have turned into a cheapskate by then.

Pearl lay across the bed almost haphazardly, as if the flood had passed and left her there. Motor mouth wide open, sawing a heap of wood. Now she noticed the stains marking the walls, which she'd overlooked in the brightness of that morning as they'd rushed forth to seize the day. Sprawling like maps of undiscovered continents, like clouds you lay back in the tall grass to watch as they drift across the sky like shapes shifting into the handsome profiles unwitting girls and boys pray every night to unexpectedly meet. Pearl lurched upward then fell back, mouthing words scarcely there. Here we are again, Rain observed, reluctantly moving through familiar paces. Reaching for her dangling legs, freeing each pinched foot from its shoe. Turning her onto one side, which she knew quieted her down or made it easier to breathe and covering her with the blanket.

She switched off the lamp and sat beside her. In that shadowed and broken silence she confronted what she had the night and morning before trusted to ignore. The voices leaking in through the walls, floor and ceiling, muttering on, shouting, whispering, laughing, sighing, screaming. The roach-powder whiff and puke stench drifting from the bathroom door. Pearl spoke without moving

I knew you were around, having fun.

Sure you did

Like when you hid behind the rubber tree plant.

You tied a good one on tonight.

I've had a marvelous time since you disappeared.

Me too. Even found my way back.

I was scared, and ready to throttle you.

Me you too.

So you took it on the lam.

Sure sounded like the thing to do.

They kept silent for a while. Pearl leaned over and reached for her smokes on the nightstand and lit up in the dark.

She cornered me. Bent my ear. I started feeling guilty. I had to give the devil her due.

Sounds like how you explained it to me once upon a time, *Render unto* and such. But we both know the Devil only cares about one thing, snatchin your soul.

You've been so unhappy.

But not only, Rain corrected.

I couldn't bear to think that the sad part might last forever. I wanted so much to

Who cares what you want?

Clearly, nobody.

That makes two of us, don't it?

Can't blame you if you hate me.

I'll get over it.

You sure about that?

Nope, not sure.

Let me know either way

I probably will.

They fell silent once again. Rain lifted her head into her lap and freed her hair from its rhinestone barrette and watched as it fell like a yoke around her neck.

I bet you had yourself a time today.

Went up ninety eleven stairs and jumped on the train. Lo and behold there's a big-time movie star sittin right next to me, *in* what's her face, *cognito*. But I took a chance to introduce myself. We had a lovely chat not so far from here, over lunch.

That must've shook down your last nickel.

We went Dutch. Come to find out I got a definite red-carpet glow about me, like Eartha Kitt, she said. And said if I make such-and-such moves that I can make the big time too. I was so thankful for the advice. She asked me to please keep her name to myself, since she did let me in on the skinny of her personal affairs, which she's been going crazy trying to keep out of the papers.

She's in good hands. By the way, *La Divina* was highly put out that we didn't show up for our appointment.

Shoot. I don't need no manicure to scratch my itch.

Dear Reflection,

time again to sit down and write myself a letter and make believe it came from You. Yep I've finaly gone crazy. But maybe not plum crazy cause there's no short circuit between us, that wire ain't never been broken. Here I am under the covers again with my trusty flashlight tryna write up all the different kind of thots which flew thru my mind before and thru it with her at the crack of dawn this morning, when POOF I was ofishaly pernounsed better off dead. I'd be delited to put down whatever coments you want to add in too like a good Crime Reporter should.

Lately all Hell has broke loose around here between me and You Know Who cause of You Know What, our so-called SECRET PLOT. Exsept I notice lately she can't walk all over me like since I was born. I wonder if some of my own super powers are finally comin out. I'm getting these messages in my mind from the four corners of the earth carrying the news. Like the ones that came up from the folks and cars down on 8th Avenue that first time I ever looked from a hotel window nineteen floors above the earth standing like a terrified giant happy to hear the good news that I might jump free in a single bound. That after I did what I came there to do she'd dissown me for good and leave me in peace. But the REAL STORY turned out to be different. A brand new SECRET jumped out the closet, Suprise! just when you're about to scratch your head like on *As the World Turns* or them other soapy shows. But I'm through with suprised, I don't care if I stay or go, cause no matter which way there's no turning back. I don't care if she don't like it.

223

That was my plan, to get up early this morning and tell her off once and for all.

I get back last night with Miss Goofy Double Ageint on that Trail Ways bus. Walk in the front door. Father says Well look who's back from the world but Mother just cuts her eyes at me with nary a word, she already heard what happened. Drag my behind upstairs took off my muddy shoes and fell out here in the bed. Wake up in the dark thinking I'm still in that BLUE ROOM in wherewasit, Brooklin. Stay up all night studying like a fool on what to say to her in the morning and how to keep my face straight in it. Even if every second I'm ready to forget the whole thing and just go on about my bizness.

I'm still working it's between the dark and light out. I hear Father pull out the driveway going to work. It's now or never. I go down and head straight for the kitchen and there she is. Sonny Boy had already came from fishin and left a mess of catfish in the sink. I come shufling in my slippers and ease up behind her. Calling myself playfull is all. Not sneaky just hopefull like in my opinyon any gal could feel like sometimes to be next to her own Mother. That she might be glad to lay eyes on them a hot second. Even tho I'm sure it's hopeless. I peek down over her shoulder into the sink. He must have left them not long before cause they're still alive them flip flopping mouths working behind them whiskers like they're trying to holler for help. Them beadie eyes looking straight through you knowing good and well what your about to do. Don't I know the feeling.

Guess I'll have to wait forever for you to speak she says. Good morning Good morning Mother I repeat right quick. I get a look like look what the cat drug in. You're determined to get in my way she says. Skrunches up her nose at me. Humph you need to wash your ass she says like it's Good Morning To You Too. Trying like she does to knock my train off the track. Course I'm used to it, it don't faze me one second. Just wish Mitsy Burton and Ada Johnson and them other highfalutin client folks who think she's so fancy and speaks so proper could hear what I hear. Right quick she desides she ain't paying me no more mind and gets back to cleaning them fish. Scares me half to death how she does it so quick. Cuts them guts out with that skinny knife then with that meat clever WHACK clean off with the head. Girl you know I can't pretend to look through all that. I aim my behind toward that hair fixing stool and fall back.

I open my mouth and take a breath and start out, Mother, the only name I've ever known to call her, what I'm sick of calling her, but cazoul like I could be starting up talking about the weather. Mother, I've been wondering lately about. Wondering what it was like. I push the words out before I get too scared to say them, WHEN YOU HAD ME. I'm thinking it's not a STUPID question like she tries to call anything I ask every time. Can't I ask since aparently I got a good reason right? HAD, ain't that a simple word for what happened right? I keep on. What was on your mind about it, your impreshins, I say. And to help that big word right then I make that Lana Turner sign I remembered last night in the mirror, with my hand like I'm reaching into a mist where you can't quite see through, I keep going. Impreshins of all different kinds I say it more proper, When you were carrying me. Work my mouth to put a smile on top.

WERE? she says grinning back in my face, You should ask what they are still. STILL she says again like she does to make sure I heard and to rub it in. Shoot, nice to know that in her opinyun I might as well still be in a diaper. Still I keep going. Before I was, I say, before I was, but I can't finish behind what she said, you know that's how she cuts you off right in your own mind. Neither one of us has time for that, she says. Then we both freeze for a second, it's like the whole entire world stops for a hot second. In my mind I can hear Jimmy explaining about fire and ice. But right then a little bird jumps up outside on the windowsill and peeks in with his little head twitching around and we both look back. Then the mouth on one of them catfish talking too like it's saying to that bird Help me. Too late, WHACK. Some way I keep on. Can't help but wonder about all that, I say.

She washes her hands and reaches in her apron for her smokes and turns around giving me a look like Oh now I'm worthy to be seen. Nope, I know that look. She's just trying to change the subject cause she's cutting her eyes looking me up and down like there's something ofensive about me. Says, What's that rag you're wearing supose to be. They call it a Chinese housecoat I say which is true. Oh she rolls her eyes and makes that retard face supose to be mine, They said so in New York and you believed it she says. The lady showed me it says MADE IN HONG KONG right here, I pull up the hem to show it. Made for some Molly in the street turning tricks, she says, shaking her head like it's a shame, like I'm a shame, and I AM. Sis remind me so I can't block it out any more, I'm a walking shame her paid LIAR. Wait no I'm working for free.

She grabs the next fish out the sink by the throat. You don't have the slightest noshion she says what the things embroided on there mean, they could say anything. Nope I admit But they're mostly flowers and I just think they're pretty and I hoped you would too when I showed you. Don't count on that rag fitting you much longer she says. Probly won't Mother, Get ready to find out for sure she says. WHACK I jump again at that sound but I keep on. Lately Mother there's so much stuff I'm wondering how it will turn out it's such a mistery to me I say. I almost start leaking again cause I know she won't tell me anything. But nobody else will either and that's why folks say It's your bed you made to lie in. Yep my big brass bed in my room of shadows twenty thousand leegues under the sea.

In my mind I'm seven miles down crossing the sand, I see the WRECK, it's the same old story. Her Pixie bottles red, blue, orange, lined up empty on the counter next to her purse alongside her appointment book and riceete book and them other things she carries around with her making her rounds from door to door. Some nights she don't get home till late then Father gets worried. Another confeshun, once I snuck downstairs and heard him calling that Carrie Austin who Mother can't stand. My friend in Christ, he said, it calms my nerves to speak with my Sister. No need to bother Mother with it he said, but I knew she'd get it out of me sooner or later. Come next day there I go, It was that Miss Carrie again, I told her. Right quick I thot, There I go again trying to get her on my side. She sipped her tea and said You think I'm a fool and can't see what's in front of me she said. Tell you like I've always told him, long as she ain't no Bride of Christlike to mine, like it was a joke but I could see the hurt in her eyes.

All that was in the olden days. Before she fired me for BURNING UP HER HOTBOX, so there all y'all I'm confesin one more time. While I know she really fired me for catching her crying when her client called to complain about the Burned Odor. But she cut me off before I could tell her what happened then the phone rang and it was him. Ricky who didn't give me time to put the canned heats out before he put pedal to the metal, Oh no he had to be on time for his poker game out at The Five Acres, I said. How come if the box was not damiged after I had scrubbed the whole inside I got fired not him. So Please save me, even if I'm stupid it's all cause she's never gave a hoot about explaining what to do or wants from me, too busy showing off for the Social Lights, I'm her talking dummy.

Now that little bird flies away like it don't want to see something about to happen. And right then she gets weak in the knees the way she does when her pressure goes sky high and slumps against the counter. But it ain't no pressure it's she's worn out with no rest from aggravation half of it she brings on herself and no pixies left to fix it. I jump up from the stool and try to catch her from falling out on the floor but she bucks back against me and knocks me back away, OH NOW YOU WANT TO BE SO HELPFUL. YOU MISSED YOUR CHANCE FOR THAT I CERTINLY DON'T NEED YOU PAWING ALL OVER ME. I sit there and while she's struggling to stand up straight and look out the window hoping the bird will come back.

Come on now dry your eyes I tell myself. Since there apparently ain't no other talking to be done stick to what you practiced in the mirror all night. Make sure to say every word you picked from Webster's clearly and correct. To stop after a period when it comes and not have your mouth keep on like a bell clapper. To at least make some kind of sense and not sound stupid running in her one ear and out the other, here I go again. I say Mother, I do firmly believe that what has been must be what it was and that what will be will be, like Doris Day says, at least I've remembered it so far. But then I start worrying about, But what will it be? Perhaps, I say, cause I like to keep that word Perhaps cause it fits my mouth and my mind, Perhaps it's just me but I bet you've thot about stuff, I mean things like that too, I say, I keep on till I'm quite frankly worried to death, wishing I knew about, how shall I express it? What's not yet. Whew right then it sounds so far so good and I'm feeling an eensy weensy bit happy but scared to feel it cause on the inside I'm turning right around hoping please that I'll never know. Too late to hope for that, she says to my surprise.

Oh Mother I know I was a fool then, I give up and say it, I remind myself every single day.

Then, now, and likely tomorrow she says, to rub my nose in it. You hardly deserve to hear it she says but long ago I was a natural born fool like you. Couldn't be satisfied with my perfectly wonderful life. All the wonderful chances I had all the wide world I'd already seen before my eyes. All the things I'd learned to do very well indeed, and all my exkwisit, I don't know she used some big ass word it sounds like that, my exkwisit friends who knew what life was worth and loved me for what I was she says. Oh no I had to prove I could be a goody two shoes, make good with some man like all the rest . Hired one and next thing I knew blown up I was, kaboom. Did I learn my lesson then? Oh no, couldn't be satisfied with the perfectly fine son I already had. Had to satisfy your Father instead, went on and blew myself up again. You might have a hard time with this one, the doctor said, with your heart trouble and all. Oh no I said. Not I, the one who could stand anything. Who'd walk through that valley from end to end and come out untouched. But you came along and my errers were soon revealed. You devoured the strength within me then you started in on my mind. And certinly we both know how it's been since. Which brings us quite up to date I'm sure, WHACK. Before I can shut my mouth I hear myself say Mother I'm so thankfull you've explained all that to me. Like I'm such a retard like she thinks and don't know what it means like I've done every time before. Guess I never really knew how you really look at me, now I see, says The Blind Girl.

But now I can't remember the rest of what I rehersed all night not even one word. Cause I can't help puzling over WHO I'm talking to here. Is it really Mother or some kinda DEVICE that looks and talks exactly like and knows everything she knows, that took her place and nobody noticed. I give her a good look up and down. My head starts to twitch around like that bird's. First I notice, how about that neck. Thick, tough to choke. Like mine. Wide shoulders like mine, except trying to carry the whole world. Thick legs, sore from standing up in kitchens day and night, not laying around half the time like a good for nothing, like me, who couldn't even learn to serve tea and crumpets. But on top of them sure feet, on the small side like mine, good for skating on thin ice. Busy hands, chop stir and next thing you know they snatch you baldheaded, knock you into the middle of next week. How mine could be if I knew what to do with myself. Head, not a stitch of good hair which is why she knows how to do with mine. Each different part of us looking alike, almost the same as when I'm sitting here looking at you. Then I see her and me today and yesterday and through the looking glass between us across the years and I hear a voice inside telling me the answer to my question and it almost knocks me down, please Granny take it back I don't want to know.

Mother I feel so different from that I bust out leaking I can't help it. Cause I can't believe you could be a fool I say like I'm saying it for the very last time. Oh no like you always say I believe it was all meant to be I say, just like that. Which proves how big a fool you really are, she hollers. Now she's the excited one how about that. You traipsed off to the big city No you sent me like I was some kinda package to deliver I answer back. So now you're a big shot you know everything she says. Turns around with that knife in her hand which makes my hair stand on end, Sis I hope you agree we don't resembell no catfish. But girl don't we know she don't need no kind of blade to carry out her nasty work. All you've ever cared for is running with every creeping low life you could find from here to eturnity she says. Heard that before, I say, what else. Whenever I care to say boo about it off you run to Father like I'm some kind of monster. Cause he don't keep reminding me that everything I say everything I do is wrong. First chance you got you took up with that no-count mush mouth after I told you to stay away, jumped up in the sack with him as soon as you thot no one was looking. Well lo and behold. Five minutes after that bastard kicked you to the curb you scrounge up another wild stranger from nowhere. Now you're knocked up and too stupid to know who's the father and too hard-headed to keep your mouth shut about it. I tried one last time to save you from yourself the only way I knew how. Behind my back, I say quietly. Behind what? she says, can't tell you a damn thing who knows what you'll say or do, I'm worried sick to think that any day now you'll run your big mouth to him and destroy everything we've worked for in this valley. So you desided to make sure I didn't, now I talk back quick. I didn't count on your gift for making a mess of everything, she says, even when it's for your own good. I catch my breath and let her carry on. Wedding bells soon to ring. Our beloved daughter is tying the knot. Wonderful news it's the talk of the town. Such a pity she's never returned very much love to us. But Lord knows you love him to death. I dare say you appear to be made for each other, such a blessing. Such a lovely picture the two of you piled up like TRASH in your little white dump in Texas. Trash now I get the whole picture. No great shakes he'll do in a pinch good enough for the likes of you.

Now I can't help but finaly say it, even if it's my own fault that it's wrong. Mother you ain't got nobody to blame for this wedding coming but yourself. You're not only a fool but a hipocrite to boot she says, as I recall YOU instegated this whole thing from the start she says. No I didn't, I say. I see that monster in her face ready to jump on me, I feel my guts coming up, I swallow to keep them down. Seems to me you have a very short memory she says. No I didn't, I say, because I feel different than you, I will never ever give her that she made me do a blessed thing. AH HA HA HA she laughs, DIFERENT, pardon me that slipped my mind, I'm scheming but you're IN LOVE she says. Yes Mother I am I say. And by gosh he's so IN LOVE with you she says. Yes we are with each other I say. Then why not tell him the truth the whole truth. I'm sure he'll forgive you for putting the finger on him in the first place, what are you waiting for. My whole truth not yours I say. What the hell she says it was true enough for you to go along with it. But not anymore I shut my eyes and just say it, count me out. She starts toard me. I feel the shock going thru my hair and all over. She gets right up in my face. You'll get the publicity you deserve. Everyone should hear about your little mistake. Then I'll just have to put your tail right out in the street, we'll see who comes to your rescue. I'm sufocating feel sick and about to faint and think what if I just grab on and throw up all over her. But I push the words stuck in my mind out thru my mouth instead. And if I break down and drop dead I say then you'll finaly be happy. I get up run out the back door just like I had to run away from that other place I couldn't stand no more.

Though the cold morning air drove through her Chinese housecoat and furry slippers to pierce to the bone, in that moment there was nowhere else she would have rather been than sitting on those wide mausoleum steps, looking back toward the house which she had once never doubted to be home, which now seemed incomprehensibly distant like a world charted yet never visited, finally standing her ground where she had always feared to linger until the morning light. Nonetheless she was thankful for the stubborn flame and useless heat of her shiny new Zippo, which she flicked open with a thumb to light another Newport, then shut with a quick trick of the wrist just as Sonny Boy had shown her how to do. *Estoy aquí, mi amor*, she thot as she dragged and puffed and recalled the summer evenings when she and none other than Zorro Casanova had sat together there and smooched and told their luxurious fortunes by the returning stars. When he would look away to the rooftops and sunset hills of the town as if he could sight across the years all his famous feats as clean-up batter, for which his grateful fans had whooped and hollered, soaring from the bat's crack over Dunn Field's left fence into the sleepy river which its first children had named *Chemung*, into those fairy-tale ticker-taped streets which lay forever beyond his reach. Oh, my rotten trampy handsome one, she thot, I missed your last inning, your last parade home before you left for the big time, and now for me it's the other twilight time. Me apart from you all, Yes all y'all who've driven me plain plum crazy, she drawled like a holy certainty. You-know-who, and you my first, and who knows if sooner or later from this one after, and after. Apart from all your comings and goings and blue bottles and bone china and blown roses and mojos and shortstops' mitts and dog tags and devices and kit bags and manicures and martinis and flims and flams and conspiracies and all the rest I've never really wanted to know what to do with, being, as you all are so fond of insisting, one without a clue. Now hear this, we're hitting the road once and for all, making our perfect getaway without getting anywhere, running headlong into the dark, seven miles under the ever-falling dust, riding the train to lost without a trace. In that last instant of twilight she heard what she'd always feared to hear there. The crowding voices of the departed, telling tales upon the wind stripping away the shell of her heretofore-true body. At last unafraid to let go, she cast her mortal frame aside without looking back and, being no longer what she once was, picked up her death and walked, stretching herself with a sigh against the long winter's rages, leaning into her first newborn footsteps. Calling out into the light of her first morning, Now, all y'all still alive and kicking, tell me, what's my name.

Harlem, NYC
December 28, 2023

Many thanks to all those who have been particularly present in my writing life. Their encouragement and inspiration over many years has imprinted itself, visibly and invisibly, upon the pages of this work.

Patti Bradshaw
Mary E. Ross
Peter Dimock
Jasper McGruder
Lee Zimmerman
Katherine Arnoldi
Mike Taylor
Lucia Dailey
Virginia Serine
Andrea Dezso & Adam Gurvitch
Robert Brink
Jay Vachon
Nehprii Amenii

Special thanks to:
Joyce Tice, Founder and Executive Director
The History Center on Main Street
61 North Main Street / Mansfield, PA

Family, friends, and the people of Chemung and Tioga Counties, New York.